BLUE AVENUE

Introducing homicide detective Daniel Turner and his troubled friend 'BB' in the first of this atmospheric crime noir series.

Summoned to identify the trussed-up, naked body of a woman found amongst a pile of garbage on Blue Avenue, Florida businessman William Byrd recognizes the victim as Belinda Mabry, the girl with whom he spent a passionate summer 25 years before. Determined to find out what happened to the woman he once loved, Byrd must revisit his own troubled past.

Recent Titles by Michael Wiley

The Joe Kozmarski Series
LAST STRIPTEASE
THE BAD KITTY LOUNGE
A BAD NIGHT'S SLEEP

The Detective Daniel Turner Mysteries
BLUE AVENUE *

* *available from Severn House*

BLUE AVENUE

Michael Wiley

Severn House Large Print
London & New York

This first large print edition published 2015
in Great Britain and the USA by
SEVERN HOUSE PUBLISHERS LTD of
19 Cedar Road, Sutton, Surrey, England, SM2 5DA.
First world regular print edition published 2014
by Severn House Publishers Ltd.

British Library Cataloguing in Publication Data

Wiley, Michael, 1961- author.
  Blue Avenue. -- (The Detective Daniel Turner mysteries)
  1. Police--Florida--Jacksonville--Fiction. 2. Serial
  murder investigation--Florida--Jacksonville--Fiction.
  3. Detective and mystery stories. 4. Large type books.
  I. Title II. Series
  813.6-dc23

  ISBN-13: 9780727897978

Severn House Publishers support the Forest Stewardship Council™
[FSC™], the leading international forest certification organisation. All
our titles that are printed on FSC certified paper carry the FSC logo.

Printed and bound in Great Britain by
T J International, Padstow, Cornwall.

For Julie, Isaac, Maya and Elias

ACKNOWLEDGMENTS

Homicide Detectives K.L. Haines and John Hinton, for driving me through the night. Judy Defonzo, for driving me through the gun barrel. Brad Way, for driving me across crime scenes. Julia Burns and Sam Kimball, for driving me through the drafts. Christine Kane, for driving me across the web. Philip Spitzer, Lukas Ortiz and Luc Hunt, for driving me forward. Kate Lyall Grant and Sara Porter, for driving me across the page and to the market. I couldn't have gotten there without you.

ONE

It's the kind of dream that's more real than waking, and when you do wake it colors your mind all day and into next week like guilty sex in which one of you gets hurt. I'm a kid again, seventeen, two years older than my son Thomas is now and seven years before I marry Susan. I'm walking on railroad tracks a half mile from my house. I'm with Belinda, my first real girlfriend. Her skin's as black as my pale ass is white and her long hair hangs down her back in a braid that swings like a metronome, a bright pink elastic band at the bottom holding the strands together, and I hope I never see a girl as pretty as her again because beauty like hers hurts too much. Our feet crunch on the gravel and the afternoon sun shines on her skin. On the side of the tracks, low-lying saw palmettos stand still in the breezeless air. Wild grape vines tug at the trunk of a diseased live oak. Mounds of kudzu rise like Indian burials. A fly is buzzing somewhere.

Belinda talks to the air in front of her, shyly. 'Dad thinks you're no good for me.'

I stumble on a creosote-stained railroad tie, catch my balance. I haven't thought of being no

9

good for her and I wonder why. 'What d'you think? Your dad right?'

She turns to me with a sly grin that rises on one side of her mouth only. 'I hope so.'

A single eye of light appears a mile down the tracks.

'Train's coming,' I say.

She squints. 'You sure?'

Sunlight glints on metal.

'Coming slow, but coming.'

She turns to face me. She unbuttons her blouse.

'What're you doing?' I ask.

She smiles. 'Sometimes you say the dumbest things.' She lets the blouse fall between the tracks, unhooks her bra and lets it fall too. She unzips her jeans and lets them slide over her hips to the gravel rail bed. She stands naked on the tracks, the sun shining on her black shoulders, her nipples erect. She cocks her head to the side.

My throat's dry. My voice catches. 'Train's coming.'

She looks over her shoulder. The train's still far in the distance but now a steady glimmer in the sun. She turns to me. 'Uh huh.'

'You're crazy,' I say and I take off my pants.

I enter her as the first dull vibrations of the approaching train shake the ground. A moment later I burst. She holds me to her. The train is close and the ground shudders. I try to pull away. I say, 'Get up.'

'Uh uh,' she says, holding me. The train

10

closes slowly and at its first whistle she comes, bucking like a terrible muscle.

I rip apart from her and crawl on to the embankment. I yell her name but she lies mesmerized by the single eye of the approaching train. I yell and reach for her but from ten feet away, maybe more. I'm scared. Too scared to go to her. Too scared to save her. She lies with her legs open. She doesn't roll away from the tracks the way she did in real life twenty-five years ago. She lies between the rails and waits for the train to take her. I open my mouth again to scream but no sound comes or, if it does, the sound of the engine, the screech of metal wheels against metal rails and the wailing whistle consume the scream and no one can hear me, not even myself. I want to go to her but I'm afraid and so I do nothing. I lie on the embankment and scream emptily into the roar.

The train takes her.

Steel crashes over her with the methodical rumble of a factory machine. The train comes and keeps coming. As far as my eyes can see, it comes. In the dream the train will never end until suddenly it does and is gone like a shadow disappearing in the afternoon sun. I crawl across the embankment, the gray and white bed stones cutting my hands and knees, and I peer at the spot where she and I were lying.

Belinda's gone. There's no blood, no skin, no hair, no fragment of bone. No clothing. No jewelry. Nothing to say that a freight train has taken a young girl's life. Not even a stain where we've lain.

I crawl down the other embankment, searching for her. She's not there and I imagine the train continuing into the afternoon, Belinda's body impaled on the front coupler of the engine like an insane hood ornament. Then I see the pink hair band that had held her braid. It's hanging from a frond of a saw palmetto.

I first had the dream on the night Susan and Thomas came home from the maternity ward. When I woke, Susan had fear in her eyes. She said I'd cried out in my sleep. A week later she moved a bed into the sunroom and she's been there ever since, showing my shame to the neighbors. I had the dream for the last time on the night before Daniel Turner – now a police lieutenant detective though I'd known him since we played football as kids – called to tell me that Belinda, twenty-five years after I last saw her, was dead.

Daniel called a couple of minutes before seven. Thomas was sleeping and Susan and I were eating breakfast on the back terrace of the Metro, a diner that fronted on San Jose Boulevard where you could hear the noise and smell the fumes of the coming day, but the terrace was trellised on three sides, bougainvillea climbed the trellises and cool water always seemed to be dripping even in the heat of day. The waitress wore a little black skirt over bare legs and I knew what I would have liked to do if the circumstances had been different. A green umbrella shaded the table though the sun hadn't yet risen above the diner roof. A plate with the remains of a poached egg and toast sat on the table in front of Susan but she was reading the menu the way she had done lately as though she might be regretting the decision she'd made and want to order something new. It was an annoying habit and I opened my mouth to say so but thought better of it.

She looked over the top of the menu and said, 'What?'

Then my cell phone rang.

'Just a sec.' I answered the phone.

'BB,' said Daniel.

'Morning, Lieutenant. Starting the day right?' For Daniel, starting the day right meant sitting behind his house on a wooden dock that stuck into Black Creek, his head shaded by the oak canopy.

'Startin' real wrong,' he said. 'I'm working a homicide on the Northside. Pretty lady about our age. Homeless man found her an hour ago in a pile of trash. Scared the hell out of him. Killer wrapped her in cellophane like a supermarket chicken. In this heat, she was cooking in the plastic.'

'Jesus, Daniel. And why're you wrecking my breakfast with the news?'

'You know the summer you spent with that black girl Belinda Mabry?'

My stomach fell. I didn't tell him I'd awakened an hour earlier from a dream about that summer. 'Yeah?'

13

'ID on the body says that's who the lady is.'

My breakfast moved back up into my throat.

He added, 'I thought you might be interested.'

I shook my head, trying to get my mind around the idea. Susan had gone back to reading the menu. I said, 'She left the city twenty-five years ago.'

'She found her way back.'

'You sure it's the same?'

'That's why I called. You want to come look? You think you'd still recognize her?'

'Yeah, maybe. Jesus, Daniel.'

When I hung up, I realized I was sweating. I wiped my hands on my pants. Susan had her eyes on her menu. 'What was that?' she said.

'Daniel Turner. A woman got killed last night.'

Her eyes rose and met mine. They were cold eyes, as if coldness could protect all that was vulnerable in her. 'Someone we know?'

'I did,' I said. 'When I was a kid.'

For a while she watched me sweat but her voice softened. 'You knew her well?'

I nodded.

'That's terrible.'

'It was a long time ago,' I said.

She nodded. 'Still.' She turned back to the menu.

The waitress stopped at the table and asked if she could take away our plates. Susan kept reading as if the waitress were talking only to me. I waved at the plates like they were insects, and the waitress cleared the table.

'Daniel wants me to identify the body,' I said. 'It could be someone else.' As if that would help Susan.

'You can drop me off at home,' she said.

Rush-hour traffic backed up at the bridge. The cars shimmered in the morning sunlight. Twenty miles off the Atlantic coast, the air smelled less of saltwater than the chemical sweetness of the downtown Folger's coffee processing plant and the paper mills upriver. Thirty years ago you couldn't drive with the windows open because of the stink, but then the mayor got smart and made the mills use filters so that the sulfur didn't knock birds out of the sky. Now you might think you were driving past a bakery if you didn't know better. The river under the bridge sparkled hard and bright in the morning sun, a motorboat cut a long *J* in the water, and I knew that peace was possible even in a city as old and rotten as this.

The highway north of the river cut past industrial lots and a big old three-story brown brick building that once was a school and then a nursing home for the indigent until a state report showed a pattern of abuse and standards of hygiene that would shock a river rat, and now had been abandoned to vines and weeds that ate into the mortar and covered the door to the front hall, which, it seemed to me, was how it should be. I exited on King Street, passed the post office, crossed over a sanitary canal and turned on Blue Avenue. The houses were wood-frame

15

bungalows, jacked off the ground on cinder-blocks. One had a rusty carport. Others had belly-high chain-link fences in front. An empty tar can lay on its side in a driveway. The little yards were sand and dirt and weed – what the world would return to when we were gone.

A quarter mile in from King Street the police had blocked the road. I pulled to the side behind a news van. A crowd from the neighborhood stood at the barrier. Most were black, though a skinny girl who I figured was Vietnamese hung at the edge and a pasty-faced white woman leaned on one of the barricades next to a tall barefooted black woman. A man from the news van stood to the side with a video camera on his shoulder. Half a block in from the barricades the police had set up a second perimeter with yellow crime-scene tape which they'd strung from a stop sign to a large tree on the corner of an empty lot, around holly bushes, along a chain-link fence and around another tree and more bushes, circling the lot and returning to the stop sign.

A young cop stood on the other side of the barricades. I went to him and gestured at the yellow tape. 'Lieutenant Turner called me,' I said. 'He asked me to come over.'

He looked like he didn't believe it. 'Your name is?'

'William Byrd.'

He took his radio off his belt and talked to someone, then waved me around the barricade. 'Hope you didn't eat anything soft for breakfast,' he said as we stepped away from the crowd. 'That spot in the shade of the oak, that's where the others've been going. If you need to.' He walked me past a half-dozen police cars and a forensic van to the second perimeter and lifted the tape for me to cross under. The sun rose over the trees and beat down on the back of my head with a sudden heat. I looked over my shoulder. The sun was as pale and hard as alabaster.

A plainclothes cop was talking to a raggedy haired barefoot black man in dirty blue pants and a sweat-stained white T-shirt – the homeless man who'd found Belinda's body, I supposed.

A dozen uniformed cops milled around, more than I would've expected for a Northside homicide. Daniel stood talking with two plainclothes cops outside a white crime-scene tent. He was a big man but with small feet that made him look lighter than he was, as if he could dance on his toes or fly. As a kid he'd had red hair but now it was white or gone – mostly gone. Beyond the tent was a fire pit full of burned trash. An assortment of chairs stood around the pit. To the side, a large dirty sheet of white foam rubber lay on the ground. Empty beer cans peeked from the weeds behind the chairs. Four officers wearing gloves were poking through the weeds for evidence.

I joined Daniel and he swung an arm over my shoulders without looking at me or breaking the conversation. He'd gone to college on a track-

and-field scholarship – shot put – before dropping out during his sophomore year. When his hand squeezed my shoulder I knew he could break it if he wanted to. 'Get the door-to-door started,' he said to one of the cops. 'Find out who parties here, who was here last night.'

'Yes, sir,' said the cop, a kid barely off his last acne. He was sweating from something more than the morning heat. 'You want us to tell the neighbors anything?'

Daniel put an edge in his voice. 'Yeah, tell them a woman got cut up and dumped on their front yard. Tell them we've never seen anything this bad. Tell them a psychopath's been driving through their neighborhood. Tell them to keep their doors locked and their handguns loaded.' He shook his head. 'No, Jerry. Keep it simple.'

The young cop's face flushed. 'Yes, sir.'

He went to do his job and Daniel mumbled, 'Christ,' forcing a smile. 'Thanks for coming, BB,' he said. He gestured at the small dark-haired woman who stood across from him. 'This is my partner, Denise Nuñez. Denise, William Byrd. Everyone calls him BB.'

She nodded. 'I know who you are.'

I looked at Daniel. He shrugged. 'Not from me.'

Then he guided me into the tent. 'Hope you've got a strong stomach this morning,' he said.

The air inside was hot and still and smelled of the beginning of decay. Flies buzzed angrily.

A forensic technician in a facemask and

gloves was leaning over a woman's body that had been stuffed inside a clear plastic bag meant for lawn waste. The woman was naked and doubled up like a diver doing a pike, her ankles over her ears, her legs tied with clothes-line around her neck. She lay on her back, her eyes staring up between her legs at the roof of the tent. The pinkness of her vagina pressed raw and swollen against the clear plastic. Her hair, which she'd ironed straight and worn long when I'd known her, was cut short into a tight afro salted with gray. Her lips turned up in a death grin. I wished I didn't recognize her. But I did.

'Yeah,' I said to Daniel Turner. 'It's Belinda Mabry.'

'No doubt?'

I retched but held my stomach down. 'No doubt.' I turned and rushed out of the tent into the open air.

Behind me the technician spoke calmly to Daniel, as if he saw this kind of thing every day. 'First glance, it looks like she suffocated. No trauma. Shortly before death, she had rough sex, probably rape. I'll tell you more after we cut her out of the bag.'

I breathed deep but the hot morning air stirred my stomach and bile rose into my throat. I swallowed it and looked up at the sun and the sky around it and wished the blue enormity could lift me out of myself. When I lowered my gaze, Daniel's partner was eyeing me. She nodded toward the tent. 'Makes me want to puke

19

and I've been doing this for eight years.'

'How do you know me?' I asked.

'Everyone knows you, BB. You don't wash off so easy.'

'I never tried to.'

'Then why are you surprised I know you?'

'Hell, I don't know,' I said and wandered toward the yellow tape. A wasp darted toward me as though the sweat on my skin were an irresistible sweetness.

The detective fell in beside me. 'Daniel says you told him you haven't seen Belinda Mabry in twenty-five years. You sure about that?'

I kept my eyes in front of me. 'Why wouldn't I be?'

'No reason. But you look distressed, more than someone might expect after all this time.' She shook her head doubtfully. 'I mean, twenty-five years is a long while. You were just kids.'

'I haven't seen her in twenty-five years,' I said.

'I guess we never get over some people. First love?'

'What difference does that make?'

She peered into my eyes. 'None, apparently.'

I stepped toward her. 'You think I killed her?'

She stepped back calmly and offered a false smile. 'No, sir. Not unless you've also killed two prostitutes.'

'Huh?'

The smile stayed. 'The sheriff's holding a press conference in an hour. Your friend's the third victim, same M.O. The other two worked the streets. I don't know about your friend. The others weren't bagged but the killer raped and suffocated them and tied them up the same. Naked and trussed. Each time, the woman's clothes have been folded and stacked next to the body. Super neat, like the killer launders and irons them after the killing. Maybe he does.'

She watched me to see how I took the news. I took it like a man. Bile rose in my throat and I vomited at her feet.

TWO

I drove east into the sun on Blue Avenue. The air quivered over the hot asphalt. A heavy woman in a faded housedress and slippers pushed an empty shopping cart on the shoulder of the road. She was no older than thirty but she limped and used the cart like a walker. She stopped in the shade of a palm tree and stared at me as I passed like I didn't belong.

I kept the windows up and the air conditioner on full until I shivered in the breeze. My dream from the previous night flooded my mind. Not what I saw in the dream, not Belinda lying between the tracks with her legs wide open as the freight train rolled over her, not my hand

21

reaching for her from too far away. The dread. The knowledge that there was nothing I could do to save her or, if there was, I wasn't going to do it.

Traffic on the return trip over the bridge was thick and I fell into a line of cars and waited my turn. What choice did I have?

Susan's Acura was gone from the driveway. She would be doing errands, none of which she would mention to me later, none of which I would ask about. Eight years ago she'd had a lover or I was pretty certain she'd had. He'd sold real estate in the neighborhood, and while it lasted Susan had shown a renewed interest in life that spilled over into the rest of our household. She'd started taking classes to get a real-estate license and I was happy for her and happy for myself too because I felt less guilty about my own habits. But I'd had a talk with the real-estate agent and the affair had ended the way these things will.

Fela, our nine-year-old tabby, sat on the front porch. Thomas had brought her home as a kitten and Susan had insisted we keep her though cats make my eyes water. As if she could sense my hatred of her and decided that she'd fool with me, Fela took to me immediately. Now she stood and stretched as I came up the steps and rubbed against my leg as I unlocked the door. I'd long ago stopped kicking her away. I picked her up against my chest and carried her inside.

Thomas was eating a bowl of Cheerios at the

kitchen counter. 'Morning, Champ,' I said. I dropped Fela to the floor and put my hand on his shoulder.

His back stiffened. 'Champ's a dog's name.'

I tried a smile and squeezed his shoulder.

He swung as if I'd jabbed him in the ribs. 'Don't do that.'

I sat on a stool next to him. 'Why are you so angry?'

He spooned Cheerios into his mouth.

I picked up a piece of cereal that had fallen on the counter and put it in my mouth, let it melt into my tongue. 'I was done being angry by the time I was your age,' I said. 'Maybe I developed early. Even when I was thirteen or fourteen, I didn't stay angry long. A burst maybe and then I would be done. I've always been a happy person, always tried to be.'

He didn't bother rolling his eyes. 'Yeah, right.'

'Anger's a waste of energy. Gets you nowhere.' I looked at the same spot in the air that seemed to interest him. 'If you don't like the way things are, take a breath, think about how you want them to be and then change them. Right?'

He dipped his spoon into the bowl, filled it with Cheerios and milk and lifted it in the air. With his other fingers, he bent the spoon-end down and released it. The spoon catapulted wet cereal on to my chest.

I grabbed his wrist. I'm a tall man, almost six foot four, not especially wide at the shoulders but big enough. Thomas also was tall and in a couple of years he'd be bigger than I was. But not yet.

He attempted to shake free but I held him. 'I thought you never got angry,' he said.

I let go of him. 'I try to be a happy man.'

'Right,' he said and slipped off the stool and out of the room.

I called after him, 'You want to go for a drive this morning?' It was a pathetic question, I knew, but he'd gotten his driver's permit and we'd found occasional peace when he was in the driver's seat and I was quiet beside him.

'Yeah, right!' he yelled again and slammed his bedroom door.

Right. I felt my anger building. So I dialed Daniel Turner's number. His partner had grilled me and I wanted to know why. *If you don't like the way things are, take a breath, think about how you want them to be and then change them.* The department receptionist said Daniel wasn't available, so I left a message asking him to call me.

At 10:00 a.m. I turned on the kitchen television and the sheriff announced the presence of a repeat killer. He stood at a podium in front of the county courthouse. No reason to stand there instead of police headquarters except the courthouse had pillars that gave him dignity and, like pin stripes on a fat man's suit, took a few pounds off him. He said that at 5:38 a.m. the police had received a call about a body on a Northside lot adjacent to Blue Avenue. Homicide detectives responded and found a woman, African-American, estimated to be between thirty-five and forty-five, deceased. The woman remained unidentified, he said.

He waited a beat and said that unusual circumstances surrounding her death resembled those surrounding the deaths of two other women, a thirty-one-year-old African-American named Tonya Richmond and a twenty-nine-year-old Caucasian named Ashley Littleton. He said that the first two victims had been sexually assaulted but warned reporters that he wouldn't tell them what was unusual about the circumstances so they need not ask for details. He continued talking as three boxes appeared on the screen, the first two showing the faces of the earlier victims with their names, the last a brown blank where, I knew, they would place Belinda's picture and name in the coming hours or days.

Ashley Littleton's face looked street-hardened, her eyes sunken, her brown hair stringy. It was the face of a long-time addict. Tonya Richmond's picture was ten years old at least and showed a smiling young woman with eyes set a little too far apart. She was wearing a blue gown that revealed breast as if she were getting ready for the prom. The sheriff noted that both had been arrested repeatedly on prostitution charges and Ashley Littleton for passing bad checks. The arrest records were supposed to reassure the public, I supposed. If you avoided walking down Highway 1 in a miniskirt at 2:00

a.m. you should be safe. Still he warned women to be vigilant and report suspicious activity to the police. So as to protect the integrity of the investigation he would take no questions from the reporters, he said, but he promised regular progress reports.

As I flipped off the TV, water splashed in the backyard pool. Thomas was taking a swim. I looked through the back window and saw him cut lazily across the water, and a longing swelled over me for a simplicity that I knew and maybe always had known didn't truly exist and I didn't trust even if it did exist. But the false memory of it did – from when I was Thomas's age and was about to meet Belinda, later when the time I spent with her would shut down the roar of others' voices, afterward with Susan for a short while, and still later when Thomas was young and wouldn't stiffen when I put my hand on his shoulder, but rather relaxed into my touch and everything seemed right in the world.

But Belinda had been gone for twenty-five years and now was dead. Ever since Thomas was born, Susan had slept in the sunroom. And, except during our occasional excursions when he practiced driving, Thomas spent most of his time alone in his bedroom writing and illustrating obscene comic books which he scanned and put online for his friends and hid from Susan and me.

I got my cell phone, checked the memory and dialed Daniel Turner's cell number. He answered on the third ring. 'Hey, BB.'

26

I kept my voice even. 'Did you ask me to identify Belinda because you thought I might've killed her?'

'No,' he said, though he didn't sound surprised by the question. 'You knew her. We wanted a quick ID and we didn't want to pull a relative into the circus if we could avoid it.'

'Your partner seemed more interested in me than that.'

'That's because you're an interesting man, BB.'

'I try not to be.'

'You can't undo history,' he said.

'But you don't think I'm involved in this.'

'Are you?'

'Jesus, Daniel.'

'No,' he said, 'I don't think you're involved.'

'Your partner said the killer leaves the women's clothes in a neat pile by the bodies.'

'She shouldn't've told you that.'

'Does he leave their wallets too?'

'How do you know that?'

'Don't treat me like an idiot,' I said. 'You knew Belinda's name and you said there was an ID on her body.'

He paused for a moment. 'Yeah, he leaves the wallets on top of the clothes. Cash is still there, credit cards too. And IDs – driver's licenses, a community college ID on the second victim.'

'What was the address on Belinda's driver's license?'

'No way, BB.'

'I want to pay respects to her family,' I said.

27

'Uh uh. You stay away from this now.'

I'd been in the middle of it since I was seventeen years old. 'You involved me when you called me this morning.'

'Now I'm uninvolving you.'

'Uninvolving isn't a word,' I said.

'Now it is. It's what I'm doing to you.'

'I'll find out her address if you don't tell me.'

'I don't doubt it,' he said and hung up.

I stared at the phone in my hand. Thomas came in through the back and disappeared into his bedroom, closing the door behind him. The sharp-sweet smell of chlorine lingered in the air.

I stared at the phone some more.

Then I dialed a number that I hadn't dialed in eight years and in the meantime I'd tried to forget but never could and, depending on your perspective, that was a good or a bad thing.

A man's rough voice said hello after the first ring.

'Charles,' I said.

'BB,' he said warmly, as if we'd talked twice a day.

'Can you meet?'

'This about Belinda Mabry?'

The police hadn't announced her identity and I guessed only a handful of people knew it. Even if he did know that Belinda had died, he shouldn't know that I knew. 'How did you hear?'

'Don't ask dumb questions.'

'Meet me at Best Gas?' Best Gas was my

28

independent gas station, named by the Lebanese man who'd once owned it before selling it to my dad. I owned three other stations too, a Shell and a couple of Exxons, but I treated Best Gas as my office.

'Give me twenty minutes,' Charles said and hung up.

As I stepped out the front door Susan pulled into the driveway and got out of the car. Two grocery bags sat on the passenger seat. I went to her and kissed her. 'I'm going to check the stations.'

'Mmm,' she said and looked at me close. 'Was the dead woman your friend?'

Sweat beaded on my neck. 'Yes.'

'I'm sorry.'

'Me too.' I kissed her again and she held me awkwardly, so I pulled away. 'I'll be back in a couple hours.'

She watched me go as though she feared I was leaving forever. 'We have dinner at seven with the Lindseys,' she said.

I had no idea who the Lindseys were. 'I'll be back early.' I tried a smile and she tried one too.

Best Gas and Food Mart was on the side of a marshy stretch of a disused Westside highway, a mile from a coal-burning power plant that produced electricity for Jacksonville and the five surrounding counties. Why anyone built a gas station there I never figured out. Maybe the builder had expected power plant workers to stop at shift changes. I guessed my dad had bought it for the same reason that I spent more time there than at any of my other stations. Solitude and silence. Few cars stopped for gas, which I kept priced well above the city average, and only a few more stopped to buy a drink or a six-pack from the refrigerated cases. I'd hired a quiet, slow-witted woman to run the cash register on dayshift. She would nod hello when I came in and never bothered me when I went into the office in the back.

I pulled into the lot a few minutes after eleven and parked in the back. On my way to the office I grabbed a Pepsi from the refrigerator and a package of Doritos. Charles had already arrived and had his feet on my desk. He wore faded blue pants, black steel-toed work boots and a soft white cotton shirt with silver buttons. I couldn't remember ever seeing him in anything else, whether he was sitting in church or grinding the tool end of a screwdriver through the back of a man's hand. I also couldn't remember ever seeing a spot of sweat or dirt on his shirt. His boots had the flat blackness of well-worn leather and were always clean.

Twenty years back, when he'd approached me to offer his services shortly after my first troubles, he was already gray-haired and leather skinned. At that time I would have put him between seventy and eighty. I still would've put him between seventy and eighty when I'd last seen him eight years ago. I would put him between seventy and eighty now as he sat in my office. He was a medium-sized man, about five ten and no more than 175 pounds. He had soft blue eyes and a fat red scar that descended from the bottom of each eye, tracing the trail that tears would fall if he cried. He'd never explained the scars to me and I'd never seen him cry.

Except for the clothes and scars, you could find men who looked like him helping themselves to extra servings of pudding in retirement home cafeteria lines. His age and size caused many men who were twice as big and a third as old to underestimate him. He was the strongest, meanest man I'd ever met. He took bigger, younger men apart with his bare hands or, if he was feeling lazy, a fishing knife – the same knife he used to fillet the mullets he caught illegally with a cast net from a riverside retaining wall.

If you asked him a question he didn't want to answer, which was most questions, he would talk in circles. He would say, 'At my age I've got nothing to lose.' So I would ask, 'How old are you, Charles?' He would answer, 'Old enough I've got nothing to lose.' Or I would ask, 'Where'd you get so mean?' He would say, 'In the war.' I would ask, 'What war?' He would say, *'The* war.' *'The* war is World War Two,' I would say, 'and you may be old but you're too young for that.' He would shake his head and answer, 'Every war is *the* war to those who were there.' So I would ask again, 'Which were you in?' Without a smile, he would answer, *'The* war.' Most of the time I remembered not to ask unnecessary questions.

31

He winked at me as I stepped into the office, his way of saying I was late.

'How you doing, Charles?' I said.

'How'm I ever doing?'

'Right.'

'So Belinda Mabry's dead,' he said.

'She is,' I said.

'And Daniel Turner asked you to identify her. A hell of a thing to do.'

'Yes.'

'And you didn't kill her?'

'I wish you wouldn't say that.'

'I've got to ask, that's all, so I know what this is.'

'You already seem to have all the information,' I said. 'You should know I didn't kill her.'

'No,' he agreed, 'you didn't.'

'No.'

'Because I suspect you would've called me to help if you had.'

'I didn't even know she was back in town,' I said.

He eyed me up and down. 'You going to give me that Pepsi and sit down or you going to stand there icing your hand?'

I tossed the Pepsi to him, dropped the bag of Doritos on the desk and sat. Slats of sunlight shined through the window blind like heat from a vent.

Charles twisted the cap off the Pepsi and said, 'So what d'you want to do about it?'

'I don't know for sure. I guess I want to get the guy.'

'You guess?'

'Yeah, for now.'

He raised his eyebrows. 'You're going to have to do better'n that. A guy who does what he's done to Belinda is a messed-up individual. If you're only *guessing* you want to get him, he's going to get you instead. You know that without my telling you.'

'All right. I'm not guessing. I want him,' I said.

'That's more like it. Any thoughts about where to start?'

'Sure. Work backward to the killer from the victims. Belinda. The police have her driver's license and know where she lives. Daniel Turner won't tell me though.'

'When you last saw her, twenty-five years ago, where was she headed?' he asked.

'North to Chicago. Whole family went.'

'Because of you and her.'

'That was part of it,' I said.

He nodded. 'So we find out where she was staying since she came back and how long, and we make a visit. What do you know about the other dead girls?'

'Just what they said on TV. That plus the killer leaves the bodies in the same position, lying on their backs naked with their ankles tied over their heads. And he has a clean fetish. Washes their clothes and stacks them neatly by the bodies.'

'We'll stake out the local dry cleaners.' He didn't smile when he was being sarcastic so I never knew for sure. He reached to the floor and brought up a black leather bag, removed a Hi-Point nine-millimeter pistol and gave it to me. 'Disposable, in case you need it.'

'I'd prefer to get the guy alive,' I said.

'Yeah, right. I've loaded it with eight plus one. If you can't take him down with that I figure you'll be dead already.'

I shook my head and handed the pistol back to him. 'You know I don't like guns.'

He smiled with bleach-white teeth and cocked his head to the side. 'You're insane is what you are.' He put the gun back in the bag and took his feet off the desk. 'I'll get Belinda's address,' he said. 'You see what you can do about the other two.'

We got up.

'How's your wife?' he said. 'Still sleeping in the sunroom?'

'That's a private matter, Charles.'

'There's no such thing as private. There's only what's known and what can be known. How about the kid?'

'Thomas is fifteen,' I said. 'He's angry with the world.'

'Better'n him letting the world roll over him.'

'He's mostly angry at me.'

'Better'n him letting *you* roll over him.'

'He draws pornographic comic books,' I said.

'That's not good.'

'Maybe he can make a living from it,' I said.

'He's fifteen. Give him time.'

'What were you doing at fifteen?'

34

'I'm unusual,' he said.

Charles wasn't quite a private investigator. At least he didn't have a state license to be one. I'd checked. He also had no other full-time job. He called himself retired and said he'd moved south because he'd heard the fishing was good. But when I'd spent time with him, he would sometimes disappear for weeks and on occasion he'd come back with a fresh wound that needed healing. He got paid well for his work. I'd paid him too though he'd tried to refuse. He'd said he recognized in me a fellow spirit and that worried me more than a little.

'Yeah,' I said. 'You're unusual.'

THREE

In this town if you wake up on a bright, hot summer morning with the need for a white girl, you can find what you desire on a stretch of Philips Highway that runs past strip clubs, auto body shops and cheap motels. Starting around nine in the morning, girls wander alongside the highway like they're looking for a bus stop and the last of them don't leave till three a.m. when their pimps pick them up for the ride home or the industrial park by the airport.

It wasn't yet noon and the sheriff had said on TV that Ashley Littleton was white, so I cruised

Philips Highway looking for a long-timer who might've known her. A young heavy blonde in faded black Lycra pants and a long white T-shirt walked along the shoulder with uneven steps as though something was wrong with one of her legs. A skinny man in jeans and a black sleeveless T-shirt walked fifty yards or so behind her. Maybe he was her pimp, maybe a friend who'd agreed to keep an eye on her, maybe a customer who was biding his time until she agreed to do him for the ten or twenty bucks he carried in his pocket. Half a mile farther a woman walked alone. Her hair was black, a dye-job, and her face was pretty. Too pretty. Probably a cop working vice. After the intersection at Emerson two more blondes stood talking on the roadside. One of them, wearing a shimmering short blue dress, had a face scarred from acne or something worse and a left eye that drooped. The other, in jeans and a sports bra, had the sallow cheeks of an addict. I slowed to the side.

The one with the blue dress and pocked face looked north and south and when she saw nothing that worried her she wandered over to my passenger-side window and leaned her head down.

'Hey, BB,' she said, then opened the door and climbed in. A pinpoint of sunlight reflected off the passenger-side rearview mirror and shone on her blue dress like a metal instrument that could sear a hole.

I drove south.

'How've you been?' the girl asked.

36

I didn't answer.

I pulled into an abandoned Chevy dealership. My dad had bought a car there when I was a kid, a gleaming burgundy Monte Carlo with a black vinyl roof, and I remembered walking through the showroom stroking my fingers across the high-polished hoods and breathing the smell of new carpet and automobile upholstery. Now beer cans, crushed Styrofoam cups and ripped cardboard boxes littered the concrete lot behind the main building.

'How's your wife?' the girl said.

'Don't be mean, Aggie.' I pulled into the shade of the building and cut the ignition. Above, sparrows darted in and out of a nest they'd built between the wall and a drainpipe.

'OK,' she said. 'Fifty bucks if you want it in the backseat. That's ten bucks cheaper than it used to be but I'm not getting younger.' She looked hard at me. 'Neither are you, BB. You OK?' She had a way of talking too fast, one word tailing into the next. At first you might mistake the habit for the effects of coke or meth but it was just her way.

'I don't want sex.'

'Then you're sure as hell not OK. Take me back where you got me.'

'You know a girl named Ashley Littleton?' I asked. 'She might've hooked along here?'

'Oh, shit, BB. The cops've been asking about her. She never hooked this strip, not that I know of. What d'you want with her?'

'You know about her though?'

37

'I know the cops said she's dead. And I know what everyone else is saying. The man that did it was fucked-up violent. I'll tell you what I say every time I hear that. Every man I've ever known was fucked up, including you, BB, and half of them were violent. So what am I supposed to do with that information?'

'Get off the street,' I said. 'Meet nicer guys. What else are people saying? Where did she hook?'

'Some say over by the arena. Why d'you want to know?'

'That's black. Ashley Littleton was white.'

'Don't tell me. I didn't make her work there,' she said.

'You hear about the other girl? Tonya Richmond?'

'Yeah, met her once or twice. She was nice but tough. The sonofabitch that killed her had to hit her with something bigger'n a knife. I once saw a guy tell her he wasn't going to pay her and she took that boy apart. Had to carry him away in an ambulance.' She eyed me nervously. 'You sure you don't want anything? I can use my hand.'

I shook my head. 'No, thanks.'

'You going to pay me?'

'Yeah, I'll pay. What else did the police say?'

She smiled like she was unsure about taking money for nothing. 'They wanted to know who I'd seen Tonya with. But she didn't hang out here much. She mostly hung at the arena too. And they showed me a picture of a green SUV

38

and asked if I'd seen Tonya get into a car that looked like it.'

'Had you?'

'Uh uh.'

'Did they tell you what the driver looked like?' I asked.

'Not after I said I hadn't seen the car.'

I sat back and thought.

'Why's this matter to you, BB?'

I ignored the question. 'What was Tonya known for? Did she do more than the other girls? Anything special?'

'Depends how much you paid her, I suppose.'

'Bondage? S and M?'

'Tough to do when you're working on the street. But if a guy had a room and would pay for it, sure, why not?' She looked at me hard. 'You're not getting off on this, are you, BB?'

'How about the other one, Ashley Littleton? Did she do anything special?'

'Look, BB, no one hooks on the street if she's got choices. Either she's got a face like mine or a habit so bad that the clubs and services won't hire her. What d'you have to do with this?'

'I don't like what this guy's doing,' I said.

'No one does. But what do you get out of it? Why you?'

'Why not?' I pulled out my wallet and gave her two twenties and a ten. 'I'll give you a ride back.'

As I turned the key in the ignition, I heard another car crunch over the pavement, its engine just above idle. In the rearview mirror, a police cruiser flipped on its cherry lights.

I cut the engine.

The cruiser pulled at an angle against my back bumper and two officers in short-sleeved uniforms got out with their service pistols drawn. They looked in their mid-twenties and both had short black hair and wore sunglasses.

They stopped a few steps from our doors and the driver said, 'Get out of the car and keep your hands where we can see them.'

'Fuck,' Aggie said and we got out.

'Turn and put your hands on the car roof,' the driver said.

He and his partner felt us for guns, knives, or other weapons. Aggie and I locked eyes, hers twitching as the officer frisking her ran his hands up the inside of her legs and stopped where her panties should have been.

'Driver's license,' the cop on my side said when he was done. He smelled of sour sweat. I gave him my license and he climbed inside the cruiser and got on the radio.

His partner said to the girl, 'I recognize you.'

'Yeah, you too,' she said. 'You like it between the tits, right?'

'Shut up,' he said and squeezed her so she hurt. He glanced at me. 'You shut up too.'

I smiled at him.

'You're a pervert,' he said. Then to Aggie, who still had her hands on the car roof, clutching my fifty dollars, he added, 'Stay like you are.' He went to the cruiser and got in next to the driver.

40

We stood in the midday sun, no sound except the hum of the police engine, the whoosh of traffic on the other side of the Chevy dealership and the occasional flutter of wings as sparrows flew past. After a few minutes the officers got out of their cruiser together.

The driver came to me and handed me my license. 'What were the two of you doing back here, Mr Byrd?' he said, as if he already knew the answer.

'We needed a private place to talk.'

He shook his head and gestured at Aggie. 'You usually pay a whore cash money to talk with you?'

'Depends on what we talk about.'

His partner said, 'You're a smart ass, Mr Byrd.'

'Just telling you what it was.'

The driver said, 'I'll tell you what it is. Next time we find you back here with or without a girl we run you in to the station. You can explain that to your wife and your friends at church.'

'But this time you're letting me go?'

He nodded. 'Get out of here.'

I shrugged. 'Get in,' I said to Aggie.

'Uh uh,' said the other officer. 'She goes with us.'

'I don't think so,' I said, but she was already moving toward their car.

The officer said, 'It doesn't matter what you think, Mr Byrd. She goes with us.'

I stepped toward him but Aggie looked at me,

41

pleading. 'I want to go with them, BB.' Then with a little smile, she said, 'I don't have a lot of choices.'

The driver opened the back door to the cruiser for her.

She started to climb in but turned to me. 'The guy you're looking for is bad, BB. Worse than you think. Leave it alone.'

I looked at her. 'Do you know who it is?'

She clasped my money and climbed into the backseat. The cop who'd frisked her climbed in with her and shut the door. The driver leaned against the cruiser and said, 'It's time you got moving, Mr Byrd.'

I went north on Philips, the air quivering and thinning above the hot pavement the way plastic film does above a flame before catching fire and melting away. The Hart Bridge, leading over the river to the arena, looked like it was made of blue matchsticks. I wondered if Aggie had meant only to tell me the obvious, that the person who'd killed Ashley Littleton, Tonya Richmond and Belinda was dangerous, or if she knew more than she'd let on.

I drove behind the arena to Bridier Street and parked across from an empty parking lot and a pink two-room bungalow with boarded-up windows. Knee-high weeds and dying palm trees lined both sides of the street. Halfway up the block a man sat smoking a cigarette on a concrete wall. No one else was out.

I leaned against my car, waiting. I knew that eyes were watching. In this neighborhood someone was always watching. A few minutes passed and the screen door on the pink bungalow swung open, showing a shadow as dark as the inside of a man's throat. A light-skinned black woman stepped on to the front porch, looked up and down the street and headed my way. She wore black high-heeled platform sandals, tight black shorts and a striped, strapless halter top. She had a short afro, a round, childish face, and a bruise above her left knee so big and dark I could see it from across the street.

She came to me, stood close and said, 'Hey.' Her eyes were glazed with something that looked like desire but wasn't.

'Hey,' I said.

She nodded at the bungalow. 'I got a room and a bed and I don't give a fuck what you do to me.'

'What's your name?' I asked.

She smiled at me with the whitest teeth I'd ever seen. 'Call me whatever you want.'

'I want to call you by your name.'

She didn't like that so well. 'Then call me Evelyn.'

'OK, Evelyn, I've got a couple questions—'

'Uh uh,' she said and her smile was gone. 'You want to fuck me and pay me, I'll talk to you while we're fucking. But I ain't gonna stand here talking in the hot sun.'

'You know someone called Tonya Richmond or maybe a white girl called Ashley Littleton? You ever hear of a woman named Belinda Mabry?'

'Fuck off,' she said and turned toward the pink house.

I grabbed a wrist. 'These women are dead. They—'

A big, dark-skinned black man barreled through the screen door of the house. I let go of the hooker's wrist but too late. She screamed as though I'd broken her hand, and the man kept coming.

He pointed at the house and shouted at the girl, 'Get inside!'

Before I could climb into my car the man was in front of me. His head was clean-shaven, perspiration beaded on his scalp, and a long scar reached upward from his left ear as if someone had tried to crack him like an egg. He wore long yellow nylon shorts that hung low off his hips, yellow gym shoes and a black T-shirt.

He stood close to me, chest to chest. 'What you do, you touch her like that?' He had a Caribbean lilt. I stepped backward and he came after me, jabbing my chest with his forefinger. 'I cut your throat you touch her like that.' I was a couple of inches taller but he had thirty or forty pounds of muscle on me.

I stopped backing away. 'Would you have cut my throat if I'd walked inside the house with Evelyn?' I asked.

He looked momentarily surprised either that I'd called him on his game or that I'd said the hooker's name. 'Ain't none your business what I do. Nobody grab what's mine.'

'You watch TV this morning?' I said.

'Huh?'

'Did you watch TV this morning? The sheriff was on. He said that someone's been killing girls like Evelyn. Two at least, maybe three.'

He looked at me with interest for the first time. 'What that got to do with me?'

'I'm looking for the killer.'

He eyed me like I might be crazy. 'And who you s'posed to be?'

'I'm just a man.'

He laughed derisively. '"Just a man." You a fucking fool, is what you are. You get back in your Lexus and drive home to your family. "Just a man." Jesus!'

He turned toward the pink house. I apparently wasn't worth his anger.

I stepped after him, kicked hard and his feet flew out from under him. He fell to the street. When he tried to get up, I kicked his head. He went down again, rolled over and stared at the sky. His sweaty forehead was smeared with dirt and dust. Blood trickled from his bottom lip.

After a moment his eyes found mine. 'What's the matter with you?' he said. 'You crazy?'

'Yep, I'm crazy.' I kicked his ribs, kicked his head.

He covered his face with his hands and yelled, 'All right! What you want?'

My foot connected.

'Jesus!'

I stooped low to him, looked up and down the street. The man who'd been sitting on the con-

45

crete wall was gone, probably calling 911. If not him, the girl inside the pink house was. I had a couple of minutes, no more. 'Two girls disappeared in the last month,' I said. 'At least one of them was working in this neighborhood. That's Ashley Littleton. A white girl. The other one was black. Tonya Richmond. Last night another woman got killed. Her name was Belinda Mabry and she was a friend of mine. A good friend. I don't know if she was hooking. I don't know what she was doing. But she's dead and, as you say, it's made me crazy. The police think the man who killed my friend also killed the other two. I want to know who did it.'

He moved his tongue around the inside of his mouth as if checking for loose or broken teeth. He spit blood and saliva on to the pavement. 'I know Ashley. She was a sad girl, always looking for something.'

'Who was her pimp?'

'Nah, I can't tell you that. I tell you and that man come looking for me. I'm small time. I got Evelyn and her sister. Bread and potatoes. I don't fuck with big-time guys.'

I cocked my fist above his face. 'I want the man's name.'

He shook his head. 'Go ahead, get it over with. Anything you do's no worse than what he do to me he find out I tell you his name.'

I relaxed my fist. 'A big-time guy was running a broken-down whore like Ashley Littleton?'

'She wasn't always broke down. Till about

46

three months ago, she did escort. Private parties. Weekends in Nassau. But then she started with the drugs and the drugs started fucking with her head and she was on the street like the rest of us, except she was prettier than most and sometimes her man still pick her up for a special gig with his friends or paying customers.'

'What do you know about Tonya Richmond?' I asked.

'Never met her. Word is she was new to the street. Don't know what she did before and don't care.'

'Belinda Mabry?'

'Never heard of her neither.'

He said it too fast and I wondered if he was lying and if he was, why, but sirens were approaching from the distance, so I said, 'What do you know about the guy who's killing them?'

'Rumors. Just rumors.'

'Like?'

'Like the man drive a green Mercedes SUV. Like he do some nasty thing to the girls after he kill them. Sick things.'

The sirens were a couple of blocks away. I stood and opened the door to my car.

'What else?' I asked.

'That's all I know. Maybe I don't even know that.'

I slid into the front seat.

'Hey,' he said looking at me from the pavement.

47

'Yeah?'

'Next time you come here I cut your throat.' Blood between his teeth, he grinned at me.

FOUR

On July afternoons the air gets heavy and electric, the blue sky darkens from the west, and lightning storms split the tedious peace. Thunder shakes the roof and your heart skips a beat though you've sat through a thousand storms like this over the years. Raindrops the size of nickels hit the pavement. Steam rises. After a half hour or an hour the clouds break and the sun shines again and the air is cool and the ozone smells sweeter than springtime. You can stand outside your front door and suck the sweetness into your lungs and it will make you happy for a while. Then the water evaporates in the heat and the world begins to bake again.

The rain started falling while I was standing in the open service bay at my Shell station. Wind whipped the dampness through the opening and softened the heavy guitar music that the kid I'd hired to change oil and tires played on the garage stereo whether he was working or inside flirting with the cash register girl. I'd told him three times that I didn't like the music and when he'd ignored me I'd stopped telling him.

Lightning flared above the strip mall across the street and a blast of thunder shook the air. My heart leapt. The girl inside at the register laughed. I let myself smile.

My first time with Belinda, a hard summer rain had fallen. We'd snuck from our houses, met in a park by the water purification plant, and were walking on a woodchip path between a circular brick building and a stand of scrub pines. She'd worn a brown cotton dress with a print of something on the front, a flower maybe, maybe a bird. Before the rain she'd carried a closed umbrella and as we walked our hands never brushed, our skin never touched. We were afraid to touch when we were out of doors in the daylight, even on a deserted path between a windowless brick wall and trees that fell away into swamp. Walking together was enough. It was for me.

A sudden wind had broken the still air and the rain had come hard. Belinda opened the umbrella and it blew back in the wind and when she straightened it, it wasn't big enough to cover us both. We ran for the brick wall as if it could shelter us and we huddled under the umbrella as best we could. She turned to me. Her eyes were large, black, almost as wet as tears. We kissed and I pulled away.

Touch was dangerous.

She whispered, 'Fuck 'em if they can't take a joke.'

She pushed me against the brick wall and came to me. She was half my size and twice my

49

strength. She slid a hand into the top of my jeans and a desire unlike any I'd ever known consumed me like an open mouth. I took her against the wet brick wall and the rain flew sideways against us and stung our bare skin.

A '95 Dodge Charger pulled into the Shell station, rainwater slicking off its back tires. The car was red with a wide gray stripe extending from front to rear. Ten years ago a man had dropped off the car for a tune-up and new set of tires and had never returned to get it. I ducked through the rain and climbed into the passenger seat. Charles shifted into drive and touched the accelerator.

I peered through the rain-smeared windshield. I said, 'With that hood stripe, I feel like I'm riding in a skunk.'

'Not my fault,' he said. 'You sold me the car.'

'If I remember, I gave it to you.'

'Same thing. Nothing in life comes free.'

'Mmm,' I said. 'Where was she living?'

'Big fancy house on the Intracoastal.'

'She had money?'

'Apparently.'

'So she wasn't hooking?' I asked.

'I don't know what she was doing. But if she was hooking she was doing it for the kink. From what they tell me she and her husband had a live-in cook, a gardener and a thirty-eight-foot Fairline tied to the dock behind the house.'

I knew better than to ask who told him this.

'She was married?'

'Was,' he said. 'Man named Jerry Stilman. Married fourteen years ago, then eighteen months ago he had a heart attack. He was a big man. Had a big heart attack.' Charles cut the steering wheel and we merged on to the highway toward the beach. 'What did you find out?' he asked.

'The guy who's doing this might be driving a green Mercedes SUV. The hookers and pimps I talked to might know who he is but if they do they're scared.'

'Might, might, might.'

'No one was very happy to talk with me.'

'Hmm,' he said and I knew that for Charles, a person's unwillingness to talk was no excuse for not getting the facts.

We drove past wetland pinewoods, highway-side developments with matching houses and community pools, a shopping center and more wetlands. A long low concrete bridge rose over the Intracoastal Waterway, a slow saltwater river ebbing and flowing around marsh-grass islands and stands of marsh trees. The rain eased as we came off the bridge, took the first exit and drove south on a well-groomed, tree-lined street past stucco houses built on a single architectural plan, then more stucco houses built on another architectural plan.

The developments gave way to single-design mansions constructed on roads named after sea-birds. Charles cut the wheel and we turned on to Great Egret Way, a short dead-end street sided

51

by a canal that extended through the marsh to the waterway.

The last house on the street was a peach-colored two-story stucco with terracotta tiles on the roof and balconies on both sides of a dark-wood grand front door. A long, straight, neatly raked gravel path, sided by flowering plumbago bushes, cut to the front steps across a sweeping front lawn. A pair of young live oaks grew on each side of the path.

We pulled up the driveway and parked outside a triple garage. The yard and house had the look of a place maintained for absent owners. The lawn was cut short and the beds were weeded and blooming but there were no cars on the driveway, no toys or outdoor furniture on the lawn, no flag in the bracket by the front door, no mat on the doorstep, no sign of the living. I pushed the doorbell and listened to the chime echo through the house.

A light-skinned black man in his mid-twenties opened the door. He wore khakis, a pink golf shirt and no shoes. 'May I help you?' he asked, his voice soft.

Charles said, 'You the cook or you the gardener?'

'Neither,' the man said. 'Who are you?'

A voice from deep in the house called, 'Who is it, Terrence?'

I recognized the voice though I hadn't heard it in twenty-five years. Belinda's brother, Bobby. I called past the man who'd opened the door, 'Bobby, it's William Byrd.'

Bobby Mabry emerged from behind the man he'd called Terrence, put an intimate hand on his back and said, 'I'll take care of this.' Terrence eyed me and Charles, and disappeared into the house.

Bobby stepped into the door in white shorts and a white T-shirt. His Nikes had never touched dust or dirt. 'What do you want?' he asked. He was a small man but lithe and strong with a scalp shaved close and a short neat beard. He wore a gold cross stud in one ear and a thin gold chain around his neck.

I reached a hand to shake his, but he ignored the gesture. I said, 'Still mad after all this time? Takes too much energy to stay angry so long.'

He shrugged.

'I heard about Belinda,' I said, and his anger seemed to break.

'Yeah, the police left an hour ago. I need to...' He broke off, seemingly uncertain what he needed to do.

'You going to invite us in?' I asked.

Bobby looked at Charles, his eyes fixed on the tear-trail scars. 'What happened to you?'

'Long story,' said Charles.

'Looks like you cry acid. Me too, today,' Bobby said, and turned to me. 'What the hell, come on in.'

The foyer rose to a large pewter chandelier and a vaulted ceiling above. A black marble floor surrounded a three-tiered marble fountain. A broad stairway wrapped around the back wall. Bobby led us to the living room, which

53

faced through large windows across a pool patio, down a sloping backyard and to a private dock and the Fairline motor cruiser. The living-room sofas and a pair of upholstered chairs were white. So was the carpet. Framed prints hung on the wall – colorful scenes of a jazz club, a dance floor, a northern city street.

'Sit down,' Bobby said, and I took one of the sofas. Charles went to the window and stared at the drizzle and gray sky. Bobby sat across from me. 'What do you want, BB?'

'I didn't know Belinda was back in town. Until I heard today...'

'Yeah, the detective said you identified her. I suppose I should thank you.'

'Unnecessary,' I said.

'So what do you want?'

I didn't know exactly. 'You've been living here with her?'

He nodded. 'Since her husband died.'

'And the man who opened the door?' I asked.

The faintest smile crossed his lips. 'Sure, him too. A happy little family, except Belinda was kind of broke up since Jerry died. But losing men always did that to her. Me too. You remember that.'

I let that pass. 'What did she do all these years?'

'After you fucked us up?' he said.

'I'm not here to fight with you, Bobby. I loved her. You know that.'

'Took her a long time to get herself back together.'

'After she did, it looks as if she did all right for herself.'

'She did OK.'

'What did she do to get all this?' I asked.

'Real estate mostly. Chicago's South Loop. They bought when it was black and sold as it was turning white. Lot of things have changed in this country but not the color of property.'

The man who'd opened the front door came into the room, eating yogurt from a plastic container. He sat in a chair, his legs tucked under him.

'What did she do for all these years?' I asked again.

'Nothing unusual,' Bobby said. 'Finished high school, went to college. She started law school but she dropped out. Unlike you, she lived a quiet life.'

'What do you know about how I've lived?'

He shook his head. 'You don't think our family kept an eye on you? Especially for the first ten years or so. Since then we tried to forget you. But you've had a way of popping up just when we've thought we were rid of you.'

'Like the undead,' Charles said as if he were talking to the window.

'Return of the repressed,' said the man with the yogurt.

Bobby put his hands behind his head and stretched. 'So after she dropped out of law school, she got involved in grassroots politics in Chicago, feeding the inner city, community organizing. That lasted until she met Jerry. The rest you know. They bought property and sold it. They made money.'

'They have any children together?'

'Belinda and Jerry? Nah. I think Jerry had a problem. Not something they were comfortable talking about.'

'What brought them back here?' I asked.

'Tired of the north? Our mom died seven years ago, our dad five.'

Nothing he'd told me gave me a clue about why Belinda had gotten killed alongside two bottom-rung hookers. She'd lived a straight life if Bobby was telling the truth, a life with a couple of lows and some good highs, like the lives of most of us.

Bobby said, 'You still haven't told me what you want.'

'Is there going to be a funeral?' I asked.

'Yeah, there's going to be a funeral. What do you want?'

'Why would someone kill her?'

'I don't know,' he said. 'What else?'

I sighed. 'I want to get the asshole who did it.'

Bobby shook his head and lowered his eyes as if he'd known the answer all along. 'Fuck you, BB.'

'What?'

'Fuck you. You didn't do her any good when she was alive. What good d'you think you're going to do her now?'

I didn't think I would do her any good. I thought I could do this for myself. 'I'd like to help.'

'You can't help her,' he said. 'Maybe a long time ago you could've. No one needs your help now.'

'I'm going to get whoever killed her,' I said.

He stood and said, 'Get out of this house.'

He said it calmly but I knew the skin on Charles' neck had tightened. I could feel it from across the room. I stood and offered Bobby my hand again, and again he refused to shake it. 'Good to see you, Bobby,' I said.

The man on the white chair ate his yogurt as Bobby led Charles and me to the front door.

Outside on the front step, Charles turned and faced Bobby. 'Was your sister whoring down-town?'

Bobby's eyes lit up with anger.

'Charles,' I said.

'Someone had to ask it.' He sounded disgusted. 'Hell if you were going to.' He looked at Bobby again. 'Was she?'

Bobby looked for a moment like he might attack Charles. But he saw something fearsome in Charles' eyes and scarred face. He turned to me. 'Thanks for coming by, BB. But don't come again, OK?'

We walked toward the car. 'Well, that was a waste of time,' Charles said.

'What? You would've beaten information out of a grieving brother?'

'Good to hit them when they're already soft,' he said. 'Anyway he didn't look like he was grieving too much.'

The rain had stopped and the sun had broken

57

through a cleft in the clouds. The gray was a tattered fabric, with holes and fissures showing blue sky. Steam rose from the asphalt driveway and odd spots on the lawn. Rainwater dripped from the eaves of the house.

Terrence, the yogurt-eating man who'd opened the front door, leaned against the hood of Charles' car.

Charles said, 'Get off it.'

The man stayed where he was. 'She wasn't hooking.'

'Off,' Charles said and headed for the car but I stopped him with a hand on his shoulder. As far as I knew, Terrence was only Bobby's plaything and his words meant nothing, but a weight on my chest lifted.

'How do you know?' I asked.

'The first year after Jerry died she never went out. In the last six months she started dating again. Some nights she stayed over with the men but mostly she came home.'

I looked at him closely. There was something in his face I didn't trust. 'How long've you and Bobby been together?'

A smile curled on his lips. 'I've known him my whole life.'

'You're living together with him here?'

'I'm living here, yes. It's my house.'

'I don't understand.'

'My name's Terrence Stilman.'

I squinted at him. 'You're their son?'

He shook his head. 'Belinda's.'

'But Bobby said—'

'Jerry wasn't my father,' he said. 'I took his name when my mom married him.'

I felt dizzy. 'How old are you, Terrence?'

He smiled. 'Twenty-four.'

As I did the math, Charles laughed. It was a dirty laugh. 'Jesus Christ, BB. Somebody give me a cigar.'

Terrence said, 'You didn't know about me?'

My head spun. 'Belinda didn't ... Why didn't you get in touch with me?'

'She said you were gone. Out of it.'

I stepped toward him. 'No, I was never gone.'

He slid off the car and stood facing me. He was seven or eight inches shorter than I was and stood with his shoulders squared as though he were preparing for pain.

'I was never gone,' I said again.

He frowned and threw a wild punch. His hand connected with the side of my cheek and I felt blood rise in my skin. His eyes looked scared – of me or of what he'd done to me, I didn't know which. I backed away and he slid off to the side. Charles moved into his path, started toward him.

'No,' I said. 'Leave him alone.' I put a hand to my cheek and brought blood away from the split skin. 'Why'd you do that?' I asked him but once he'd cleared Charles he ran toward the house. By the time the front door slammed, Charles had climbed into the driver's seat.

I climbed in beside him. 'Don't bleed on the upholstery,' he said.

We went out the same way we'd come in, the

59

sun shining through the leaves and glimmering on the wet pavement. The skin under my right eye was swelling and my head pounded. The punch hadn't been enough to make my head ache. But Terrence's words had. I tried to get my mind around them. He looked like Belinda but I saw nothing of myself in him. The idea that he was my child seemed like a joke or a trick. I was *gone*, he said. *Out of it*. Out of what? Out of everything and he didn't want me in. I understood his anger. But I couldn't see him as my child. It seemed too much and my head hurt to think about it.

Charles drove with his eyes straight ahead on the road. 'So you going to tell me?'

I said, 'What's to tell?'

'What happened between you and Belinda that got her family so pissed off at you?'

FIVE

The first rock went through the Mabrys' window three weeks before they moved in. My friend Christopher threw it. I handed it to him. As the window shattered I felt a release as though the world's tension had been locked inside the frozen pane and the breaking allowed me to breathe. It was the summer before our senior year in high school and Christopher had taken to sneaking out at one in the morning and breaking into cars and houses if he knew that the owners were away. Some nights I snuck out with him but I stood on the sidewalk while he rifled an automobile console for change and cassette tapes or I hid in the shadows while he broke into the darkness of an empty house. I was a coward then and at heart I always will be.

As soon as the Mabrys bought the house, word had spread in the neighborhood that a black family was coming and Christopher and I started our petty vandalisms. It wasn't just that the Mabrys were black. It was that they were from Milwaukee and new in a neighborhood where homes had generally passed from one generation to the next for a hundred years or more. The night after we learned that they'd bought the place, Christopher and I blew up their mailbox with M-80s. We'd heard that four of them equaled a stick of dynamite but that seemed a bit much so Christopher taped two together and I lit the fuse.

On the day that the Mabrys moved in we stood across the street with rocks in our hands. But we didn't throw them. Belinda climbed out of the car first and looked across at us. The rock fell from Christopher's hand. I gripped mine tighter.

'Oooeee,' Christopher whispered. 'I'm going to nail *that* girl.'

We crossed the street as Belinda's parents and her brother Bobby got out.

Christopher went straight to Mr Mabry and

61

shook his hand. 'Welcome to the neighborhood,' he said.

I stood in front of Belinda and made the only sound I could bring to my tongue. 'Hi.'

That was the first time I saw the little tight-lipped smile that rose on one side of her mouth and told me this girl owned the world and everything in it. Twenty-five years later I still saw that smile in my dreams. She said, 'You've got a rock in your hand.'

I looked at my hand, surprised to see the rock there. I held it to her. 'You want it?'

Her smile broke into a full grin. 'No, I don't want your rock.' She turned and walked to the house.

Her father, who'd moved his family south when Allstate Insurance transferred him, watched Christopher and me with a mix of confusion and appreciation as we carried suitcases from the back of the station wagon to his family's front porch. His wife caught his eye once or twice with a look that said, *See, it's going to be all right*. They'd replaced the broken windows before moving in but they still needed a new mailbox and the spray paint on the driveway wouldn't come off until they sandblasted it.

Christopher started working on Belinda right off. He all but stood under her window singing love songs with a steel guitar. He'd hang out on her front porch flirting with her in the morning and go back for more after dinner. In the middle of the day he'd find me and tell me again, 'I'm

62

going to nail that girl,' though when I asked about his progress he had none to report. He tried to convince her to sneak out with him in the middle of the night but she made excuses, mostly involving her father who may have been an insurance man but was big enough to break her neck if she ever tried something like that and had told her so. Now and then I would go with Christopher and stand on the porch with him and Belinda. She would look at me and laugh and say, 'When're you going to bring me another rock?'

One night early in August she agreed to sneak out to meet Christopher. That afternoon I went with him to Walgreens to buy a box of Trojans.

'You even kissed her yet?' I asked outside the store.

He looked at me like the jerk I was. 'I'm not interested in kissing,' he said.

'What makes you think *she's* interested in even doing that?'

'Why would she sneak out with me if she isn't?'

He had a point but I quietly decided I would sneak out that night too.

A family two doors up from the Mabrys had a screened-in poolside cabana that they used for barbeque parties on evenings when the mosquitoes were bad. Inside were two thickly cushioned reclining deck chairs that could be lowered, pushed together and made into a bed. Christopher decided that was where he would take Belinda, and I slipped in with him when the sun set and helped him fix the chairs and watched him put the condoms in a cabinet that the family used for candles and bug spray.

I said good luck and goodnight and I ran home through the backyards. My feet and legs never had felt so light and strong and never have since. The moon was half full and rising, the sky was clear, the heat of the day was gone and the grass had a smell like urgency. I felt happy. I didn't know why but I did, as if I knew in my bones and muscles that something was about to happen that would change my life forever.

A little after midnight I returned to the cabana and hid in the shadows of a camphor tree which was the kind of place where I seemed to spend most of my time when I snuck out at night with Christopher. In my hand I held a rock the size of a split brick.

At one o'clock I heard voices. Christopher and Belinda were coming, holding hands, talking in whispers though no one but me was awake to hear. Christopher did most of the talking and Belinda laughed a pitch higher than I'd heard her laugh before. She was nervous, excited.

They went into the cabana and Christopher removed a candle from the cabinet and lit it. He stood and kissed Belinda. It was a kids' kiss, maybe Belinda's first, nervous and awkward, but then it became something else as if they were relearning an old memory. Standing in the cabana Belinda opened her mouth and seemed to give herself to him.

Christopher's hand reached to the bottom of her T-shirt and lifted it up her back and over her head. She removed her bra for him and he kissed her again now on the breasts and she ran her fingers through his hair and raised her face to the top of the cabana. From the shadows I saw the tight-lipped smile that rose on one side of her mouth and it made her look like she had power over all that happened in the night.

Christopher's hands descended to her shorts, caressing, and worked on the front button. Belinda put her own hands on his and pushed them away gently. For a minute he returned to her breasts but then tried the shorts again. She backed away from him and shook her head no. He laughed a quiet, uncertain laugh and stepped after her, pulling her to him, kissing her on the lips and neck. She stood with him until he attempted the shorts again, and she pushed him away and reached to the floor for her bra.

Before she could stand he was on top of her. She struggled and made sounds like a hurt animal and he finally got the shorts button and pulled the shorts off over her legs. He held her down and struggled with his own pants until he had them at his knees and he was ready. But by that time I was coming in behind him through the screen door, stepping quietly, easing the door closed against the latch.

Christopher whispered to Belinda, 'It'll be all right,' and I lifted the rock and brought it down on the back of his head.

He hung in the air above Belinda the way a cut tree does before gravity does its work, and he fell face forward on to the cabana floor. Belinda lay in the soft light of the candle and the half moon shining through the branches of the camphor tree, and she looked at me like I was the strangest, most unexpected creature she'd ever seen. So I showed her what I'd used to knock out Christopher and I said, 'I brought you another rock.'

Christopher never knew what had hit him or if he did he never said. But I took his spot on the Mabrys' front porch and the August days passed in a sweep of heat and haze. Mr Mabry didn't take to me the way he'd taken to Christopher, though. Maybe Christopher had fooled him. Or maybe Mr Mabry saw that when I was with Belinda I meant it, and if a fast-talking kid like Christopher was worth keeping an eye on, a kid who was in love was dangerous. Two weeks after I knocked out Christopher I kissed Belinda for the first time under the humming porch light in front of her house and the next day when I knocked on her door her father answered and said she wasn't available and wouldn't be, so I could stop coming around and bothering her.

We met secretly. She would walk out with Bobby to a park and while Bobby shot baskets or wandered by himself we would disappear into the shadows of a picnic shelter. The Friday before school started we met alone at the water processing plant a half mile from her house and she gave herself to me in the rain. I didn't ask her to. She offered herself and I took her.

The first day of school and every day after, Bobby found trouble. He was skinny and black and the other boys sensed he was gay even if he didn't know it yet and they beat the hell out of him. One afternoon in September the janitor found him in a classroom two hours after school ended and he said he was hiding but they accused him of breaking in and stealing a teacher's money from her desk and they suspended him for two weeks.

Christopher had continued his night-time outings and had mostly stopped coming to school and Belinda told me that during the suspension Bobby had started hanging out with him and a couple of his friends.

When I found Christopher I shoved him and said, 'What are you doing? Bobby's a loser. Don't mess with him.'

Christopher laughed and shoved back. 'Who says I'm messing with him? He's a good kid. I like having him around.'

'Bullshit,' I said.

He gave me a grin that told me something was up but said, 'He's OK. What do you care if I hang around with him? You're busy with Belinda.'

That was true. We'd found a spot in some trees between the water purification plant and the railroad tracks, a clearing where someone had left a sleeping bag and empty beer cans. We cleaned the clearing and spent our afternoons there while Bobby was getting beaten up or breaking into classrooms, and afterward I walked Belinda home along the tracks.

'Leave him alone,' I said to Christopher. 'He's got enough trouble without you.'

He flipped his fuck-you finger in my face and I laughed because what else was I supposed to do?

Christopher had figured out a new trick. There was a strip mall near his house and on Saturday mornings he would stand in the parking lot near a liquor store. Sooner or later someone would come out with a bag, put it in a car and go into the bakery next door. Christopher would be inside the car before the front door of the bakery swung closed and that night we would have a party. Christopher would feed Bobby shots until Bobby was puking in the bushes, passed out on the floor, or dancing naked on the back lawn and we all had a good laugh.

Everything was fine until the Saturday before Halloween. In the morning Christopher had stolen a couple bottles of vodka from the backseat of a BMW. I'd told him I was skipping the party and I'd met Belinda in the clearing after dark. A little before eleven I walked her back along the tracks. When I got home I sat on the front sidewalk unwilling to let the evening end. The night was cool and clear and I felt as happy as I'd ever felt. With the concrete beneath me and the dark all around, the earth seemed a solid enough place to live, a good place, a place where I knew what to do.

I closed my eyes under the stars. Then footsteps, light and fast, startled me. I got to my feet, unsure what was coming, and Belinda crashed into my open arms.

She was crying. In that first moment, I thought her father must've figured out that we were meeting and I felt the same strange mix of fear and release that you get when you realize you've cut yourself and the blood rises through the skin but the pain hasn't yet come.

'It's all right,' I said and I thought I heard in my own voice the adult I would become.

She shook her head, sobbing. 'He's in the hospital.'

'What?'

'My dad took him. Bobby. He was bleeding.'

Her words made me dizzy. 'What happened?' I asked.

Her eyes found mine and even in the darkness they glistened with angry tears. 'They raped him.'

'Bobby? Who did?'

'Christopher and his friends.'

'No,' I said but I felt it was true.

She nodded, her lips twisting. 'He was bleeding.'

I pulled her to my chest and she sobbed. We stood like that for a long time until her breathing slowed and her body relaxed into mine like a child easing toward sleep. I kissed her forehead and she looked up at me, calm.

69

She said, 'Kill him.'
'What? Who?'
'Christopher. Kill him. For me.'

I didn't kill him.

Of course.

Bobby spent a week in the hospital. I don't know what his injuries were and never wanted to know. The hospital kept him isolated from the other kids on his floor – maybe because of the nature of his hurt, maybe because he sometimes lost his head and screamed, or that's what Belinda said. When I visited he was quiet but like someone whose tongue and teeth had been pulled out, not like he had nothing to say. Belinda sat in a chair by his bed looking as if her anger had only grown since she'd found me on the sidewalk.

'Hey, Bobby,' I said.

His eyes flicked to mine and back to the white bed sheet. He had an IV in his arm and his hospital gown was decorated with variously colored teddy bears. The shade on the window was pulled and the fluorescent light gave his skin a greenish hue.

'Sorry ... about this,' I said.

Mr Mabry was standing outside the hospital room talking with a black cop about the same age as him.

'You're going to pursue charges,' the cop said. He was telling, not asking.

'No,' Mr Mabry said, as though he were saying no to the world, no to God, no to the rest of his life.

The cop sounded desperate. This was about more than the rape of one fourteen-year-old black boy. 'The kids that did this ... they're animals...'

'No,' Mr Mabry said again.

Belinda looked at me. She mouthed two words. *Kill him*. Bobby's eyes rose to mine. His eyes questioned me and I knew that Belinda had told him what she'd asked me to do.

I said, 'Take care of yourself, Bobby,' and left the room.

I found Christopher at his house. His mother and father worked and he hadn't told them he'd stopped going to school, so he would leave the house in the morning and circle back once they were gone. He would get high, lift weights, or watch TV until the rest of us came home. He answered the door, wearing exercise shorts and a sweaty T-shirt, his muscles pumped.

He grinned. 'What's up?'

I hit him in the chest and stepped into the front hall. Sun shined through a decorative window above the door and the house was clean and bright and smelled like laundry soap.

'Hey, what's wrong?' he said, backing away.

'You put Bobby in the hospital.'

He shook his head. 'He put himself there. We got drunk and he wiggled his ass at us. What were we supposed to do? If you'd been there you'd've done him too.' I hit him again and he pushed back. 'Don't do that!'

'Bobby's a little kid,' I said.

Christopher looked at me with scorn as though I'd fallen in his eyes. 'He's a faggot nigger. Get out of my house.'

I could've killed him then. My dad had bought a Ruger .22 after a string of robberies at the gas stations, and he kept it loaded on his shelf. I could've gotten it and shot Christopher.

But I did nothing. I went home and stayed there.

When Belinda came back to school I asked her to meet me in our clearing but she didn't come. I went night after night by myself hoping she would come and then one night I brought a Bic lighter and lit the drying grass. I wanted to burn the grove of trees. I wanted her to see the flames from her house. I wanted her to smell the smoke.

But the fire smoldered for ten minutes in the grass and went out.

At the beginning of December the Mabrys put a For Sale sign in front of their house. At school Belinda told me they would be moving north over Christmas vacation.

I said, 'I don't want you to go.'

She looked at me with her one-sided smile and now I saw sadness in it. She said, 'It's not up to you, is it?'

I guessed that was it for us but the afternoon before they moved Belinda knocked at my front door and asked me to walk with her. We went up to the railroad tracks and that afternoon I told her I loved her and she told me she loved me too. That was the last time I saw her alive.

SIX

'That's a bunch of shit,' Charles said and he dropped me off at the Shell station.

I drove home a little after seven. The sky had cleared and the sun had clocked hard to the west. In another hour it would descend into the flat North Florida pine forests as if it meant to incinerate them. Before Thomas was born Susan and I sometimes sat in lawn chairs on the east bank of the river and watched as the sun turned orange and grew huge as it neared the horizon, then dropped under, watched until the sky went black and left us feeling small and helpless except for the little pleasure we could give each other.

I parked behind Susan's Acura and let myself in through the front door. Voices and laughter came from the back of the house. *Damn*, I thought. Susan had told me we would have company. The Lindseys, whoever they were.

I went through to the kitchen and out to the pool deck. Thomas was sitting at the edge of the pool, his legs hanging in the water. Susan sat at the patio table with a couple in their late twenties. Susan and the man had empty margarita glasses, the woman a mostly full glass of water.

He wore loose gray cotton pants, sandals and an untucked blue cotton shirt. His black hair was cut short, he had glasses and had gone a couple of days without shaving. The woman wore a loose, flowery cotton dress and sandals. She was almost pretty, with long, dark, curling hair and a face that was only a little too flat. She looked like she might be a few months pregnant.

They smiled at me and the man stood to shake my hand. 'Michael Lindsey,' he said. 'And my wife, Hannah.' His voice sounded of the north.

We shook hands. 'William Byrd,' I said. 'Sorry I'm late.'

He gave me a nod that forgave everything. 'Susan was explaining the neighborhood to us.'

Susan said, 'They've moved from Michigan. He teaches political science.'

He nodded. 'And Hannah does translations.'

I asked, 'Are you pregnant?'

She exchanged a glance with her husband. 'Four months,' she said.

'It's a great neighborhood to raise kids,' I said. 'I'm going to get a drink. Anyone need a refill?'

Susan and Michael lifted their glasses to me and Hannah said, 'Susan tells us you always keep a pitcher of margaritas in the refrigerator.'

'Not everyone drinks coffee in the morning,' I said, and turned to Thomas. 'D'you want anything?'

He kicked his legs slowly in the water and shook his head.

'Great neighborhood to raise kids,' I said again and went for the drinks.

We grilled salmon on the patio. I said, 'Mom left Dad when I was six years old and moved to Arizona when I was seven.'

The Lindseys listened sympathetically.

'I didn't hear from her until I was thirty, when she started sending Christmas cards. Signature only. No note. I sent her cards too. Signature only. We haven't moved beyond that. I don't know if we ever will. I don't know if I care, though I suspect I do more than I let on to myself.'

Hannah nodded. She'd given up on her glass of water and was sipping from her husband's drink. Thomas stared into the air looking stoned, though unless he'd slipped something into his mouth between bites of salmon, he was just bored. Susan had heard my stories before and continued eating as if I weren't there.

'Dad owned four gas stations. Different brands. Two Exxons, a Shell and an independent. When I graduated from high school he said he didn't want me to follow him into the business. He had aspirations for me if not himself. I didn't feel particularly ambitious either but I went to college because I had no good reason not to. Dad died of a heart attack at the beginning of my sophomore year. I stopped going to class and by January I was home again, sole proprietor of four gas stations and the house where I grew up. I dragged Dad's mattress and bed frame into my room and filled his

75

closet with my clothes. After a year and a half I changed the utility bills to my name. That same year I met Susan and we got married eleven months later.'

Susan reached for her glass, looked annoyed that it was empty and said, 'Would you get more drinks?'

I went to get them but stopped inside the door. Susan spoke quietly. 'None of that's true. You'll hear the stories about BB sooner or later and we might as well be the ones to tell them. BB left college at the beginning of his sophomore year but not because his dad died. In September of that year BB went to a football game. They were playing Rollins College and were supposed to win easily. But Rollins surprised them.

'A group of Rollins kids, including three from Honduras, had come to the game in a van and afterward were celebrating at a bar before driving back. Some of the locals took offense and decided to beat up the Hondurans. The other kids from Rollins watched, and so did the rest of the locals. Then BB stepped into the fight. Five men were attacking the kids and he just took them apart. The Hondurans slipped away but BB didn't stop beating the men until the police pulled him off. One of the men died and another had his neck broken. The police charged BB with homicide but the newspapers and television news publicized the circumstances – one against five, defending the brown-skinned kids – so the District Attorney dropped the case. But that was the end of college.'

'Hmm,' said Michael Lindsey in a way that made me smile.

His wife said to Susan, 'You married him knowing this?'

I stepped outside. 'It's why she married me.'

Susan looked at me. 'The drinks?'

'Ah, the drinks,' I said and went to make them. I stood in the air conditioning under the bright kitchen light, my head lightly stirred by the alcohol, and felt the coldness of the house. Thomas carried in his plate and left it on the counter.

'Hey,' I said softly.

He frowned at me. 'Hey,' he said and headed to his bedroom.

When I returned with the tray Hannah gazed at me with a mix of curiosity and fear and I thought I knew what that kind of look could mean for me if I wanted it to. 'Why wouldn't you tell the truth?' she said.

I said, 'If truth doesn't get you through the day, what good is it?'

'The truth *does* get you through the day,' she said. 'It gets *me* through it.'

'Then you've got easy truths,' I said. 'You want to know mine?'

She looked uncertain. 'I do.'

I took a drink from my glass. 'OK, the truth is I liked beating those five guys.'

Susan said, 'Don't, BB.'

I waved her away. 'It may have started because they were hurting some kids who'd done

77

nothing to them, but it didn't end that way. I wish it didn't feel so good but it did. If the police hadn't stopped me I would've killed all five.'

She nodded as if she heard stories like mine every day but her eyes showed worry.

Her husband said, 'So you crossed the line for the wrong reason and you enjoyed it. So what? You saved the kids. The bigger evil would've been watching and doing nothing.'

'That's what some of the newspapers said. The others said you shouldn't justify vigilantism. Otherwise people will make a habit of it.'

He showed his palms as if to say that he'd won the point. 'But you didn't make a habit of it, did you?'

'Who says I didn't?'

He laughed uncomfortably and Susan asked, 'Who'd like coffee?'

After the Lindseys went home, I stood outside on the dark patio and listened to the tree frogs trilling and the breeze blowing through the leaves. The backyard dipped from the pool until it reached the edge of a pond. Fifty years before my dad was born this part of the neighborhood had been a brick quarry which the owner flooded after the clay deposit thinned. He'd parceled the land around the quarry and sold it as waterfront property, and now a neighborhood preservation society sold plaques that homeowners could tack next to their front doors, celebrating the historical architecture as if we hadn't built

78

our houses on the banks of an open pit. As a kid digging in the backyard I'd unearthed clumps of pink-gray clay, cool to the touch, coated with sandy soil which I'd washed away under a garden hose. I'd formed the clay into bowls that I gave to my mother before she went away and once an ashtray that I gave to my dad.

After my mother left us, but before she moved to Arizona, she'd rented an apartment above a dry-cleaners a half mile from our house. One summer afternoon, too young really to know where I was going, I went from the house without telling my father and found the apartment. She'd arranged my clay bowls in the front window as if beckoning me to her. When I rang the buzzer, she answered the street door wearing a bathrobe and brought me upstairs. A man was in her bedroom – a dark-skinned white man, or a fair-skinned black man, or a Mexican, I don't know what. Something. I don't remember. But I remember his dirty sweat, which cut through the smell of dry-cleaning solvent from the store below.

My mother spoke to me. Words of anger. Words of love. Words that told me I was far from home and should never wander outside alone. Something. I went to the windowsill, picked up a clay bowl and dropped it on the floor. It broke into a dozen pieces. I wanted her to hold me, or to yell or hit me, but, eyes on mine, she crossed her arms over her chest and gave me the plainest, flattest look I'd ever seen, a look that said she didn't care. I took another bowl and dropped it. The man came into the living room, wearing a towel around his waist, and she told him to go back to the bedroom, but he didn't. He stood in the doorway and eyed me like I was a curiosity. I picked up another bowl and broke it.

'What the hell,' the man said and came after me.

My mother told him to stop but the man ignored her again.

I swept the other bowls from the windowsill before he reached me, but then he was on top of me, his sweating, stinking arms around me. Why were his arms around me instead of the arms of my mother, the arms that I desired? I grabbed a piece of a broken bowl from the floor and tried to stab him in the eye. The shard went into the skin below his cheekbone and he staggered back, blood on his face, on his chest, on the towel, which now was coming loose from his waist.

My mother came to me and I felt a wave of relief. I moved toward her, too, unafraid, wanting – needing – the safety of her touch.

She slapped me across the face. 'You little bastard!'

I feel the sting of it now.

Then she said something that made no sense to me at the time, and though I understood both its general and particular meaning when I was a teenager, its full meaning still was – and remains – elusive, partly because I was never sure that it was true. She said, 'You have choices.'

Susan came out of the house and stood beside me. I put my arm around her waist and said, 'That was a nice evening.'

'You're a jerk,' she said, not unlovingly.

'Come to me tonight?' I asked. I'd asked her hundreds of times since Thomas was born and she'd never come. I said, 'I need you.'

'I wish you did,' she said. 'I don't think you need anyone.'

'That's not true.'

'Tell me about the woman who died,' she said.

I thought about Belinda on the railroad tracks. I thought about her telling me that her family was moving north. I thought about her dead flesh pasted against a clear plastic lawn bag on an empty lot on Blue Avenue. 'I can't,' I said.

Susan pulled away. 'Good night, BB.'

My keys were on the kitchen counter. The light in the sunroom was off and Susan was sleeping or at least quiet. Music played in Thomas's bedroom and his light remained on, probably would be on all night as he drew the adventures of one of his pornographic superheroes. I grabbed the keys and went to my car.

A quarter mile from my house a chocolate shop stayed open until eleven p.m. on summer nights, selling ice cream to couples who'd come out of the movie theater next door. I parked outside and bought a half-pound box of chocolate almonds from a counter boy in braces.

Lee Ann lived in a pink one-story house in a

Southside neighborhood of similar houses, most of them in need of a paintjob and new gutters. Her yard was a carpet of low-lying azalea bushes that bloomed like purple and white fire in late winter and looked ragged the rest of the year. I'd known Lee Ann since high school. Over the years she'd worked as a waitress, an interior designer and a life coach, but mostly she'd survived on the dollars and change left on her night table afterward by men like me.

I parked at the curb in front of her house and walked the path through the ragged azaleas. She answered the door, barefoot, wearing red shorts and a white blouse, looking like she'd been waiting for me. She had tight curly red hair, heavy thighs and small, childish breasts. The living room was dusty, the upholstered furniture worn, a stack of magazines on a credenza, a pile of unopened mail next to it.

Lee Ann looked at the chocolates as though she'd never seen anything like them before and was unsure what to do with them. 'You don't have to do this, BB,' she said.

'Hey, chocolate's the greatest gift.'

She swallowed a yawn. 'I thought donating a kidney was the greatest gift.'

'You don't need a kidney.'

'I don't need chocolates either.'

'Fine.' I took the box from her, dropped it on the floor, pulled her to me and unbuttoned her blouse.

'I heard about Belinda Mabry,' she said.

I shook my head. 'Don't.'

'OK,' she said and pressed her mouth to mine.

After we finished she laid her head on my sweaty chest. So much in her house was old and dusty, but the bed sheets smelled fresh, and lying in her bed was luxurious. She said, 'If I ever really *did* need something from you, would you give it to me?'

'Like what?'

'Something big.'

'Like a kidney?'

She nodded. 'Something big.'

I thought about it. 'No.'

A little after three a.m. I drove home. Heat lightning flashed in the west and showed a slate-blue sky between thin yellow clouds. I let myself in through the back door. Thomas's room was dark and he'd turned off the music. Only a kitchen light remained on. I went to the refrigerator and opened the door but decided I'd already had enough or more than enough. I closed my eyes, breathed deep and listened to the refrigerator hum. When I needed sex I got it on the side and always with a deep stain that didn't fade until I started desiring again but there was nothing to help that. I'd lived with it for fifteen years. I would live with it for another thirty if I needed to.

But now I would sleep.

I set the keys on the kitchen counter and saw a note from Susan. It said that Daniel Turner had called from the police station at midnight and he needed to talk right away.

SEVEN

Tomorrow, I thought. *Or the next day*. I climbed the stairs, stripped off my clothes, folded them, stacked them on a chair next to my bed and climbed in.

I dreamed about clear sheets of plastic – waves of it spread over a hot, bare landscape, thin as film, like trash bags slit down the seams and then stitched together. Naked bodies writhed under the plastic – legs, arms and breasts desperately pressing upward, mouths seeking air. But there was no air, no breath, and they clawed at the plastic in the pain and thrill of orgasmic asphyxiation.

Who were they?

Belinda.

The two prostitutes who'd died like her.

Lee Ann.

Others too.

Women I'd known or not known.

I watched from above and knew that I could remove the plastic if I chose to, but I chose not to. It was the kind of dream that was more real than waking. The women screamed and the sound rang in my ears like sex.

I woke to a bright room. The sun had risen

while the women gaped at me through the clear plastic with desperate, bulging eyes. Daniel Turner stood at the side of my bed looking like he hadn't slept and was angry about it. Susan stood at the door.

'Morning, Lieutenant,' I said.

'Why didn't you call last night?'

'Get out of my house.' I said it as politely as I could.

He sighed. 'I left a message.'

'I was busy.'

'Doing what?'

I glanced at Susan and back at Daniel. 'Fucking.'

Susan disappeared from the doorway.

Daniel frowned. 'Jesus, BB.'

'What else am I supposed to do at one in the morning?'

He shook his head. 'What happened to Bobby Mabry yesterday?'

'What do you mean? I talked to him. You knew I planned to go to Belinda's house.'

'Then what?' he asked.

'Then nothing. I told him I was sorry about Belinda.'

'And then?'

'I left,' I said.

'You didn't return?'

'Why would I? What's this about?'

He looked hard at me. 'Someone burned the back of his hands. Three spots on each hand. Like with cigarettes. Like stigmata.'

Charles, I thought. He must've gone back.

85

'What?' Daniel said.

'Nothing. When did it happen?'

'The call came in at eight-forty-eight.'

'I was here all evening,' I said. 'We had company. The Lindseys. New neighbors.'

He nodded as if he was relieved.

'Bobby said I did it?' I asked.

Daniel shook his head, disgusted. 'He's not saying. Baptist Hospital cleaned and bandaged the burns, wrote him a prescription for Percodan and let him go. He wouldn't tell the officer what happened. Said it was an accident, as if he could do that to himself. But Belinda's son said you and a friend had stopped by in the afternoon.'

'This is true.'

'Care to tell me who you took with you when you went visiting?'

'I'd rather not,' I said.

'Jesus, BB. I don't know what the hell you think you're doing.'

'Fact is I was trying to sleep until you broke down my door.'

'I didn't break down your door and I don't plan to. But you know you've got to stay away from this.'

'Yes,' I said, 'you've told me twice.'

He shook his head again and started toward the door.

'Daniel?' I said.

He turned back reluctantly. 'What?'

'What's this I hear about the killer driving a green Mercedes SUV?'

'Fuck you, BB.'

The sun shone through the open shades and heated the bed sheets and I lay on the mattress, listening to Daniel's footsteps descending the stairs. It was the kind of sunlight and dry warmth that could lead to a lifetime of complacency. When the front door closed I picked up the phone and called Charles. He answered on the second ring.

I said, 'Someone ground a lighted cigarette into Bobby's hands.'

'Hmm,' he said as if the news didn't surprise him. But news never seemed to.

I asked, 'Any idea who would do that?'

'I don't smoke,' he said. 'Can't stand the smell of burning tobacco.'

'It didn't have to be a cigarette. It could've been a heated metal rod.'

'Not my style. Can't stand the smell of burning flesh either.'

'If you didn't do it, who did?' I asked.

'Damned good question,' he said. 'You ready to go out?'

He'd never quite said that he hadn't burned Bobby but I supposed I'd gotten as much from him as he was going to give. 'What d'you want to do?' I asked.

'I got the addresses for the hookers. Ashley Littleton and Tonya Richmond.'

'That's something,' I said. 'Give me an hour, and I'll pick you up.'

'Do me a favor on your way?'

'Sure.'

'Buy me another pack of cigarettes?'

'Not funny, Charles.'

I showered and let the smell of Lee Ann eddy into the drain, worrying about Charles' tendency to go off plan, even if his approach did usually work better than mine. I shaved and got dressed in jeans, a light blue button-down cotton shirt and loafers. Susan had made lemon muffins and left a plate of cold scrambled eggs but her car was no longer in the driveway. I poured a cup of coffee and sat at the counter.

Thomas came in wearing shorts and a Miami Heat jersey. He got orange juice from the refrigerator, bit into a muffin and stared at me as he chewed.

'What?' I asked.

'Did you know that woman who was killed?'

I nodded. 'Belinda Mabry. I knew her when I was about your age.'

His eyes were worried. 'Why did the police need to talk to you?'

'They didn't,' I said. 'Daniel Turner asked me to identify her.'

He ate another bite, swallowed hard and asked his real question. 'Does he think you did it?'

'D'you think he would?'

He shook his head uncertainly. 'No.'

'No,' I agreed, 'he doesn't think I did it.'

He looked relieved.

'Come sit with me,' I said.

He hesitated, then came.

I slid the plate of cold eggs between us and we

ate breakfast together in silence, though I guessed his head was as full of troubled voices as mine. When I was done, I said, 'I try to be a good father to you.'

'I know,' he said.

'I find it difficult.'

'I know.'

'I'm sorry,' I said.

He shrugged.

Charles lived in a brown ranch-style house on a tree-covered two-acre lot in the wetlands between town and the beach. He'd put a chain-link fence around the edge of the property and an electric gate across the driveway. He left the gate open most of the time but a closed-circuit security camera pointed through it toward the street. He didn't mind visitors coming but wanted to know that they'd arrived.

A little before ten I drove into the driveway and through a yard carpeted with palmettos, ferns and dead and rotting leaves. Spanish moss hung from oak branches. A scrub pine tipped in the sandy soil and rested against a stand of other trees. The yard was a little chaos of neglect but Charles knew if a leaf shifted or a twig snapped.

As I pulled up he came out the front door, holding a calico cat, set it on to the ground, glanced once toward the canopy of branches and leaves as though he were wondering if we would have rain, and climbed into the car. The calico walked across the driveway lazily, then shot into the brush as if it saw something living that needed to be dead.

'You look exhausted,' Charles said.

'I had a late night.'

He fixed his eyes on me. 'Is that a good thing?'

'Just the way it is. Where to?'

'North into Arlington,' he said. 'Tonya Richmond's mother, father and little sister still live in the house where she grew up.'

'Want to tell me where you found that out?'

'Want to tell me what you were doing last night?'

I glanced at him. 'I was getting laid.'

'So was I,' he said. 'By a friend who likes to talk.'

Eaton Avenue ran north–south through a neighborhood of flat-roofed prefab houses, aluminum carports and yards that got more care than they probably deserved. It was a hanging-on neighborhood with well-tended flower gardens, newly washed cars on the lawns and a park with a single tennis court. The Richmonds lived in the biggest house on the block, a blue prefab on to which they'd added a screened porch. They'd built the house sideways to the street and planted cabbage palms and holly bushes that mostly blocked it from view.

The heat of the day was rising and the air was bright with too much sun and heavy with humidity. The neighborhood was quiet except for the hum of window air conditioners and the distant buzz of an electric saw. A cracked concrete walk led to the front door.

Charles rang the bell and we stepped back the way that magazine salesmen do to show they're no threat.

A young woman with a narrow face and blemished black skin answered the door. She wore green shorts and a pink T-shirt that said *Lollipop* in gold sequins. She carried a baby boy on her hip. She looked suspiciously at Charles and me. 'What d'you want?'

'Miss Richmond?' Charles said.

She nodded.

'Are you Tonya Richmond's sister?'

She tried to shut the door but Charles seemed to float across the front steps and kicked it open.

The woman stepped back, stunned. 'What d'you want?'

'We'd like to talk,' I said. 'I've lost someone too.'

'Nothing to talk about,' she said. 'Tonya was a crack whore. Crack whores die like crack whores live.'

'Please,' I said.

A female voice asked from behind the woman, 'Who's there, Deni?'

The woman kept her eyes on Charles and me. 'No one, Mama.'

A heavy, graying woman stepped into the door, wearing a loose faded-blue dress. 'Who are you?' she said.

'My name's William Byrd,' I said. 'I'd like to talk with you about Tonya.'

91

She fixed her eyes on Charles. 'What about you?'

'I'm with him,' he said.

'You're spooky looking,' she said. 'Come on in – why not?' Her daughter glared at her, but the older woman frowned at her daughter's worry. 'What're these boys going to do to me that hasn't already been done?'

We followed her into her living room. A brown foldout sofa and two matching easy chairs stood on green wall-to-wall carpet. A window unit blew a cold stream of air but the room was hot anyway. A coffee table had been pushed against a wall with a memorial to Tonya Richmond arranged on top of it. A framed five-by-seven stood in the middle – the same picture that the television had shown during the sheriff's press conference. Tonya wore a blue gown that revealed some breast but not so much that you ever would've guessed what would become of her. A votive candle stood on either side of the picture, burning though the room was bright with sun, and a drying white carnation, riddled with brown streaks of decay, lay on top of a pile of hand-written notes.

'Have a seat,' the older woman said to us. Her daughter sat across from Charles, bouncing her baby on a leg. 'Now,' the older woman asked, 'what do you boys want?'

'The man who killed your daughter also killed a close friend of mine,' I said.

'A close friend?' said the girl with the baby, making the words sound dirty. 'Another crack whore?'

'A woman I loved,' I said to the older woman.

'The police've been here,' she said. 'We talked to them, told them everything. What else is there to do?'

Charles smiled. The baby caught the smile and laughed.

'The police'll do their job,' I said. 'They might even catch the man who did it.'

'Then why would you want to come into my home and bother me while I'm grieving?' Her voice held no anger, only pain.

I shrugged. 'I can't help myself.'

The woman seemed to consider that, nodded to herself. 'What d'you want to know?'

The baby grinned at Charles. He offered his finger and the baby clutched it. It seemed useless to warn the baby of the danger.

'Did you know much about what Tonya was doing?' Charles asked.

The woman tipped her head toward her daughter. 'Deni knew. I knew only a little.'

'Knew she was a crack whore,' said Deni.

'Do you know who her pimp was or who was selling her the crack?' he asked.

'Same man. Beat her up if she didn't stand on the corner for him. Beat her up if she bought drugs from someone else.'

'What's his name?' Charles asked.

'Ashawn,' she replied. 'Lives in a room at the Gator Lodge on Philips Highway though he's probably cleared out now that the police are asking questions.'

'Does Ashawn have a last name?' Charles asked.

'Just Ashawn.' She pulled her baby's hand from Charles' finger.

'What did Tonya tell you about her customers?' he asked. 'Did anyone scare her?'

She laughed. 'Anyone that wants sex with a crack whore is scary. No one knows that better than a crack whore herself. Yeah, everyone that ever paid Tonya to get in his car scared her.'

Mrs Richmond listened to this with a strange calm that suggested she'd heard worse.

A tinge of rot – from the carnation, I guessed – caught in my nostrils.

Charles asked Deni, 'Did Tonya tell you about any men in particular?'

'Yeah, every time we talked. But no one stood out as scarier than the others.'

'What about Ashawn?' he said. 'Did he ever arrange anything special for Tonya? With guys who wanted something unusual?'

Deni shook her head. 'Ashawn's a little guy. Got no imagination for that kind of thing.'

'That's not true,' said Mrs Richmond. 'He sent Tonya to the Bahamas for a party. She thought she'd hit the big time.'

'It was Jamaica, Mama. And that wasn't Ashawn. It was Ashawn's friend, Darrin. Yeah, she went to Jamaica three, four months ago. For a big party. Came back hurt.'

'Hurt how?' I asked.

She looked disgusted. 'How d'you think? They tore her.'

94

I glanced at Mrs Richmond.

She said, 'Tonya was my daughter. If you can hear it, I can.'

I asked Deni, 'Do you know if they tied her up?'

She laughed bitterly. 'They did everything. And you want to know the sad thing? They paid her good money, so she would've gone back for more. That's what a crack whore does. A man tears her and she asks for more.'

The baby reached for Charles' finger again.

'Where can we find Ashawn's friend?' he asked.

'Darrin? He manages a club called Little Vegas off Cassat Avenue on the Westside.' She glanced at me. 'He's tall like you. But better looking. If you go to Little Vegas you won't miss him.'

Mrs Richmond said, 'Don't say Deni sent you.'

'I don't care what you tell him,' Deni said. 'Darrin's a punk, just like Ashawn.'

Mrs Richmond looked at the baby on Deni's lap and smiled pleasantly. 'Darrin and Deni used to be together.'

Deni looked at the baby too and seemed surprised to see him holding Charles' finger again. 'Just a punk,' she said and pulled the baby away.

I asked, 'Do you know if Tonya was friends with Ashley Littleton?'

'She the one you knew?'

'No. I knew Belinda Mabry.'

'Tonya knew Ashley a little from Little Vegas, but she just met the Mabry woman.'

'Did she? How did that happen?'

'They met in Jamaica,' she said.

The heat of the room closed on me. My throat felt dry and the carnation rot caught in it. 'At the party?'

'No, at church.' She rolled her eyes. 'Yeah, at the party. Where the hell else?'

Charles asked, 'Was she working the party too?'

She shrugged. 'I believe she was a guest. Tonya said some of the men brought dates. Tonya said she seemed out of place, like she hadn't done this kind of thing before. Said she got into it eventually though.'

'What did getting into it involve?' I asked, though I knew that I didn't want her to tell me.

Deni's smile showed no interest or pity. 'She didn't say exactly. But the lady apparently enjoyed herself.'

Charles asked, 'Did Tonya say who Belinda's date was?'

Deni shook her head. 'Just another boy with money. They all had money. They were drinking expensive liquor and had more coke than Santa Claus. Nice cars. Big house by the beach. Swimming pool.'

I tried to place Belinda at such a party but couldn't see it.

'What else?' Deni asked.

'Why would anyone want to kill your sister?' I said.

'I don't know why anyone would want to have sex with her, much less kill her.'

I glanced at Charles to see if he had more questions.

He shook his head, stood and said to the older woman, 'Thank you, Mrs Richmond.' He smiled at Deni. 'Beautiful baby. Don't ever let him go.'

When we stepped outside, the heat was dizzying. Somewhere in a nearby tree a locust wound up like a high-pitched electric motor. In the car, I turned on the air conditioner and hot air shot into our faces.

'What do you think?' I asked and pulled from the curb.

'I think you went in there like a little boy lost in the woods.'

I considered that and considered the oppressive heat of the Richmonds' living room as Tonya's sister told us stories about Belinda. 'I don't know if I've got the stomach for this.'

'Fine,' he said. 'Drop me off at my house.'

I drove to the corner. On the stop sign someone had spray painted a black number three under the word Stop.

Stop
3

'What the hell does that mean?' I said.

Charles rolled down his window, spit and rolled it up. 'What's anything mean?'

I accelerated through the intersection. 'Where did Ashley Littleton live?'

'You sure about this?'

I've been sure about very few things in my life. 'Where does she live?'

Ashley Littleton shared a rental with a roommate in the Spring Park neighborhood, a lower-middle-class triangle between the Interstate, the beach road and a cemetery. It was a single-story yellow-sided house with brown shingles, awnings over the windows and pulled shades. A car with a canvas cover on it was parked in the driveway. Beyond the car was a chest-high white metal fence. A brown dog that looked part boxer lay inside the fence against the gate. The dog pulled to its feet as Charles and I walked to the front door.

No one answered the bell.

'Who's the roommate?' I asked.

'Girl named Brianna Sumner. She's half Thai. Works as a bartender. Sometimes hooks.' He stepped off the front porch and peered through a window where the blind met the sill. 'Come on,' he said and headed toward the driveway.

The dog stood on its hind legs against the metal gate and growled as Charles and I approached. Charles stooped so he was face-to-face with it, and it bared its teeth, its gums black, its eyes wide, shining and mean. Charles reached his hand through the bars. The dog lunged at it, canines flashing, but with a flick of the wrist Charles hit its muzzle so hard it made a crack and the dog tumbled on to its back. It scrambled to its feet, ran three or four yards from the gate and stood warily watching

Charles.

Charles unhooked the gate and swung it open.

'What are you doing?' I asked.

He stepped into the backyard, leaving the gate open for me.

There were no trees, no shade. Empty water and food bowls stood on the concrete by the stairs to the back door. Against the back wall, tomato plants grew in plastic containers next to a potted hibiscus with three big red flowers. Charles climbed the stairs and knocked on the door. When no one came he took a single step back and kicked the door. The bottom panel broke inward. He shook his head as though the door had failed to do its job, reached through the gap and popped the lock.

'We could've come back when she was here,' I said.

'Would she let us search the house?'

'Guess not.'

The back door led into a kitchen that needed painting and smelled of spoiled food. Dirty dishes from a long-ago breakfast were stacked in the sink, and a cockroach scuttled across the counter and behind the faucet. Charles glanced around the room and went to a pile of mail and newspapers on the kitchen table. He leafed through it as though he were sorting for bills and handed me a stack of three advertising postcards, the kind that businesses hire kids to slip under your windshield wiper at the movie theater or mall. The postcards promoted a two-for-one-drinks ladies night at Little Vegas.

Charles wandered into the living room and I took the hall to the bedrooms. The first was Ashley Littleton's and showed signs of having been searched by the police. The dresser drawers were open a crack, the closet door wide. A framed picture stood on the dresser, showing Ashley Littleton and two girls who might've been her nieces or much younger sisters. If she'd kept other pictures on the dresser or boxes of belongings on the closet shelves, the police had impounded them. I slipped the solitary picture from the frame.

The second bedroom door was shut and as I pushed it open I smelled something animal-like and dirty. Flies were buzzing. It was the same buzzing I'd heard when Daniel Turner showed me Belinda's body, and my stomach turned and the picture of Ashley Littleton slipped from my fingers even before I saw Brianna Sumner naked and bloody, her feet bound over her head with clothesline, dead on a bare mattress.

My throat made a choking sound, and Charles came from behind me.

He heard all he needed to know. 'That's not good,' he muttered.

I ran through the hall to the bathroom, my body sweating, my stomach turning as if I had something inside me that needed out or I would die too. I ran cold water over my face and held my cold hands over my eyes. When I managed to stand and look in the mirror, my reflection seemed for a long moment to be that of a man I didn't know, as though the shock of seeing the dead woman could change my lineaments inside and out.

I went into the hall. Charles was inside the dead woman's room and I stood for a while outside her door, unwilling to look in, unwilling to see again what I had already seen, listening to Charles moving around the body, opening and shutting drawers and closet doors. The picture I'd dropped was at my feet and I picked it up, folded it into quarters and crammed it into my pocket.

When Charles stepped out of the bedroom he looked at me carefully, assessing the damage, then walked toward the kitchen. 'Nothing in her room,' he said. 'At least nothing that means anything to me.'

I followed him out the back door on to the stairs. The dog lay near the fence, watching us. Sunlight glinted off the metal banister and heat radiated from the walls of the house.

I pulled my cell phone from my pocket.

'What're you doing?' Charles said.

'Calling Daniel Turner,' I said.

Charles shook his head. 'What good'll it do? He already thinks you're in this too deep.'

I opened the phone and dialed.

He said, 'I'll let the police know and keep you out of it.'

'Yeah?'

He nodded.

'Fine.' I snapped the phone shut and we went down the stairs and to the gate.

'Hold on,' Charles said. He went back to the

stairs, picked up the two dog bowls and disappeared inside. A minute later he came out with water and refrigerator scraps – salami, a chunk of cheese, a clump of congealed noodles. He set the bowls on the concrete and the dog came from the fence and circled, its eyes fixed on Charles, until Charles stepped away. Then it approached the dishes and lapped at the food.

'That stuff'll make a dog sick,' I said.

Charles headed to the gate. 'Not on my conscience.'

EIGHT

Thunder rang in the roof beams. I steadied my beer bottle and lifted it to my lips.

As I'd driven home, a storm had blown in over the river, dropping splinters of lightning into the wind-whipped water. The rain had started suddenly, pelting the windshield and blinding me to the world, and I'd wondered if it wasn't better this way but I'd flipped on my wipers and headlights like a good man. In the driveway I'd sat in the car with the engine off, cocooned in water that was streaming over steel and glass, until the heat inside rose and I'd gotten out and sprinted the fifteen steps between car and front porch. Now I sat on a kitchen stool with a Coors on the counter, my clothes heavy and cold with rainwater, our cat Fela sitting on the counter, watching me, and I wondered if I gave a damn.

Charles didn't. I knew that for certain. He did what he did because it was all he knew. He fixed what needed fixing. He broke what needed breaking. He thought about nothing else.

Outside, a gust tore through the oak tree, scattering leaves and Spanish moss and tossing a branch into the swimming pool. Rainwater poured off the roof and collected on the patio.

Charles first came to me after I attacked the men who were beating up the Honduran kids. I'd bonded out of jail and gone home to my dad who'd said little and stared at me as if I were a stranger in his house. For ten days an ankle monitor kept me inside until the newspapers declared me a hero and my lawyer convinced the judge I presented no risk. I offered to help at the service stations but my dad gave me the cold stare as if to say *you're none of mine* so I spent my days golfing or at the beach. Whenever I went out, a red Mercury Capri followed me. I wasn't surprised. For every letter to the editor supporting me, another said I should be hung by my neck. The TV news had reporters tracking my behavior. The parents of the man who'd died had filed a civil suit, which my lawyer said would mean investigators watching everything I did so I needed to be good.

I was eating lunch at Worman's Deli when a man, somewhere between seventy and eighty, got out of the Capri. Charles. He walked into the restaurant and sat across from me at my table. He said, 'You fucked those boys up good.'

I ate a bite of hamburger and pretended he wasn't there.

He said, 'Not a lot of guys who can take down five men, kill one and break another's neck. Takes a special kind of guy to do that. It's not about strength but I suppose you already know that. It's not about being a great fighter either. It's about focus.'

The waitress came to the table and Charles said, 'Give me what he's having.'

I took ten dollars from my wallet and gave it to her. 'For my bill.'

When she left, Charles said, 'You can't run away from it. God knows I tried.'

'I don't know what you're talking about.'

'Yes you do,' he said. 'You know it and it scares you. It scared me too when I first discovered it in myself.' He leaned across the table. 'I'll tell you something I've told no one else. It scares me still. But that doesn't mean I can run from it.'

I looked at the fat red scars that descended from his eyes. 'What happened to your face?'

'A whole lot of crying,' he said.

'Looks like someone raked you with a knife.'

'Could've been that too. By the time you're my age you'll look like me or worse.'

He was angering me but I was determined not to show it. 'Why do you think you know me?'

104

'Because I do.'

I laughed at him. He was a lunatic.

He shrugged and said, 'Some men are born forsaken.'

The waitress returned with my change and a receipt and put them on the table.

I asked Charles, 'What do you want from me?'

He shook his head. 'It's not what I want from you. It's what you want from me. I can teach you.'

'Thanks,' I said, 'but I don't need your help.'

'Yes you do,' he said. 'It'll be clear when you no longer need me.'

'Yeah? How's that?'

'That'll be the day that you try to kill me.'

I stood. 'I've got enough trouble already without you following me around, all right?'

I was willing to wait for an answer. He took my receipt, printed on it with a ballpoint pen and slid it across the table. It said *Charles Tucker* and included a phone number. 'Call if you need me,' he said.

I said, 'I never will.'

Susan came in as lightning struck with a crack that sounded like something had broken in the sky and land. The kitchen lights flickered. Susan was wearing a yellow cotton dress and though her hips had widened in recent years I wanted them still. 'Come here,' I said and she came. I held her and kissed her forehead.

She said, 'What have you done?'

A bead of perspiration had formed above her lip and I felt an impulse to kiss it away. 'Nothing,' I said.

'Don't lie to me.' She pulled away, got a beer for herself and left the room.

I poured a pool of beer on the counter in front of Fela. She sniffed it, jerked her head away, sniffed it again and lapped it up. When she was done she purred and looked at me for more.

Thunder rumbled across the sky.

I wondered if I gave a damn.

The phone rang, rang again. On the third ring I answered it.

It was Daniel Turner. He said, 'Hey, BB, guess where I am?'

'I don't play guessing games.'

His voice was shaky with anger or fear or both. 'I'm standing in the house where Ashley Littleton lived. One of the neighbors called and said a couple of hours ago two men were in the yard acting suspiciously. I thought I should check things out and when I did I found Ashley Littleton's roommate dead. Same as Ashley Littleton, Tonya Richmond and Belinda Mabry. And guess what else? The neighbor wrote down a description of the car that the two men got out of. A white Lexus. He got the tag number too.'

'Shit,' I said.

'I know enough about a dead body to tell you this girl didn't die in the last couple of hours,' he said. 'But I sure as hell would like to know why you were in her house and I sure would like to know if you've ever been here before.'

'First and only time,' I said. 'I went to see if the roommate could tell me anything about Belinda's killer.'

'You're a fool, BB.'

'I know that without you telling me.'

'The neighbor said you were with an older man.'

'That's true.'

'You riding with Charles Tucker again?'

I admitted I was.

'Jesus Christ! I thought you were done with that eight years ago.'

'I thought so too.'

He said nothing. The rain drummed on the roof.

'Daniel?' I said.

He sighed into the phone. 'This is going to be messy,' he said. 'You'd best come into the station, make yourself available, tell your story, do it without a lawyer.'

'You think that would be best, huh?'

'I do, BB. I do.'

'Then I'll come right in,' I said and hung up.

We kept a laptop computer plugged in on a shelf under Susan's cookbooks. I typed into it, finished my beer and went back out through the rain to my car.

Christopher had been in and out of my life, mostly out, since the autumn when he attacked Bobby Mabry. I'd last seen him four or five summers earlier at a Suns minor league game. We'd been polite, the way you can be a couple of decades after a terrible pain, and he'd introduced me to his wife, a mousy woman he'd married after he'd cleaned himself up. The latest word was that they'd divorced and he'd remarried and moved to the beach. Google put him in a new housing development between the Intracoastal and the ocean.

The company that built the development had put up rows of white two-story stuccos, each with a two-car garage and a matching mailbox at the curb. The lawns were well tended and the palm trees looked fresh from the nursery. I walked through the rain to Christopher's door a little before six and pushed a bell that sounded like the chimes of a grandfather clock.

A blonde thirteen- or fourteen-year-old girl answered and called for Christopher, who came to the door in white shorts and an unpressed Oxford cloth shirt. He didn't look surprised that I'd shown up. 'BB! It's great to see you. Come in – get out of the rain, for God's sake.'

I stepped into an overly air-conditioned front hall and followed him into a living room. The girl who'd answered the door went to the next room and started practicing on a piano.

'What's up?' Christopher asked. His face had filled and fattened with time and had the uneven glow of a man who'd spent too much time in the sun or with a bottle, or both. He hung his bottom lip open in a smile which made him look friendly and a little slow. I didn't remember him doing that when we were kids.

I asked, 'You hear about Belinda Mabry?'

'Yeah, yeah. Saw it on the news. Terrible.'

A blonde woman came into the room. She wore jeans, flip-flops with bright red toenails and a Hawaiian shirt. His face lit up when she entered. 'Linda, this is BB – William Byrd – a childhood friend. He also knew Belinda Mabry.'

She smiled, said she was glad to meet me and acted like a woman who'd escaped in life without a lot of damage. I wondered how Christopher had ended up with her. 'Have a seat, BB,' she said. 'Can I get you something to drink?'

'I'd love a beer,' I said and she left us alone.

Christopher's stepdaughter hit a wrong key and started again. 'So what can I do for you, BB?' he asked.

'When I think about who might've wanted to hurt Belinda, you come to mind.'

He looked at me with friendly amusement. 'You're still whipped on her, aren't you? It's been twenty-five years, BB.'

'You don't need to tell me how long it's been.'

'I moved on,' he said. 'I figured you did too. I'm sure she did.'

'How would you know that?'

'I could tell,' he said. 'I had dinner at her house when she moved back. She was living a different life.'

It made no sense that she would've invited him to dinner. 'How did that happen?'

'What? My going to her house? She called and asked me.'

I shook my head. 'Not after what you did to

Bobby.'

'I grew up, BB. Belinda did too. That's what most of us do. We grow up.'

My talk with him was souring my stomach and I wanted to be away from his new house and new life. 'No one gets over something like that,' I said. 'That's not part of growing up.'

He looked at me hard and I resisted the impulse to turn away. 'The day before she and her family moved to Chicago she came to my house. Did you know that?'

'No.'

'She had a knife. Nothing very serious. A kitchen knife. When I opened the door she tried to stab me.'

'I believe that.'

'I took the knife from her but she got me in the shoulder,' he said. 'I still have the scar.'

'You earned that scar and more.'

Again he looked at me hard. 'And then I fucked her.'

'What do you mean?'

'I fucked her. We were both pretty miserable.'

'You raped her?'

'No.'

'She let you – after what you did to Bobby?'

'Yeah,' he said. 'She helped me clean my shoulder and then I fucked her on the bathroom counter.'

'I don't believe it.'

He had a sadness in his eyes. 'I've always been grateful to you.'

'For what?'

'She said she asked you to kill me. You didn't do it.'

'I probably should have.'

'Probably.'

His wife brought us a couple bottles of Miller Lite and sat on the couch next to me. In the next room his stepdaughter played the piano. I knew I'd made a mistake in coming. Everything Christopher said confused me. He gave his slack-jawed smile to his wife and said, 'It took me a long time to get my head together. My first marriage was one step. Linda's been another. You know what? I've been blessed.'

I asked, 'What was Belinda's husband like?'

'Flashy clothes and a lot of gold. You know the type. I didn't much like him but she looked happy. What do you think, Linda?'

'Mmm,' she agreed.

'They made their money in real estate?' I asked.

His slack-jawed smile stayed. 'That's what they said.' He glanced at Linda and again at me. 'But before I cleaned myself up I spent plenty of time around people who got rich fast, usually on drug money. Belinda's husband had that look. Their house did.'

'Belinda too?'

'Maybe. I'm not saying that's how they got their money, just that they had the look.'

'You think that's why someone killed her?'

He shook his head. 'I don't have any idea. I figure it was random. The other two women who were killed, Belinda wasn't like them.'

'Listen to the news tonight. There's been another killing – the roommate of one of the other women. D'you think that's random too?'

'I don't know what to think,' he said, 'and to tell the truth my thinking about it won't do a lot of good.'

There was something aggressive in his slack-jawed smile. I stood, downed the last of the beer and set the bottle on the coffee table. 'Thanks for the beer, Linda,' I said.

She smiled up at me. 'Come by any time, BB.'

Christopher walked with me to the front door and we stepped outside. Light rain was falling and heavy clouds had brought an early-evening darkness. The air smelled of cut grass and the sharp, salty rot of vegetation in the swampy marsh at the edge of the subdivision. Christopher held out a hand to shake. 'It's good to see you, BB.'

I shook it and asked what I knew I shouldn't. 'When you saw her, did Belinda mention me?'

He looked at me evenly. 'No.'

I stepped into the rain and looked back at him standing barefoot on the front step. 'It's a nice house,' I said.

He gazed up at it as if he was surprised to find himself there. 'It's Linda's. Colleen got ours when we split so I moved in here. Furniture's Linda's, pictures on the wall are hers, ice cream in the fridge is hers.' He laughed. 'I'm a tenant. It's not so bad though. Neighborhood's nice. There's a community pool.' He pointed at an identical house across the street. 'They're Pakistanis and so are the people next to them. The family to the left is Mexican and next to them is too. You've got to drive a block and a half before you find an American. Not that I'm complaining.'

'You're blessed,' I said.

He smiled. 'I tell myself that every fucking day.'

NINE

When I pulled into the driveway, the front porch light was on and the house was quiet. The evening sky was violet, the clouds breaking apart. As I got out of the car, I looked up until I found Venus, then breathed deep and felt the tension ease in my chest. So Belinda had called Christopher when she'd moved back. So twenty-five years ago in a fit of anger and confusion they'd had sex. So she'd lived a life that I hadn't imagined. It made no difference. I was who I was. I would do what I would do. A frog trilled in the holly bushes as I climbed the porch steps.

There was a puddle of something slick on the porch tile in front of the door – slick and red with a cluster of white globules. Blood. And whatever the white stuff was. My heart raced. I fumbled with the house key and shoved it into the lock.

Susan and Thomas were in the kitchen. Susan had been crying but now had a fiery anger in her eyes. Thomas was pale.

'What happened?' I asked.

Susan pointed at the kitchen sink. A decapitated cat lay in a cardboard box, her striped gray fur soaked and darkened with blood. It was Fela.

'What the hell happened?'

Susan said, 'We heard her shriek.'

'Cats don't—'

'She *shrieked*.'

'Jesus.'

'We went to the front door,' she said. 'I thought maybe a possum ... but she was lying on the porch. She was...' Susan pointed at Fela to explain what she was.

'That's it?' I said.

She nodded.

I held my arms open to Thomas. 'Come here.'

He looked at my face as though I were a stranger, turned away and stumbled out of the room. I started after him but Susan said, 'Let him go.'

I went to the sink and stared at the cat. The bright kitchen lights made her look cold in death. 'Where's her head?'

'I don't know. We looked in the bushes and on the front lawn.'

'Damn.'

'What have you gotten yourself into?' she said.

'What do you mean?'

'People don't cut off the heads of their neighbors' cats,' she said. 'This has something to do with you.'

I guessed she was right but I looked at her like she was insane. 'This is a sick kid pulling a sick prank. That's all. Probably someone Thomas knows.'

'Don't you dare blame Thomas.'

'I'm not blaming him.'

'You said you were done with this. Eight years ago you did.'

'I told you the truth,' I said.

'Because I can't take it again. You know that.'

'When did you hear Fela yowl?'

'*Shriek*,' she said. 'Twenty minutes ago. A little more.'

'No one was outside when you opened the door?'

'Yeah, a man was dancing on the lawn with a butcher knife in his teeth. I forgot to mention him.' She shook her head bitterly. 'No. No one was outside. There was a car at the corner.'

'What did it look like?'

She looked angry enough to hit me but she sighed. 'Damn it, BB, you're doing it again.' She followed Thomas out of the kitchen.

I went outside and across the wet lawn, got a shovel from the tool shed, left it by the quarry pond and returned for Fela. She felt heavier dead than alive and as I carried the blood-soaked box into the dark I resisted an impulse to hug her to my chest. A couple of paces from the pond I dug through the grass and a layer of sand into the dark dirt below, and I lowered the box into the hole. I tried to pray but felt foolish, so I shoveled the sand and soil over Fela's body and tamped the grave with my shoes and hands. My hand found a clump of clay, the kind I'd pulled from the backyard when I was a kid. The clay was soft, warm and wet, and I squeezed and kneaded it as if I was restoring circulation to a dead limb, then dug into the grave with my fingers and pulled out more.

I carried the clay inside and washed it in the kitchen sink, the sand mixing with Fela's blood, swirling into the drain. The bright cold kitchen dizzied me, so I took the clay to the counter and sat. In the glare of the overhead lamp I rolled a piece of it between my palms until it formed a ball. With my thumbs I shoved a hollow into one end as if there were an invisible sphincter that needed opening. I pinched and worked the clay until thin walls rose around the thumbhole.

Thomas came in and watched me from across the room. 'What are you doing?' he said as if it was something dirty and embarrassing.

I pinched a crescent moon into the rim of the bowl, then another, and said nothing.

Thomas watched, frowning, then came to the counter and reached for the clay. I thought he meant to knock it from the counter but he scooped some into his hands. He sat at the counter with me, rolling the clay into a ball,

116

shoving his thumbs into it. He pinched the walls thin and smoothed the exterior and interior with his fingers until he'd formed a bowl more perfect than mine.

'Where'd you learn to do that?' I asked.

'I didn't,' he said.

I looked at him. 'You're going to be all right,' I said.

He nodded.

At ten p.m. three clay bowls – one of mine and two of Thomas's – dried on a piece of newspaper and Thomas had disappeared into his bedroom. An empty Coors bottle stood on the counter next to the bowls.

I could drink another beer, go upstairs, climb into bed and lie awake through half the night. I could go to the sunroom, explain myself to Susan and ask her again to forgive me. Or I could go to Lee Ann's house, pull her into bed and stick my thumb inside her like she was a ball of clay. I got up, found the telephone and dialed.

Charles answered. 'Hey,' he said as if he knew it would be me.

'D'you want to go to Little Vegas?' I said.

We drove across the river in Charles' car, the windows wide open, the warm night air rushing in. The headlights of oncoming traffic flared on the windshield and disappeared behind us. The city had laid an ornamental rope of violet neon lights along the guardrail on the next bridge downriver, and warm purple clouds glowed on the flat water. I closed my eyes.

'You should've shown the cat to me before you buried her,' Charles said.

I opened my eyes. 'Why?'

'The way a man kills says a lot about him. Did the cut start on the left or right? If it started on the left and he killed from behind, which he did since no one wants to get scratched in the face by a dying cat, he's right handed. If it started on the right, he's a lefty. Did he do anything else to her body? Did he leave marks that tell you about his special kind of sickness?'

'He didn't *leave* anything. He *took* her head.'

'It'll turn up sooner or later.'

'I know.'

For a minute we drove without talking.

'We could dig her up,' he said.

'No, sir.'

Traffic thinned as we drove into the Westside. If we skipped the Cassatt Avenue exit we would soon be in a pine forest instead of at Little Vegas.

I asked, 'Do you think Christopher could have killed Belinda?'

'No.'

'He tried to hurt her twenty-five years ago,' I said. 'He knew she was back in town and knew what she'd been doing.'

'Give it up, BB,' Charles said, which I guessed was his way of telling me what Christopher also had told me. *Grow up*.

'Maybe you're right,' I said.

'I am.'

Lit by overhead spotlights, Little Vegas, a brown single-story cinderblock structure with a tinted glass door, stood by itself on a piece of property next to a strip mall. A black awning stretched from the door and dim lights, manufactured to look like gas lamps, hung on either side. A stunted cabbage palm tree stood sentry along the sidewalk. A half-dozen cars and pickups were parked in the parking lot. A large neon sign advertised *Little Vegas Gentlemen's Club* and a small sign under it said *More Parking in Rear*.

A short, fat black man stood outside the door in black shoes, black linen pants and a black linen shirt unbuttoned to show graying chest hair and a thin gold chain. He gave us a look-over, said, 'Good evening, gentlemen,' and opened the door.

'Not much of a bouncer,' I said to Charles as we stepped inside.

'You're wrong,' he said.

My eyes adjusted to the dim light. 'Not much of a club either.'

The floor was concrete, painted yellow and stained with beer. The walls were milk-chocolate brown. Cheap track lighting, filled with red and blue bulbs, lined the edges of the ceiling, a string of Christmas lights was tacked to the wall behind the bar and a disco ball hung at the far end of the room. There were no women in the place. A black bartender stood behind the bar. Five black men sat on stools at the bar. Two more sat at one of the three tables in the room.

The bartender, a barrel-chested man with short hair and a neat goatee, approached Charles and me. 'Twenty-buck cover and a two-drink minimum,' he said.

I smiled at him. 'Why the cover? There're no girls.'

He extended a hand for our money. 'They'll be here in an hour or so.'

I kept my wallet in my pocket. 'Is Darrin here?'

'Twenty bucks and a drink order,' he said.

I fished out the bills and ordered a Coors, Charles a vodka on ice.

When the bartender gave us our drinks I asked again, 'Darrin here?'

'Yeah, in the back.'

Charles said, 'We want to talk to him.'

'I didn't think you wanted to suck his dick. What about?'

I'd seen Charles break the bones in a man's hands for less than that but he took a long, slow sip of his vodka and gestured the bartender close with his index finger. He whispered to him and the bartender's head popped back an inch. He walked around the end of the bar and disappeared into a back hallway.

'What did you tell him?' I asked.

'I told him who I am,' Charles said.

I laughed. 'Yeah? And who's that?'

He laughed too and took another long drink.

The bartender came out again a minute later and pointed at me. 'You go on back.' He gestured at Charles. 'But you stay here.'

Charles shrugged. 'Then give me another drink.'

The hallway led to a closed door. I knocked and opened it into an office. Darrin – a tall, thin black man with close-shaved hair – sat behind a steel desk. He was twenty-five or thirty and, as Tonya's sister had said, he was good looking. He pointed at a chair across the desk from him.

'Who are you?' he asked.

I sat. 'William Byrd.'

The office smelled of ammonia the way rooms in places like this did after someone had cleaned them of the sweaty smells of sex. Behind Darrin, a window and a door faced the back parking lot. 'I understand you've got questions about a couple of my girls,' he said and I heard barely controlled rage in his voice.

'Tonya Richmond and Ashley Littleton.'

'But you're not a cop?' he said.

I shook my head. 'I guess I'm a friend.'

'Tonya and Ashley had no friends. If they did I would've known about them. And you sure as hell ain't *my* friend.'

I said, 'I knew one of the other women who was killed. Belinda Mabry. I'm trying to find out what happened.'

His rage seemed to dissolve. 'Yeah. It's terrible. You know I used to be with Tonya's sister. I've been hurting with this. Tonya was trouble. She was heavy into coke and meth, but she was one of mine, you know? She was my baby's aunt.'

'So you pimped her to a party in Jamaica.'

His face fell. 'Look at me. This is what I do. I run a place you couldn't rent as a storage locker except we've got girls like Tonya and Ashley who hang out here. If they're straight enough to show up. And look at what Tonya was. If I hadn't put her on a jet to Kingston, she would've been out on the highway doing it for dime rocks.'

'You know what bothers me?' I said. 'When someone justifies himself by saying that the world's a bad place.'

'I've heard of you before, Mr Byrd. It seems to me you're a hypocrite.'

'I may be that,' I said. 'But it still bothers me. My own self-justification may even be *why* it bothers me.' In his eyes I saw uncertainty, which was a kind of darkness I especially despised. I asked, 'Did you also send Ashley Littleton to Jamaica?'

He shook his head. 'It's time for you to leave.'

'Tell me about Belinda Mabry,' I said.

He stared at me silently and we listened to the music and laughter from the bar. Then he said, 'Nothing to tell. Never met her myself.'

'She was in Jamaica too.'

He looked like I'd poked him. 'The news says she was a nice lady. The Kingston party wasn't for nice ladies.'

'Then who asked you to send Tonya Richmond?'

He shook his head again. 'No, sir. I can't tell you that. These are private people. I put Tonya on a plane and she came back. A couple weeks

122

later she got killed. Jamaica's got nothing to do with it.'

'I need to talk to whoever asked you to send her. If Belinda Mabry was there too, something bad happened at the party.'

He nodded regretfully. 'I'll call and see if it's OK for me to tell you his name.' He picked up the phone and dialed.

When the person on the other end answered, Darrin said, 'I've got William Byrd here. He has questions about Jamaica.' He listened uncomfortably and said, 'He knows that Tonya was there and thinks Belinda Mabry was too.' After another silence, he hung up and said to me, 'I'll give you his number.' He opened a desk drawer, but instead of a pen and paper he pulled out a black pistol and pointed it at my chest.

I knew I should feel fear, but I felt an old familiar calm. 'You don't want to do this,' I said.

He shook his head. 'You're wrong. I do. Anyway I don't have a choice.' He motioned with the pistol barrel. 'Get up.'

I stood.

'I'm sorry about Tonya and Ashley,' he said. 'About Belinda Mabry too.'

He took me out through the back door. My feet felt light on the gravel parking lot. Charles would be inside drinking his vodka and feeling the normal effects of gravity. I said, 'My friend will be upset when he realizes I'm gone.'

'I wouldn't worry about him,' Darrin said.

123

He guided me around the side of the building. The short, fat bouncer had Charles' face pressed against the cinderblock wall. Charles stood with his feet at shoulder width. His body was taut, ready to spring, but the bouncer held a silver revolver against the skin behind his right ear.

Darrin stepped around them to an indigo-blue Silverado pick-up. He popped the locks and handed me the key. 'You drive.'

I shouted, 'You all right, Charles?'

'Hell, yeah,' he said. His voice held no fear and more than a little pleasure.

TEN

The old money in Jacksonville lived in Ortega, a riverside neighborhood three miles from Little Vegas. Lawyers and judges lived there and doctors who left home for medical school and came back to occupy the family houses. Live oaks whose trunks had fattened on summer rains for two or more centuries shaded the yards. In the past thirty years realtors had sold houses to families from the North in almost every neighborhood in the city, but not Ortega. If Ortega families had no children who wanted their houses, they sold them to the children of friends and the neighborhood was as corrupt as ever and smelled like jasmine blossoms.

Darrin held his gun against my ribcage and directed me through the dark streets until we reached McGirts Boulevard, which abutted the muddy banks where the Ortega River spilled into the St. Johns. When we reached a long brick wall, Darrin pointed at an open gate and said, 'In there.' A black driveway snaked past oaks to a large orange-brick house. Heavy branches shaded the yard against the moonlight and soft floodlights, positioned in a garden, illuminated the exterior walls from beneath as if the house were a painting that the owner wanted visitors to admire.

On the front porch Darrin rang once and the door opened to a large man with a heavy face, straight salt-and-pepper hair and bright blue eyes. I recognized him. His name was Don Melchiori. He was a city councilman who managed to position himself next to the mayor whenever news cameras covered a press conference. The newspaper had featured him recently in a series on historical preservation.

He looked me over and nodded into the front hall. We followed him into a living room with a white carpet, a large sofa and matching chairs upholstered in blue seersucker. An ornate mirror hung over a marble fireplace. He held his head forward and low, the way large men sometimes do as if the weight of their big skulls has become burdensome. 'Now what's this all about?' he said.

'I'm William—'

'I know who the hell you are,' he said. 'Why were you at my bar asking about Tonya Richmond?'

'Little Vegas is yours?'

He said, 'I own a piece of it. Is this a problem?'

'Only if you tell the manager to hire a girl for a sex party and then the girl gets killed.'

He stepped close to me. He was at least a hundred pounds heavier than I was. Suddenly he butted his forehead into mine. The blow staggered me and when my vision cleared he was crossing the room to the fireplace and a warm trickle of blood was running from my head on to my cheek.

Melchiori spoke to Darrin. 'I'm sixty-one years old and still on a daily basis people surprise me with their stupidity. I wake up every morning and I think, "There's nothing difficult here. Nothing complicated. A man with a third-grade education should be able to figure it out." But inevitably before lunchtime someone manages to prove that I've overestimated humankind. Often it happens before breakfast. Then all day long it happens again and again and again.'

A drop of blood fell from my cheek on to my shirt. I asked, 'What happened in Jamaica that got Tonya Richmond killed?'

Melchiori spun and fixed his eyes on me. He looked at my forehead and my cheek, then dug a white cloth handkerchief out of his pocket and threw it at me. 'Don't bleed on the carpet,'

he said.

'What happened in Jamaica?'

He came to me, got close again, and I guessed he expected me to back away but I didn't. 'Nothing happened in Jamaica,' he said. 'We had a party. We had a good time. Then we came home.'

'Why was Belinda Mabry there?'

He glanced at Darrin. 'Same reason as the rest of us. For the party.'

'And now she's dead and Tonya Richmond's dead and—'

Melchiori's fist shot into my stomach and the air punched from my lungs. I sank to the white carpet and sat looking up at the big man. A hard kick in his knees would put him on the carpet next to me. I glanced at Darrin. His gun pointed at my head.

Melchiori said, 'Tonya Richmond was a prostitute, the lowest kind. Sooner or later a girl like that gets killed. Belinda Mabry liked risky sex, the riskier the better. Sooner or later she had to get hurt. I don't like coincidence any more than you do, Mr Byrd, but they both put themselves in harm's way. That's not coincidence. That's bad judgment.'

'And how about Ashley Littleton?'

He stared at me with icy eyes and said, 'I know nothing about her.'

'I think you're lying,' I said.

Melchiori stood over me and shook his head sadly as though I were a small and bothersome creature. 'You show bad judgment too.'

'Who did Belinda Mabry come with to your party?'

A little smile formed on his big mouth. 'Now why would I tell you that?'

'Because you don't want me to break your knees?'

For a big man he moved quickly. He kicked me in the ribs. I tried to grab his foot but was much too slow and the air punched out of my lungs again. As I fought for breath, he said, 'You want to know about Belinda Mabry, you should ask her son. He spends all his time begging free drinks at Little Vegas.'

Belinda's son, I thought. *And mine.* I said, 'He drives in all the way from the Intracoastal to go to your club?' Talking hurt.

'Comes in four or five nights a week.'

'Why would he do that?'

He looked at me again like I was slow. 'Jesus, I kicked you in the ribs, not the head. I suppose he likes the girls.'

'He could find better clubs close to home. Clubs where girls actually show up.'

'Maybe he likes to slum. Like his mother.'

I lunged for his legs but he neatly sidestepped me.

I looked up at him. 'Did you kill my cat?'

He glanced at Darrin with a smile. 'Maybe I did get him in the head.' He glared down at me. 'Why in the world would I kill your cat?'

'I don't know. Why in the world would you headbutt me and punch me in the stomach?'

'Because you're a pain in the ass, Mr Byrd.

128

You ask questions you shouldn't ask.'

'Who brought Belinda Mabry to the party?' I asked.

'Ah, fuck you.' He turned to Darrin. 'Get rid of him.'

But as Darrin came for me another man stepped into the room, an old man with tear-stain scars under his eyes and a spotless white shirt buttoned up to his neck. 'Good evening, gentlemen,' Charles said.

Melchiori looked annoyed. 'Who are you?'

Charles nodded toward me. 'His friend.'

A deep laugh erupted from Melchiori's chest. 'This old man is your backup?' he asked, then said to Darrin, 'Get these scumbags out of my house.'

Charles reached down, unzipped his zipper and pulled out his penis.

'Huh,' Darrin said.

Melchiori was furious. 'I'm going to tear your head off.'

'He's crazy, Mr Melchiori,' Darrin said but Melchiori was already coming at Charles.

Charles started to piss. Melchiori froze, so angry he couldn't move, and watched a heavy stream of urine splatter on his white carpet. Charles pissed for a full minute and more. Then he shook his penis and tucked it into his pants.

Melchiori, his face flushed, looked at the ruined carpet, made a choking sound and came at Charles again. But he'd lost his inner balance. As Melchiori stepped up to him, Charles shot a fist into his stomach and an elbow into his face. A bone cracked – Melchiori's nose or jaw – and he started to fall. Darrin fired his gun at Charles. The bullet hit Melchiori's shoulder.

Charles caught Melchiori against him, hoisted him to his chest. Melchiori was twice Charles' size but Charles held him as though he were stuffed with cotton. If Darrin wanted to shoot at Charles again he would have to shoot through Melchiori's body.

Charles whispered something in Melchiori's ear and stepped toward Darrin, clutching the big man to him. Darrin tried to get an angle on Charles but couldn't find the shot. Charles stepped closer. 'Put the gun down,' he said calmly.

'Fuck you,' Darrin said and dodged to the side.

But Charles turned with him, dancing with Melchiori. Melchiori's eyes had turned glazy and saliva was running on to his chin.

'Fuck,' Darrin yelled and turned for the door. 'Run,' said Charles calmly. 'Run, run, run.' Darrin did.

Charles laid the big man on the carpet. Melchiori's leg rested in the pool of urine. He stared at the air above him and rasped to no one in particular, probably Charles and me both, 'I'm going to kill you.'

Charles came to me. 'You all right?'

'Scratches and scrapes,' I said.

'Then get up.'

He gazed around the living room, spotted the handkerchief Melchiori had thrown at me and used it to lift Melchiori's phone off the receiver. He dialed 911 with a knuckle. When the operator answered, Charles said, 'Gunshots on McGirts Boulevard,' gave Melchiori's street address and hung up.

He looked down at Melchiori. 'You'll live,' he said, 'though you might regret it.'

Melchiori rasped, 'Fuck you.'

Charles asked me, 'You want to burn down the house?'

Melchiori flinched but said nothing and we left him and went outside to Charles' car. Darrin's pickup truck was gone. As we pulled out of the driveway I rolled down my window and listened to the night. Tree frogs chirped in the branches. A small airplane, invisible in the darkness, tore gently across the sky. There were no sirens.

I asked Charles. 'What did you whisper to Melchiori when you caught him?'

'I told him I'd kill him if his blood stained my shirt.'

'You're a crazy old man.'

'That's what makes me so lovable,' he said.

'Yeah, to other wolverines.'

As we turned from McGirts on to Grand Avenue and crossed the Ortega River, a police cruiser flew past, its lights flashing.

'Melchiori says that Terrence Mabry hangs out at Little Vegas,' I said.

'Then we'll need to talk to your boy again.'

'Don't call him my boy.'

'OK.'

We rode quietly for a while and I said, 'The

131

pissing thing. I've never seen that before.'

'I've never done it before. I wanted Melchiori to know this city isn't his own. Not even his house.' He turned the corner on to Roosevelt Boulevard and squinted up at a road sign. 'And besides' – he shrugged – 'I needed to piss.'

ELEVEN

I first called Charles' number two weeks after he wrote it on the back of a Worman's Deli receipt. The brother of the man whose neck I'd broken had tracked down my address and shown up at my front door with a couple of friends. My dad had scared them off with his Ruger and afterward had called the police, who'd told him there was nothing they could do unless he got a judge to issue an order of protection or actual violence was committed. And I was a problem in the community anyway so why didn't he get me out of town until the trial? After lying low for a few days, the brother and his friends waited one morning until my dad drove away from the house, then crossed the yard with tire irons which they used to demolish the front door. By the time the police came, they were gone. We hung a new door. Two days later the brother and his friends returned and demolished it too.

When I called and explained the situation, Charles asked, 'You sure you want to stop them?'

They'd scared me out of my mind. 'Of course.'

'Because once you stop them you can't start them again.'

I didn't know what that meant. 'I'm sure,' I said.

'All right then.' He sounded pleased. 'I'll pick you up tomorrow at noon.'

'What for?'

'Be in front of your house,' he said. 'I don't like to wait.'

A few minutes before twelve the next day, a brown Buick sedan with a white vinyl roof pulled into the driveway. Charles sat at the wheel, dressed in his bright white shirt, buttoned to the top, his hands and tear-scarred face looking freshly scrubbed. 'You ready?' he asked as I climbed in.

'For what?'

He hit the accelerator. 'The rest of your life.'

We drove into a rough scrubby wetland east of downtown where loggers had cut and pulped pines in the first decades of the twentieth century. It was early October but the sun was high and hot and we kept the windows up and the air conditioner streaming cold.

Charles left the highway and drove for a quarter mile on an asphalt strip and, when the asphalt ended, a sand and dirt road that wound through pines and cypress. The road ended at a clearing. At the far end was a wooden shack that you could use as a hunting blind, and to the side were four posts as thick as telephone poles, the bottom ends buried in the ground, the tops rising eight feet or so into the air. Chained to three of the poles were the brother of the man whose neck I'd broken and his two friends. Charles had stripped off their shirts and shoes and the morning sun had baked their faces, chests and shoulders red. I didn't know what else Charles had done but they seemed stoned, barely able to keep on their feet. They didn't look at us, didn't seem to know we were there.

'When I called you I didn't mean this,' I said. 'I just wanted to stop them.'

Charles looked at me straight. 'I'm stopping them.'

'We've got to let them go—'

'It's too late for that,' he said.

Charles walked toward the men. I stood where I was and yelled after him, 'Why did you bring me here?'

'This is for you,' he said. 'Not me. As far as I'm concerned I don't even exist except for you right now, my friend.'

So I followed him across the clearing. He said, 'If you stand outside, shivering bare-chested all night long in the cool swamp air, and then sweat in heat like this without water for six or seven hours, you'll start hallucinating.' He stepped up to the brother and slapped his cheeks twice. The man groaned but his eyes never focused.

134

Charles went to the other men and slapped them too. Flies swarmed around the third man's belly.

'Give them something to drink,' I said.

Charles narrowed his eyes at me. 'Now? Are you crazy?'

He went to his car and opened the trunk. I moved close to the brother. His breath stunk like nothing living.

I whispered, 'I'm sorry.'

His brown eyes, bloodshot and glazed, brought me into focus. He looked hurt and confused, as though someone had pulled a terrible joke on him and he was just figuring out the damage. He pursed his lips and I thought he would speak to me but he tried to spit. He was too weak and his mouth too dry. Thick flecks of saliva fell on to his chin.

Charles came back with a small pistol and held it against the man's temple.

'No,' I said quietly.

'Yes,' he said and pulled the trigger.

The man's head jerked and fell against his chest and the gunshot echoed through the trees like cracking wood. The wound barely bled.

'Just enough to do the job,' Charles said to me or to himself or to no one at all. That turned out to be his first lesson. Shed no more blood than necessary. Don't break a sweat if a task doesn't require exertion. Save your energy because sooner or later you'll need it. *Do just enough to do the job*.

He went to the second man and shot him in

the head, then to the third and shot him too. The sound bounced through the trees and passed into the distance and he said, 'There's no such thing as a clean killing but you can do a lot to reduce the mess.'

Bile rose in my throat and I stooped, trying to settle my stomach.

Charles went to the car, put away the gun and returned with a shovel. 'In this soil you'll hit water in about two and a half feet. Set a body in the hole and cover it properly and it'll rot away in a year. In two years you can use it to compost a rose garden and except for metal fillings and maybe a tooth or two, you'll never know the difference.'

Vomit rose from my belly and I pitched forward on to my hands and knees and let it come out as if I could rid my insides of the guilt of these three men's deaths. I stayed on my hands and knees long after I was done, rocking forward and back.

Charles waited until I stopped, then stuck the blade of the shovel into the soft dirt in front of my face and said, 'Best thing for that is work.'

He sat, his legs crossed under him, while I dug the hole. When I was done we heaved the bodies into the ground and shoveled dirt over them. Charles tamped the grave flat and solid with the back of the shovel blade. Afterward he said, 'These guys have disappeared. No one will ever know where they went. But everyone will know what happens to men who mess with you. People will fear you now.'

He walked to the car and I followed him, dropped the shovel into the trunk and got in beside him. I vowed that afternoon to reject every lesson Charles tried to teach me and, most of all, to let the fear that I could inspire turn to dust. I vowed to forget I'd met him and forget the part of me that was like him.

At one-thirty a.m., my ribs aching where Don Melchiori had kicked me and my forehead throbbing where he'd butted me, we pulled into my Best Gas station. My night manager, an Indian named Atul Mehta, put down the *Car and Driver* magazine he was reading and his smile fell away when he saw my bloodied face.

I shook my head. 'Just a small accident, Atul.' I went to the display of bandages, aspirin and cold medicines that we kept behind the counter and took two packages of gauze and a box of Band-aids. Charles helped himself to a Pepsi from the refrigerator case.

In the bathroom I stripped off my blood-stained shirt and stuffed it in the trash, damp-ened the gauze pads in the sink and cleaned my face. The wound on my forehead bled again so I tamped it until the skin looked moist and pink, and I put a Band-aid over it. There was nothing I could do for the bruises rising over my ribs. I went to my office and put on one of the Best Gas T-shirts that I kept in a box in the closet. When I came out, Charles and Atul were talking about a Ferrari pictured on the front cover of *Car and Driver*.

Charles nodded at me with a little smile as if he approved of how I'd cleaned up. 'Home?' he asked.

'Home,' I agreed.

Charles drove fast and smooth, and riding with him even in the daytime felt like getting caught in a rushing dream. I closed my eyes and may have slept because when I opened them again we were crossing the bridge a half mile from my house. I said nothing but watched Charles drive. He breathed slowly and looked calm as though restfulness for him was jetting over a bridge at ninety miles an hour.

When we pulled on to my block, two police cruisers were parked in my driveway and the lights were on inside the house. For a moment I panicked. Had the man who'd killed Fela come back and harmed Susan and Thomas? But I realized that if that were the case there would be more activity – more police cars, emergency vehicles and television news vans. No, the police were there for me, not for them.

Charles must've come to the same conclusion. He slowed his car and stopped two houses from mine. 'I can't go with you,' he said.

'I know.'

'Don't say any more than you need to,' he said.

'You don't have to tell me that.' I climbed out of the car.

'Call me in the morning,' he said, hit the accelerator and was gone.

* * *

138

Susan and Thomas sat in the living room with Daniel Turner and two other officers in uniform. Susan had on cotton pajamas and Thomas the jeans and black T-shirt he'd worn all day. Susan and Thomas looked relieved to see me, Daniel and the others less so. 'We heard you were in an accident,' Susan said.

'You talked to Atul?' I said.

'When Daniel came, I called the station and asked Atul to let me know if you showed up.'

'And asked him not to tell me that you were looking for me?'

Daniel nodded, 'At my request.'

'I'll have to fire him,' I said.

Daniel shook his head, disgusted. 'Where have you been?'

'Out for a drive.'

'You told me this afternoon that you would come right in to the station.'

'A long drive,' I said.

One of the uniformed officers asked, 'Without your car?'

'I went with a friend.'

'Charles Tucker?' Daniel asked.

I saw no reason to answer.

Daniel glared at me.

I held my wrists toward him. 'You going to arrest me?'

'Calm down,' he said. 'I'd like you to come in and talk voluntarily.'

Thomas said, 'Don't do it, Dad.'

Susan and I stared at him.

'Not without a lawyer,' he said. 'Not unless

they arrest you.'

Daniel spoke to him gently. 'We don't suspect your dad of anything. We just want him to help us straighten out a few facts.'

'You could do that here,' Thomas said and I realized he was afraid that I was guilty of something terrible.

'It's OK,' I said to him but told Daniel, 'Thomas is right. We can talk here. I'm not hiding anything.'

Daniel shook his head. 'Your life is nothing if not hiding.'

I sat next to Thomas on the sofa. 'I've got nothing to hide.'

One of the uniformed officers said, 'What happened to your forehead?'

'I'd rather not say.'

'If you don't help, I'll have to arrest you, BB,' Daniel said. 'You know I don't want to do that.'

'On what charge?' I asked.

'You decide. Assault and battery: Bobby Mabry's burned hands. Breaking and entry: Ashley Littleton's house.' He glanced at Susan and Thomas, then back at me. 'Suspicion of murder: Ashley Littleton's roommate, Brianna Sumner.'

He didn't mention the shooting of Don Melchiori and that came as a relief. I said, 'None of that's true except the breaking and entry if you want to stretch the point.'

'We could charge you and hold you for a couple of weeks while we make sure you're clear.'

140

I considered my options and said to Susan, 'Why don't you and Thomas get some sleep. This might take a while.'

She stayed in her chair.

I leaned toward her and said as politely as I could, 'Please get Thomas the hell out of here.'

She frowned but held her hand toward Thomas, who ignored it. He stood on his own and shook his head at me. He left the room and Susan followed him.

Daniel nodded to one of the uniformed officers, who opened a notepad and readied a pen. Daniel said, 'Did Charles Tucker burn Bobby Mabry's hands?'

'I don't know,' I said. 'He didn't tell me.'

'Did you ask him?'

'More or less. He said he doesn't like the smell of burning flesh. Why don't you ask Bobby Mabry who did it?'

'Maybe we've already done that,' he said. 'Maybe he told us that Charles Tucker's responsible.' He watched me closely.

I said, 'What else d'you want to know?'

'I want to hear what you know about Charles.'

'Charles is a hard man to get to know.'

'Fine,' he said. 'Was Brianna Sumner still alive when you and Charles broke into her house?'

'First, I'm not saying that I broke into her house. Second, you saw her body. She'd been dead a long time.'

'OK,' he said, 'so why does a killer come for

141

her? He's already killed her roommate and so killing her comes at a high price. Until her death the other killings looked random. Now we know they're not. What makes killing her worthwhile?'

'I don't know.'

'Then I'll tell you my theory,' he said. 'Brianna Sumner knew the killer or was in a position to figure out his identity. When the killer first murdered her roommate, he felt comfortable letting her live. Two weeks passed after Ashley Littleton's death before he came for her. So something happened in the last twenty-four or forty-eight hours that worried him.'

'That much seems obvious,' I said.

He frowned at me. 'That something involved one of two people, or both. Maybe it involved Belinda Mabry. If Ashley Littleton had a connection to Belinda, and the killer suspected that Brianna Sumner knew about it, then killing her would become an easy choice.'

'Sounds reasonable,' I said. 'Who's the other one?'

'You,' Daniel said. 'I pulled you in to identify Belinda's body and you started poking your nose into everyone's lives like the idiot-bastard you are. You might've poked your nose in too deep somewhere and made the killer nervous. Maybe the killer thought that if you got to Brianna Sumner, as you eventually did, she would tell you something she shouldn't.'

'The killer would've known that you would talk to her too,' I said. 'Why wouldn't that worry him?'

'Ashley Littleton was a hooker. Brianna Sumner had a dirty record too. The charges were three years old, but still. Prostitutes and their friends don't like to talk to the police, especially if their pimps – or well-connected customers – are threatening them. But a prostitute might talk to you, especially if you're traveling with Charles Tucker. So, let's go with the second possibility. What have *you* done? Whose life have you poked your nose into? Who have you made nervous?'

If I told him about Little Vegas or the trips to Jamaica that the dead women took, he would make quick tracks to Don Melchiori, and then Charles and I would be in trouble. Anyway, he was asking what I'd done that could have led to Brianna Sumner's killing, and I'd learned about Little Vegas and Jamaica after she was killed. I said, 'Over on Bridier Street by the arena I talked to a hooker and her pimp. They're working out of a boarded-up pink bungalow or were when I went by there two days ago. The pimp told me about some rumors. For example, that the killer drives a green Mercedes SUV. I had the feeling he knew more than he was telling me. It's possible he got word back to someone.'

'What're the hooker's and pimp's names?' Daniel asked.

'The hooker said her name was Evelyn. I didn't get the pimp's name. He's a bald, black guy and talks like he's from the Caribbean.' I watched the officer with the pen scribble on the notepad. 'Is it true about the Mercedes SUV?'

'Might be,' Daniel said. 'One of Tonya Richmond's friends saw her climb into one early on the day she was killed. Another girl says she saw a green SUV cruising the street where Ashley Littleton got picked up for the last time. But there're a lot of SUVs in this city and more than a few of them green. What else can you tell me?'

'When I went to Belinda's house, Bobby Mabry said she and her husband made their money in real estate. I didn't believe it.'

Daniel said, 'Her husband was Jerry Stilman and it's true he owned property in Chicago. But he also trafficked drugs. Spent twelve years in federal after a tire blew outside of Atlanta on one of the trucks he owned. A search of the truck turned up a hundred and fifty kilos of cocaine, heading from Miami to Chicago. The DEA says that when Stilman decided to sell his property and move from Chicago he did it in a hurry. The guy I talked to seemed to think someone forced him out.'

'So did drugs cause the killings?' I asked.

'We've thought about it and probably not. Ashley Littleton and Tonya Richmond were junkies but small time and no more interesting than a thousand other junkies in town. And drug-related killings usually don't include the kind of quirks this killer has.'

The air conditioner turned on and a cold breeze brushed over me. For a moment I wished that I was still outside riding through the hot night with Charles. I said, 'The Miami to Chicago trip takes you right through here, and Ashley Littleton and Tonya Richmond might-'ve been junkies but they would screw anyone who wanted to screw them and that could've made them attractive to guys higher up the ladder.' The Jamaica party also showed that Tonya Richmond was screwing above her pay grade and the pimp on Bridier Street had said that until recently Ashley Littleton had done private parties and groups, so she probably was still sometimes screwing above herself too, whether in Jamaica or elsewhere, but I didn't say so to Daniel. Instead I said, 'I think you should look into the drugs.'

He nodded as if I might be right. 'Anyone else you've been hassling since we found Belinda dead?'

'If I listened to you, I'd think I'd been hassling everyone I met,' I said.

'Do you think the killer is worried about you personally?' he asked.

There was a headless cat buried in the back-yard that told me the killer was, and a rib-kicking city councilman too. 'Nothing I can think of.'

He shook his head. 'How about your cat?'

I smiled. 'Susan told you about Fela?'

He nodded.

I said, 'I'm guessing it's one of the neighborhood kids.'

He didn't look like he believed it either. 'You'll let me know if someone returns the rest of her or sends a message?'

'Of course.'

'Of course. For your own good I'm asking a couple of officers to keep an eye on you and your house.'

'No, thanks,' I said.

'Think about Susan and Thomas – their safety.'

'They're fine,' I said. 'We're safe.'

'I don't need to ask for your permission,' he said.

I looked in his eyes, this man I'd known since we were kids. Back then I would've told him that he was being a jerk or I would've punched him and we would've scrapped until we were dirty and bloody. I said, 'Do what you've got to do.'

I watched as Daniel and the two officers backed out of the driveway and pulled away, their car tires crunching on the pavement, their tail lights fading into darkness. The night was clear and I looked at the stars. In the winter sky, Orion would hang overhead in the early morning but he was gone to wherever he went in the summer and the night seemed to lack a center. It was a sea of stars whose names I didn't know.

I closed the front door and yawned. My ribs ached and the throb in my forehead had receded into a low, dull pain. I flipped off the living-room lights and stumbled into the kitchen.

Susan and Thomas were sitting at the table, tired eyed and silent. I knew they'd heard everything we'd talked about in the living room.

'It's late,' I said. 'You should be in bed.'

'Damn you, BB,' Susan said. 'What gives you the right to do this? It's none of your business. It's none of Thomas's and mine. But you drag it into our house.'

I looked at Thomas. 'What do you think, Champ?'

'My name isn't Champ,' he said. 'I think the cut on your forehead is bleeding through the Band-aid.'

The light in the kitchen was too bright and I felt a pit in my stomach that was like hunger or longing. 'Do you want me to stop?' I asked him.

One side of his mouth twitched. 'I don't think you could even if I did.'

'You're a smart boy,' I said. 'Now go to bed. We can talk more in the morning.'

He walked to the doorway, stopped, and looked first at Susan and then at me. 'I don't want you to stop,' he said.

'Goodnight, Thomas,' I said.

He left the room.

Susan glared at me and when his bedroom door closed she said, 'You'll destroy us.'

'What's left to destroy?'

'You'll destroy Thomas,' she said.

'I hope not.'

'He cares so much about what you think about him and what you do.'

I felt heat in my face and neck. 'I don't think so.'

147

She stood.

I said, 'It doesn't have to be this way.'

'Doesn't it?'

I shook my head. 'Spend the night with me,'

She looked in my eyes, pleadingly. 'And that would make it better?'

'Maybe it would,' I said. 'It would be a beginning.'

Her hardness fell and I thought she might for once consent to be together but she said, 'Why do you ask me when you know it won't happen?'

'Because even after everything, I love you. God knows why but I do.'

A small sad smile appeared on her lips. 'Goodnight, BB,' she said and left the room.

I stood in the kitchen alone and thought about what I could do to make myself feel better. I could throw a counter stool through the glass on the French doors to the backyard. I could punch holes in the kitchen wall with my fists. I could drive to Lee Ann's house, wake her, and fuck her until we were hurt and exhausted.

I stood in the kitchen and breathed deep, my lungs pressing against my injured ribs, breathing in and out, waiting in vain for my adrenaline to come down. I stood like that for a long time before climbing the stairs to my bedroom where I crawled into bed and prepared myself for bad dreams.

TWELVE

At a quarter to ten the next morning the sound of a lawn mower woke me. Sunlight shined soft and warm through the shades and a single dust mote caught the light and glimmered in the air like a tiny daytime star. The smell of frying breakfast sausage made its way from the kitchen into my room.

The nightmares had never come. My sleep had been hard and dreamless and the morning felt calm, a time in which to forget the storms of the previous evening. But when I moved to get up, pain stabbed me above the ribs and I fell back to the mattress, sweating. I probed the bruise where Melchiori had kicked me. No ribs seemed to be broken so I tried again, slowly rocking myself on to my feet and straightening my back. I shuffled to the bathroom and faced the mirror.

The bruise extended from the middle of my belly to below my left nipple, cloudy as the Milky Way, darkening where Melchiori's heel had struck me. But my forehead looked good. No bruise – just a half-inch-long scab where the skin had split. The spot on my cheek where Terrence had hit me two days ago was only a scratch. I sucked in a deep breath and lifted my arms cautiously above my shoulders and then above my head. My face paled but my legs remained steady. So I showered, letting the hot water sting the skin on my back, and dressed in jeans and a loose cotton T-shirt.

Downstairs, Susan was eating breakfast at the kitchen table. She offered me her cheek and I kissed it and smelled soap and shampoo.

'Good morning,' she said and looked into my eyes with a warmth that seemed to me borne of our having survived a hard night.

'Did you sleep?' I asked.

'A little. You?'

I nodded. 'Surprisingly.'

I sat with her and ate and she handed me the sections of the morning paper that she'd finished reading but I left them on the table and watched her. She gave me a mild look and I knew better than to tell her again that we could live differently, so I asked, 'What are you doing today?'

'Showing a house on Old St Augustine.'

'Want to have dinner out tonight?'

'With Thomas?'

'If he'll come,' I said.

Again she smiled. 'OK.'

'He still sleeping?' I asked.

She nodded. 'He stayed up until dawn drawing a new comic book. It was a rough night for all of us.'

I heard something to hope for in the word *us*.

When Susan left I read the paper. The front-page headline said *Fourth Woman Killed*. The article described Daniel Turner's discovery of Brianna Sumner's body in her bedroom after a neighbor called about suspicious activity. A police spokesman said that all four killings involved sexual assault and asphyxiation and without naming specifics added that details in this killing resembled those in the earlier three. The article said the suspicious activity that the neighbor observed involved two men who the police had decided weren't responsible for Brianna's Sumner's death, though anyone with information concerning these men was encouraged to contact a citizens' hotline. The reporter had interviewed the neighbor, a man named Bruce Serikos. Brianna Sumner and Ashley Littleton had been quiet and friendly, he'd said, and sometimes when they were out of town he'd taken care of their dog. He mentioned nothing about prostitution, nothing about drug addictions.

The article included photographs of the four victims along with short biographies. Tonya Richmond had wanted to be a model. Ashley Littleton, who was the daughter of a well-liked captain of a Mayport shrimp trawler, had completed a certificate program in accounting, loved dogs and had gotten married and divorced before she was twenty. Both had records for drug possession and prostitution. Brianna Sumner had worked as a dancer and bartender and she had a two-year-old son who lived with his father. Belinda had been born in Milwaukee, moved to Jacksonville as a teenager, left for Chicago – where she'd gone to college, worked as a community organizer and gotten married – and then moved back south. The newspaper said that Belinda's husband had been a real-estate developer but said nothing about his conviction for drug trafficking or about Terrence.

By the time I finished reading, my calm was gone.

I looked at the Metro section. A headline at the top of the front page said *City Councilman Shot in Home Invasion*. According to the police, Don Melchiori had awakened and confronted two robbers at eleven-thirty the previous night. They'd struggled and the robbers had beaten the councilman and shot him in the shoulder before leaving empty handed. Melchiori was finishing his second term on the city council and was known for his work on the historical preservation of neighborhoods. He was in fair condition at University Hospital with non-life-threatening injuries.

I cleaned the dishes, leaving a plate of sausages for Thomas, got my keys and went into the living room. Charles and I had talked about going to see Terrence Mabry today. *My son* – an idea I couldn't get my mind around. I also wanted to see Bobby Mabry and ask him about the burns on his hands. If Charles came with me when I talked to him, Bobby probably would refuse to tell me who'd hurt him. I looked out the living-room window. Glinting in the morning sun a police car was parked against the curb two houses away. Daniel had followed through on his promise to post an officer on me.

I threw my keys on to the couch. Daniel had said the officer would protect Susan, Thomas and me, but I knew better. Daniel wanted to know how deeply I'd involved myself in Belinda's death.

So I went out the back door, across the patio and past the glassy surface of the pool. I walked down to the quarry pond and the drying mound of dirt where I'd buried Fela, then along the bank of the pond, through the neighbors' yards and up to the street. I could call Charles and ask him to pick me up but I didn't. I continued up the street and walked another quarter mile to the east until I reached the railroad tracks.

I went north on the railroad toward the water purification plant and the stretch of tracks where Belinda and I had lain on the gravel as a train bore down upon us. In the past two decades companies had built offices and cinder-block warehouses against the fence that separated the tracks from private land, and the railroad had replaced the creosote-stained wooden ties with reinforced concrete. Near the water plant, a radio station had erected a tower that looked like the steel framework for a huge church steeple. But the gravel rail bed remained the same, as did the smell of diesel and the ragged odor of flowering weeds. Memories of the days and evenings when I'd come to the tracks with Belinda flooded me. I thought about the words Christopher had spoken when I'd visited him at the house he shared with his new wife and her daughter. *Belinda grew up. That's what most of us do.* I wondered what that meant. If it meant forgetting the past, I wanted none of it.

Near the spot on the tracks where Belinda and I had sex, the chain-link fence had been bent to the ground, forming a bridge to the parking lot behind a factory that made disposable plastic plates and cups. Next to the bent fence a man was sitting on a stack of the wooden ties that the railroad had removed. He was tan and skinny, in his late twenties or early thirties, wearing brown denim overalls cut off at the knees, and no T-shirt. A dirty blond ponytail hung down his back. He drank from a sixteen-ounce can of Budweiser.

I stooped between the rails and looked northward into the heat-bent air. What was I looking for? Tens of thousands of trains had passed over the spot where Belinda and I had lain. Men like the one on the railroad ties had drunk their beer and pissed on it. Tens of thousands of rains and winds had washed the gravel clean of our presence. What was I looking for? The heat was dizzying. What did I expect to find?

'Next train don't come for twenty-five minutes,' said the man on the ties.

I didn't reply.

'You going to kill yourself?'

I said nothing.

'I wouldn't come here no more if you did.'

I walked over to him. 'I used to come to this spot.'

'Yeah, you and everyone else.'

I looked at him close. He was drunk or crazy or both. 'You come here a lot?'

He nodded the slow, lazy nod of a man who had nowhere else to be.

'Why?' I asked.

'Why the hell not?' He laughed.

'But why *here*?'

He drank from the can, squinted and said, 'Fuck off.'

'All right,' I said and turned away.

But as I walked back the way I'd come he yelled after me, 'You have choices!'

You have choices. My mother's words when I cut her lover's face in the apartment above the dry-cleaners.

Then, my mother held me down as the sweaty man put his hands on me. Blood on his face, blood on his chest, blood on the bath towel that lay discarded on the floor like bleached road-kill.

Did she have choices? Did he?

Something happened. Something amid the broken pieces of clay bowls in the apartment above the dry-cleaners, in the chemical and sweat stink of a summer afternoon. Something. I preferred not to talk about it or to think about it even. Would not, most of the time.

Did I have choices? Maybe some of the time. What if I put my hands on Lee Anne while

155

Susan slept alone in our sunroom? Did choice make a difference? The result was the same. Susan didn't have to like it. *I* didn't have to like it.

What if I chased Belinda's killer like a blind man? Did choice make a difference then?

Later on the day that I visited my mother, my father had dragged me from our house to the car, a gleaming new burgundy Monte Carlo that he'd bought only weeks earlier. He'd put me in the front passenger seat and slammed the door. He'd disappeared into the house again. The sky over the dashboard was an endless blue. My skin felt as if it would burst in the heat of the car. My father came outside again with his Ruger .22. I didn't ask where we were going. I knew, and I took a secret, childish pleasure in the violence that must come.

We drove the half mile to my mother's apartment and parked at the curb. My father didn't look at me. He checked the magazine of the Ruger, said, 'Wait here,' and climbed out of the car.

He wasn't gone long. I looked up through the passenger window to the sill where my mother had displayed my bowls. With the bowls gone, the apartment looked empty from outside, as if no one had ever lived there. I watched a woman in a green dress, carrying shirts on hangers, come out of the dry-cleaners. She smiled at me and I didn't smile back. I watched a single black bird cross the sky over the building and wondered whether its nest was near.

A gunshot, sharp and without echo, dis-charged inside the building and suddenly I felt a damp heat soaking through my underwear on to my legs.

Then my father came out of the street door and climbed into the car. He tossed his gun on to the backseat. He was sweating and panting. A sprinkle of blood covered the bottom of his work shirt. He looked at me with fierce eyes. 'You don't ever have to let anyone hurt you,' he said. 'You've got choices.'

'Did you shoot her?' I asked, uncertain whether I wanted my mother dead or alive.

'No,' he said. 'I didn't shoot her.' He pulled the car from the curb and drove us home.

I didn't know what my mother did with her lover's dead body. I didn't even know that he really *was* dead. But I'd assumed it for all these years. I never saw the man again. The police never came to our house to question my father. My mother left, alone, for Arizona less than a month later.

Thomas was eating breakfast at the counter when I came in through the back door. He wore khaki shorts and the same black T-shirt he'd had on the previous night. His hair was matted from sleep. The newspaper was spread out next to his plate and he was reading about Brianna Sumner.

'That's a sad story,' I said, poured myself a cup of coffee and watched him read.

He looked up. 'It doesn't mention you.'

157

'It shouldn't. This isn't about me,' I said. He looked unconvinced, so I added, 'I knew one of the women twenty-five years ago. I shouldn't even be involved.'

'That's what everyone keeps telling you.'

'Yes.'

He looked at the pictures of Belinda, Tonya Richmond, Ashley Littleton and Brianna Sumner and read the biographies. He said, 'I want to help.'

That rocked me on my heels. 'What?'

'I want to help you ... do what you're doing.'

'Why?'

'I don't know,' he said. 'I just want to.'

A laugh erupted from my gut, a short, hard laugh that made my ribs hurt, a laugh of surprise, not derision. 'No,' I said. 'Definitely not.'

Thomas looked hurt.

'But I've never been prouder of you,' I said. 'Never.'

'Fuck you, Dad.'

I looked at him long and perplexed. 'Don't ever say that. It's an ugly thing to say.'

He said, 'You treat Mom and me like we're children.'

'You *are* a child.'

'I'm almost sixteen.'

'Which makes you a child. Technically.'

'I'm almost as big as you.'

'Physically.'

He squared his eyes on mine in a way that nearly made me shrink from him. 'Not just physically.'

I shook my head. 'I'm sorry, Thomas.' I sipped from my coffee and went into the living room.

He called after me, 'I want to help.'

I went to the window and looked out. The police car hadn't moved. It idled in the sunshine, heat rising from its hood, like a slow beast that might rise and move when it finished warming its cold blood. The leaves on the trees were still. The sky was hot and cloudless.

Thomas came into the room and stood beside me. He was almost as tall as I was.

'Your mother would kill me if I let you.'

'She'll probably kill you anyway.'

I laughed. 'When did you grow up?'

'In May.'

'Yeah? What happened in May?'

'Nothing,' he said. 'I made that up.'

I put my hand on his shoulder. He tensed but didn't pull away. I nodded out the window and said, 'If you go out the back and walk to the driveway through the gate, you can get to my car without the man in the cruiser seeing you. Then you can back out of the driveway and pull away in the other direction. Let him follow but try not to let him see you clearly. Take him on a slow tour of the city.'

Thomas cocked his head to the side. 'I only have a driver's permit. You or Mom should be in the car when I'm driving.'

'I know.'

'You want me to drive around by myself with a police car behind me?'

'Yes.'

He thought about it and said, 'Cool.'

'Don't get carried away.'

'Anything else?'

'Yes, you can have dinner with your mother and me at Sorrento's.'

That excited him less but he agreed to eat with us.

'Take your phone,' I said and gave him my car key.

He headed to the back door with a grin, the first I'd seen on his face in weeks. He said, 'This is totally irresponsible.'

I watched from the front as Thomas backed my Lexus out of the driveway, shifted and hit the gas. Faster than I would've liked but it did the trick. The police cruiser pulled from the curb and followed.

Then I went to the kitchen and called Charles. 'Can you pick me up?' I asked.

'Twenty minutes,' he said and hung up.

THIRTEEN

Bobby Mabry answered the door to Belinda's house with bandages on his hands and stony fear in his eyes, the fear of a man who has lived most of his life afraid and still hasn't fully adapted to the condition. He glanced at the cut on my forehead, looked warily at Charles and said, 'What?'

His scalp was freshly shaved, his beard neatly trimmed, his shorts and shirt white and pressed. I asked, 'Who shaves you with your hands wrapped like that?'

'I told you not to come here again,' he said, and tried to close the door, but Charles stepped between it and the frame.

Bobby backed away from Charles into the foyer and we walked inside. 'What do you want?'

'What happened to your hands?' I asked.

He looked at Charles, frightened, but said to me, 'What happened to your forehead?'

I smiled. 'Should we start again?'

'If you want.'

'We need to talk to Terrence,' I said.

'About what? He's got nothing to tell you.'

Terrence appeared at the top of a broad

stairway that swept down to the foyer. 'I can talk for myself, Bobby,' he said. He came down the stairs in tight black jeans and an untucked rust-colored silk shirt. There was no fear in *his* eyes.

'Why have you been hanging out at Little Vegas?' I asked.

'Who says I have?'

'You've been there four or five nights a week, sponging drinks.'

He considered me. 'I like the girls there and I like the feel of the place.'

'Last night there were no girls at all and from what I can tell the girls who do work there aren't worth driving across the city for.'

'Who can explain desire?' He smiled. 'Some white boys can only get it up for black girls, right? Uncle Bobby gets it up for other boys. I get it up for the girls at Little Vegas. We all need something. Why do you care where I hang out?'

Charles spoke. 'One of the women who work-ed there died the same way as your mother.'

'Yeah,' Terrence said. 'Ashley Littleton.'

'You knew her?' I asked.

'She wasn't hard to get to know. Fifty bucks would do it. Sometimes twenty.'

Charles circled the foyer, observing and listening, then stopped at the three-tiered white marble fountain. He put a finger at the edge of the second tier so the water forked around it as it cascaded to the first tier.

I said to Terrence, 'Tonya Richmond hung out there too. The manager and her sister had a baby together.'

He nodded. 'Darrin and Deni.'

'Sounds as if there was a close family at Little Vegas,' Charles said.

'I didn't know Tonya well,' Terrence said. 'I like them trashy but not that trashy.'

I asked, 'Did you tell the police all this?'

'Of course. I had no reason not to.'

Charles said, 'Did you tell them your mother went to a party in Jamaica with Tonya Richmond?'

Terrence looked at him like he was crazy. 'What're you talking about?'

'Three or four months ago,' Charles said. 'Probably a weekend deal, maybe longer.'

Terrence shook his head. 'My mom never hung out with Tonya.'

I said, 'When we were here last time you said she'd started dating again about six months ago. Did she see anyone at Little Vegas?'

'That wasn't who she was,' he said. 'She liked established guys, guys who owned businesses, guys with money.'

'Don Melchiori?' I asked.

The councilman's name stung him but he recovered. 'She didn't date him. But she knew him and dated one of his friends.'

Charles said, 'You know that Melchiori's a part owner of Little Vegas.'

Terrence nodded, looking defeated. 'That doesn't mean she was like Tonya.'

Charles removed his finger from the fountain. He flicked it and a drop of water arced through

163

the air and landed on the black tile at Terrence's feet. 'You see what happened to Melchiori last night?' Charles asked.

Terrence gave a half nod. 'I watched the morning news.'

I asked, 'Which of Melchiori's friends did she date?'

Bobby said, 'It's none of his damn business, Terrence.'

Terrence looked at me evenly. 'A man named David Fowler,' he said. 'He works in the mayor's office.'

I asked, 'Have you heard from him since your mom died?'

He shook his head.

We'd learned most of what we'd hoped for from the visit so I glanced at Charles. 'D'you have anything else?'

He shook his head. 'I'm ready.'

I said to Terrence, 'I'm sorry for doing this.'

We shook hands and he looked like he might forgive my intrusion until Charles turned and climbed the broad stairway and I followed him.

'Where are you going?' Bobby shouted at us.

'I'm sorry,' I said.

In the hallway that extended from the second-story landing, doors opened to four rooms. With Bobby and Terrence behind us, we went into the master bedroom. Belinda's. It was a large room, painted pale mocha, with a queen-sized bed centered against one wall and a twin bed positioned under a window that faced the backyard and the Intracoastal Waterway. A line

164

drawing of a nude woman hung on the wall above the head of the larger bed. Along the third wall a wide passage led to a dressing room and bathroom. Inside the dressing room, visible from the bedroom, two large dark-wood dressers, his and hers, stood side by side. A ceiling fan spun slowly.

Charles and I went to the dressers. A framed photograph of Jerry Stilman stood on Belinda's. He was a large-faced dark-skinned black man with a tightly trimmed goatee. He was handsome, though there was something mean in his eyes.

I opened the top drawer.

'I'm calling the police,' Bobby said but didn't go to the phone.

'What's with the extra bed?' I asked.

'Jerry was a rough sleeper,' Terrence said. 'Sometimes Mom needed to get out of the way.'

The top drawer held Belinda's panties, bras and an open box with necklaces, earrings, and a wide bracelet. My heart dropped a little and I breathed in, expecting to catch the scent of a girl long gone from my life but I smelled only the cedar grain of the dresser.

Charles held up a pair of extra large men's underwear and unfurled it. 'Jerry Stilman *was* a big man, wasn't he?' He looked over his shoulder at Terrence. 'When'd you say he died?'

'I didn't. About a year and a half ago. A heart attack.'

'And your mother kept his underwear drawer stocked and ready,' I said.

Terrence looked at me and repeated something Bobby had said the last time Charles and I had come. 'Losing men was hard on her.'

I opened the second drawer, removed a green blouse, held it to my face and breathed in. Nothing.

Charles asked, 'Did the police look through your mother's room?'

'We didn't let them,' Terrence said.

'Yeah?' Charles said. 'Why?'

'I didn't want them fingering her things.'

Charles removed a black pistol from the second drawer of the other dresser. He sniffed the barrel, then tucked the gun into his waistband.

'You can't take that,' said Bobby.

Charles rooted through the drawer until he found a box of .38 caliber shells and he put it in his pocket. 'Yes,' he said, 'I believe I can.'

Belinda's bottom dresser drawer contained nightgowns and pajamas, and as I stirred them, searching for anything she might have hidden, a scent finally arose that I knew as well as my own body. My chest tugged and I recoiled from the sweetness of it.

When we finished with the bedroom we tried the next door, a home office with a big desk, two computers, a worktable, a small photocopier, a large wooden filing cabinet and a safe.

'What did they use this office for?' I asked.

'Their real estate firm,' Terrence said.

'I thought they sold everything before moving from Chicago.'

'They kept a couple of buildings. Jerry would've sold them but Mom wanted them.'

I went to the window and looked out. The Fairline motor cruiser rested against the dock, its lines hanging lazily in the water. Dark storm clouds were crossing the Intracoastal.

'What's in the safe?' Charles asked.

'Don't know,' Terrence said.

'Bobby?' I asked.

He shook his head.

Charles asked, 'D'you have the combination?'

Again Bobby shook his head.

Terrence said, 'We've scheduled someone to cut it open next week. My mom and Jerry kept the business private from me, and then when Jerry died Mom ran it on her own.'

Charles removed the gun from his belt, put in a single shell, went to the safe and aimed at the combination touch pad.

'No,' Bobby said.

'Do you know the combination?' Charles asked.

Bobby shook his head.

Charles grinned and tucked the gun in his waistband again. 'Shooting it would only make noise and a mess.'

Bobby and Terrence smiled uneasily. Terrence asked, 'What're you looking for?'

I went to the filing cabinet and opened the top drawer. 'We'll know when we find it.' The drawer held expired contracts reaching back fourteen years with nothing before then. The second drawer contained folders of bank records sorted by year, again going back fourteen years and stopping.

I pulled the handle on the third drawer. It was locked.

'The key?' I asked Terrence.

He shook his head.

'Bobby?'

'I don't know where it is,' he said.

Charles pulled the pistol from his waistband again and pointed it at the drawer.

Bobby and Terrence smiled, tight-lipped, as though the joke was getting old.

Charles fired the gun. The wood front split apart and splinters showered the room. The blast made my ears ring.

'Jesus,' Bobby yelled.

Terrence laughed, shocked.

Charles admired the gun. 'Probably more power than the job needed.'

'You could've kicked the drawer in,' I said.

'Yeah, I could've.' He picked up the shell, put it in his pocket and tucked the gun away.

The shot had knocked the drawer off its track, so I shoved it in and pulled it out until it slid open. The drawer contained only a faded nine-by-twelve manila envelope and a small leatherette portfolio. I looked inside the portfolio and found papers and letters, some with business letterheads, some with government seals. I crammed the manila envelope in with the other papers and tossed the portfolio to Charles.

'What're you doing with that?' Bobby asked.

168

'I'll return it when we're done,' I said.

He moved toward the door but Charles cut him off and pulled the pistol out of his waistband again. He loaded it with three more rounds.

'What do you want?' There was pleading in Bobby's voice.

Charles made no pretense toward friendliness or kindness. 'For you to cooperate and stop acting like an asshole.'

We went into Bobby's bedroom. Bobby had surprisingly little in it – a few changes of clothes and toiletries. It looked and felt like a guest room.

'How long have you been staying here?' I asked.

'I'm done talking,' he said.

We moved to Terrence's bedroom, the room of a kid who'd become an adult and never left home. There was a plain twin bed, a brown pressboard bookcase, a desk with a laptop computer on it, a dresser, a cabinet and a dartboard hanging on the closet door.

'Don't search in here,' Terrence said.

'Sorry, son,' Charles said.

Terrence's face flashed anger but Charles held the pistol and wore such a strangely innocent expression that you could believe that he would use it like a child who knew no better.

I searched the dresser, the cabinet, and the closet and found nothing that interested me. 'See? No reason to worry,' I said and went to the bookshelf. A line of paperback novels and a dictionary stood on the top shelf. On the next shelf were stacks of old magazines and a hand-carved wooden box, the kind they sell in Mexican tourist markets. I picked up the top magazine, an old copy of *Details*. Under it was a deeply creased magazine called *Whiplash* – with pictures of bondage and S&M on the cover.

'This what you're into?' I asked Terrence and picked it up.

About a dozen odd-shaped pieces of paper fell from between the magazine pages and snowed to the floor. Terrence had clipped out favorite pictures. A woman wearing a mask over her head and studs through her nipples landed face up. So did a woman with feet and hands splayed spread eagle, chained to a dark wall, a cut below her lip. 'What do you do? Arrange them like paper dolls?'

Terrence sighed. He moved to pick up the pictures. But Charles grabbed him.

I gathered the pictures myself, scooping them between the magazine pages, and saw that Terrence had altered some of them. He'd cut pictures of faces from other magazines or clipped them from family photographs and pasted them above the shoulders of the *Whiplash* shots. One of the faces was of a little Asian girl, no older than seven, which he'd affixed to the body of a skinny white woman with bleeding nipples. I stared at the next one for several seconds before I comprehended what I was looking at. He'd cut out a fat white woman who

170

was being doubly penetrated and had pasted on a photograph of the face of Belinda at twenty-one or twenty-two years old. Belinda's hair was shorter than when I'd first met her but her eyes were still young and hopeful. She had an open-mouthed smile as two men reamed the woman under her.

'Jesus!' I said.

Terrence said, 'I told you not to look.'

'Why did you do that?' I asked.

Terrence looked mortified but said, 'You can't control what you desire.'

'You can control what you do about it,' I said.

'Can you?' he said.

'I hope so.'

Charles mumbled, *'You* never did.'

I balled up the picture and stuffed it in my pocket. 'This isn't desire. I understand what need can do to a man,' I said. 'But I don't understand how you could make a picture like that.'

Terrence's eyes were wet with shame and anger. 'Get out of my room,' he said. 'Please.'

'I want to,' I said. 'I honestly do.' I turned back to the shelf and thumbed through the rest of the magazines. There were two more copies of *Whiplash.* I didn't shake them to see what would fall out. I opened the carved wooden box. Inside was a pair of surgical scissors, probably the ones he'd used to snip pictures from magazines, and three glassine baggies. 'Heroin?' I asked.

'Please get out of my room,' he said.

171

I closed the box and said to Charles, 'Let's go.'

We went downstairs to the front door. Bobby and Terrence looked humiliated, the way men do when you've exposed their essential nakedness. Charles looked as innocent and content as ever. I tried not to look like I regretted stripping Terrence and Bobby of the little that seemed to cover them.

Charles said, 'Let's check the garage.'

I'd seen enough. 'I'm done.'

'Come on,' he said. 'I might want to trade that piece-of-junk Dodge you gave me for one of their cars.' He walked back through the house, into the kitchen, through a large laundry room and into a three-car garage. A brown Nissan SUV and a burgundy Mercedes convertible were parked in two of the spots, both looking like they'd come straight from the carwash.

'Could anyone mistake the Nissan for green?' I asked.

'Doubt it,' Charles said.

A clean workbench with a tall tool chest and a set of shelves stood in the third parking spot. I went to the chest and opened the drawers. It held tools, though they looked unused.

Charles went to the shelves. They held vases and flowerpots, garden shears, a couple of pairs of garden gloves and a spool of clear plastic lawn bags. Charles peeled one of the large bags off the spool.

Bobby said, 'We hire Mexicans for that.'

'Shut up, Bobby,' I said.

Charles climbed into the passenger seat of the Nissan and checked the glove compartment, then got out and looked in the back. He did the same with the Mercedes.

'All right?' I asked.

'Good enough. Let's go.'

We went back through the house and out on to the front porch.

Heavy thunderheads had rolled in silently while we were inside. The green of the lawn and trees had deepened in the gloom. The air was still and humid.

'When's Belinda's funeral?' I asked Bobby.

He shook his head. 'Police won't release her body. They say it could be weeks.'

'How about a memorial service?'

'Sorry. You're not invited.'

Terrence glanced at his uncle, then me. 'Tomorrow at four. Palm Valley Baptist Church.'

'Thank you,' I said.

Bobby asked Charles, 'What are you going to do with Jerry's gun?'

'I was planning to add it to my collection,' Charles said. 'What do you think I should do with it?'

'I think you should give it back.'

Charles pulled it from his belt. 'Yeah? It won't do you any good. You've got to be able to shoot it.'

'It's not yours,' Bobby said.

'Fine.' Charles handed the gun to Bobby, butt first, setting it roughly into Bobby's bandaged fingers. He dug the box of shells out of his

173

pocket and gave it to him too. 'There're still three rounds in the magazine. Don't forget to unload it.'

Bobby struggled to point the gun at him. 'Give me the other things.'

Charles considered the leatherette portfolio that I'd taken from the file cabinet and said, 'Ah, go to hell.' He turned and walked toward his car.

Bobby fumbled with the pistol, pointed it at the lowering clouds and managed to pull the trigger. The shot cracked through the air. Charles stopped and cocked his head to the side as though he couldn't believe what he'd heard and was deciding what to do about it. He came back and got close to Bobby, who pointed the pistol at him, looking shocked at his own nerve.

'You stupid sonofabitch,' Charles said. He swung the portfolio at Bobby and knocked the pistol out of his hands. It landed softly on the lawn. A sudden cool wind gusted through the branches in the side yard and crossed the grass. Bobby turned from the gun and looked at the sky as if the storm might strike us down. The first cold, fat raindrops splashed on the neatly raked gravel of the front walk.

FOURTEEN

Charles and I pulled out of the driveway, the portfolio at my feet. Thunder rumbled high in the clouds, and then a shard of lightning tore from the sky and exploded in the air above us. I asked, 'Could it be Terrence?'

'No.'

'The lawn bags?'

'You can buy them at any Home Depot,' Charles said.

'Then why'd you take one?'

'To watch his reaction.'

'Which was?'

'He had none.' A half block away the street disappeared in a haze where rain was falling hard. Charles flipped the wipers to high and a few moments later the shower pelted the metal roof and washed over the windshield. 'On the other hand,' Charles said, 'if he's the kind of psychopath who could kill four women, he might not react.'

A gust of wind buffeted the car and rain slapped the windows. Fronds on the street-side palms swung wildly.

'How about the pictures?' I asked.

'Who can explain desire?'

'Hmm.'

'OK, the man has problems,' Charles said. 'But I've known people capable of doing what this killer has done and he doesn't impress me that way. He's not smart enough, not cold enough.'

'Not enough like you?' I said.

Charles smiled. 'Or you for that matter. Even if he is your son.'

I shook my head. 'I don't feel it. He's a stranger to me.'

'We're all strangers, sooner or later,' he said.

I looked at him. 'Even you and me?'

He kept his eyes on the road. 'Especially you and me.'

'Why did you burn Bobby's hands?' I asked.

'Don't ask questions unless you really want to know the answers,' he said.

I considered what we'd walked into at Belinda's house. The air-conditioned stillness of the rooms. The glimpses of the Fairline motor cruiser from the back windows as storm clouds approached over the water. The hot shade and the faint smell of gasoline in the garage.

I said, 'If you drive a brown SUV at night someone might see it as green.'

'More likely the other way around,' Charles said. 'At night you'd see green as brown.'

'So it isn't Terrence.'

'I doubt it.'

The rain silenced as we crossed under a viaduct beneath the highway leading back to the city. Charles drove past the on-ramp. 'Where are we going?' I asked.

'I want to see what's in the leather case,' he said.

We parked at an Applebee's restaurant and ran through the rain. The neon apple at the top of the sign glowed in the downpour. The hostess, dressed in a red polo shirt with an Applebee's button, brightened when we stepped inside. 'Hi, Charlie,' she said and gave him a hug.

Charlie. 'You've got to be kidding,' I said.

'Why?' he said.

'This where you hang out?'

'Beats Little Vegas.'

'I don't know.'

He reached for the portfolio. 'Let's see.'

We spread the papers on the table as rain smeared the windows. The letterheads were mostly from legal and governmental offices in Chicago, dating from four to five years back, though a few recent letters had come from local addresses. Four separate letters from the chambers of a judge named Glen Stanislaus in the U.S. District Court building on Dearborn in Chicago were paperclipped together. One referred to limits that the judge was placing on an interstate interdiction unit. Another, signed by a clerk, not the judge, discussed the statutes of limitations for federal offenses. Clipped together separately, two testimonials – from the congressman for Illinois' seventh state congressional district and the city alderman for Chicago's second ward – said that Stilman had a good character and had helped revitalize the city's south and west sides. In another letter, a vice president at a Jacksonville company called Tri-Quon mentioned conversations with Stilman and said he hoped they would continue to talk in the future.

'D'you have any idea what this is about?' I asked.

Charles put down the Tri-Quon letter. 'I think so. What's in the envelope?'

I opened the manila envelope that had shared the file drawer with the portfolio. It contained receipts from a foreign bank named Grüd Fortem Èenen. Most of them showed monthly payouts of $3,000, a few considerably more.

'Damned cute,' Charles said.

'What language is that?'

'*Grüd*'s the name of a town in Ukraine. Also an anagram of drug. *Fortem* is Latin for strong and also the name of a town in Belgium. *Èenen* without the accent means dine in Spanish, as in, *They cenen at Applebee's.*'

'First,' I said, 'how do you know that? Second, what does it mean?'

'I've seen it and names like it before, and it means there's an overly clever asshole at the DEA. It's a shell name. Tri-Quon's a shell company. The DEA was paying off Jerry Stilman.'

'The DEA? Why?'

A gust slapped rain against the window and the lights in the restaurant flickered. Charles squinted at the storm as if assessing it as an enemy. 'My guess is he was informing on his old buddies. If he'd been clean and buying real

178

estate for fourteen or fifteen years, the statute of limitations would've expired for drug crimes but let's say someone died during the drug years and Stilman pulled the trigger. There's no limit on murder charges. If the feds showed him that they had evidence that could put him away, he'd find it easy to talk, especially if he'd really gone clean. He'd also think moving here from Chicago would be a good idea. He'd be running away but he might make it look like retirement to his old drug buddies.'

'Why keep the bank records? Why take the payoffs at all? He could've just given the DEA what they asked for and been done with it. You saw the house. He didn't need the money.'

Charles said, 'If he didn't go on the payroll he'd have less proof that he was working on the good side if the deal fell apart. Plus the guy was a businessman. He didn't give anything away if he could sell it.'

I had the sense that Charles knew what he was talking about but I said, 'These papers could've gotten Stilman and Belinda killed. Why wouldn't they keep them in the safe?'

'If local law or the feds came into the house, Stilman would want to be able to produce the papers fast. If any of his trafficking buddies suspected him, he'd be a dead man with or without the papers. Putting the papers in a locked drawer seems just about right.'

A waitress brought two hamburger plates. 'Here you go, Charlie,' she said and squeezed his shoulder. I knew there were women who liked scarred men though I never understood why.

I asked him, 'Does the DEA have an office here?'

'They work out of an office park on Woodcock Drive. I've got a friend there. But they spend most of their time at the port.'

'Some day you're going to tell me stories,' I said.

'I doubt it.' He drank from his coffee. 'So, I'll ask the DEA if Stilman was still talking with them when he died. And if he'd really gotten away from the drugs. I'll ask where the drugs came from. Through the Caribbean? Jamaica?'

'Ask if Belinda was involved,' I said.

'Got it.'

'And what do they know about Terrence?'

'You really want to know about him?'

'Ask them,' I said.

We ate our burgers.

'So Belinda dated Melchiori's friend David Fowler in the mayor's office,' Charles said.

'You know who he is?'

'Never heard of him. But he seems like a man worth getting to know.'

The rain was still coming down hard when Charles dropped me off at home. The police car that had been parked outside during the night was still following Thomas or else the driver had figured out our game and gone back to the station to face Daniel. I felt the absence of Fela as I put the key in the door and I missed the gentle pressure I'd come to expect as she'd leaned against my legs. Inside, the house was quiet. The dry, air-conditioned air chilled my damp skin. The three clay bowls that Thomas and I had made stood on the kitchen counter.

I got a Coors from the refrigerator, sat on a stool, took a long drink, and shuddered from the cold. I poured beer into one of the clay bowls and tasted it. It had the gritty bitterness of mud. What was I doing? I picked up the phone and dialed Thomas's cell number. It rang four times and voicemail picked up. I imagined Thomas in handcuffs sitting in the backseat of a squad car. Or lying in a ditch in the falling rain, having lost control of a car he was just learning to drive. More likely, though, he had turned the radio volume high and had no idea that the trilling of the phone wasn't part of the music. I left a message telling him to call.

I went to the French doors, opened them and watched the rain pock and froth the surface of the pool. In a rain like this, anything at all – a body, an old tire, a disease – could float inches below the surface and you'd never see it. When the wind gusted, the froth skimmed across the pool and a warm mist stung my face and arms.

I worried about Charles. In the years I'd known him he'd revealed that he knew the insides of the sheriff's department, the ATF and now the DEA, and I guessed that he'd done contract work for the federal government outside of the country. But I'd never sensed that he'd done what he'd done because it was right. As far as I could tell he'd done it only because he was good at it, it paid him well and it gave him pleasure.

After he helped me during my troubles in college I hadn't ridden with him again until a year before Thomas was born. Less than a mile from my house three brothers had been playing in their front yard when a sedan driven by a balding white man had slowed to the curb. The man had rolled down the passenger window and called to them. He had a sick bear, he said, and wondered if the boys could help. On the front seat next to him sat a large yellow teddy bear, the kind you can win as a grand prize at carnival games.

Two of the boys hung back, but the youngest brother, a six-year-old, went to look. The older boys remembered him laughing as he realized the man was pulling a trick and the laughter stopping as the man grabbed him and pulled him inside. The police showed the brothers plastic models and photographs of cars, and they picked a faded yellow '81 Ford Falcon. With the help of a sketch artist they described a man with an oval face, thin hair and untrimmed beard. Four days later a woman walking her dog along the riverbank found the little boy's wrecked and naked body.

The police did nothing, or so it seemed, and so I called Charles. 'These guys always come back for more,' he said. 'They can't help them- selves.' So we drove and watched and drove some more until one morning we saw a dirty white Chrysler Cordoba. It was trawling through a neighborhood about a mile from where the boy had been picked up. A dirty white Cordoba was close enough to a faded yellow Ford Falcon. We pulled next to it and looked at the driver. He was about sixty, nearly bald, and needed a shave. In his backseat, there was an oversized yellow stuffed animal – the comic-strip cat Garfield. I couldn't control myself. I cut the steering wheel and ran the Cordoba on to a lawn. It crashed into a cluster of boxwood bushes.

We got out and beat the guy. We broke his ribs. We broke his wrist. We damaged his face.

The only problem was, he wasn't the right guy. The man who'd raped and killed the child turned up the next month two counties away in a Motel 6 with an eight-year-old boy. When the police arrested him his faded yellow Ford Falcon was parked outside. In the car they found strands of hair from the earlier crime and souvenirs he'd taken with him.

The guy we'd beaten had no police record and no history of sexual abuse. 'We screwed up bad,' I'd said to Charles.

'We didn't screw up,' he'd said. He'd seemed content to have beaten someone even if the man wasn't the right one. 'The man never explained why he was cruising with a Garfield doll in his backseat,' he'd said. 'He had no children of his own and had no reason to be there. Maybe we stopped him before he did something.'

'Or maybe he just liked Garfield.'

'So why doesn't he identify us and press

charges?'

'You've gotten too deep inside his head for that,' I'd said.

'Me?' he'd laughed. 'I thought that was you.'

There was a chirp of surprise behind me in the kitchen. Susan had come in from her real-estate appointment and hadn't expected to find me there. 'What are you doing?' she asked.

'Watching the rain. How did the appointment go?'

'Fine,' she said. 'I think they're interested. Where's your car?'

'Thomas has it.'

'What?'

'He'll be sixteen next month,' I said. 'He needs the practice.'

'Why aren't you with him?'

'Because I'm here. Tell me about the customers. Where are they from?'

'Call him,' she said. 'Tell him to come home.'

'I already left a message.'

'Damnit, BB.'

'Thomas and I agreed that you'd kill me for this.'

'Killing's too good for you.' She threw her keys on the counter and left the room.

I took another drink of beer, picked up her keys and went out through the front door.

FIFTEEN

I drove Susan's car downtown and parked at Hemming Plaza. The plaza is named for Charles Hemming who raised a sixty-foot memorial to the Confederate dead with a life-sized bronze sculpture of a soldier facing south from the top. Once in the early 1960s, men with ax handles and baseball bats gathered around the monument before beating a group of teenagers who were staging a sit-in at a Woolworth's lunch counter. Behind the bronze soldier's back stands a four-story white-granite building constructed a hundred years ago as a Cohen Brothers Department Store. When the store went out of business the city council bought it and renamed it City Hall.

I rode the elevator to the fourth floor and asked a uniformed police officer at a reception desk where I could find a mayor's aide named David Fowler. 'Office of Special Events,' he said and pointed at double glass doors at the end of the corridor.

On the walls inside the doors hung poster-sized photographs of crowds gathered in a big green tent for a jazz festival, yachts decorated bow to stern with Christmas lights for Venetian

Night, fireworks over the St Johns River and floats in a Veterans Day parade. They were nice pictures, but it seemed to me that older, indelible images of the city's past remained just under the surface of the walls, like old water stains that eventually would bleed through no matter how many times maintenance workers painted them over. In one, the owner of the Monson Motel poured muriatic acid into an all-white swimming pool after black protesters jumped in, just to show that they could. In another, a pulp and paper mill pumped stinking fumes into the air and noxious effluent into the river. In an earlier, fainter image, orange groves covered the land at the south of the city before the first train bridge was built and everyone moved on – an image of when this still was paradise if you were white and survived the cholera, though if you were black no hospital would admit you no matter how sick you were so you died at home or amid the blossoming trees. Or earlier still, when a fire started after a cinder lit drying moss in a fiber factory and burned the whole city down, leaving the bones of houses and businesses, owned by white and black both, protruding from the dark river dirt. Only a nickel-sized yellow stain might remain from the Spanish, French, English and Timucua Indians coming together for hundreds of years to kill each other.

I walked past a series of other doors until I found one with a placard for David Fowler, Head Events Coordinator. He sat at his desk, talking on the phone. He was in his early thirties, tall, thin and white, with curly blond hair and wire-rimmed glasses. Except for the blond hair and glasses I could imagine someone thinking he looked like me at thirty. Beyond his desk a plate-glass window looked out at the plaza. A horizontal shot through the rain would catch the bronze soldier between the shoulders.

When I tapped on the door, Fowler held up a finger, asking me to wait a moment, but I walked in and sat in a chair across the desk from him. He looked annoyed, said, 'I'll need to call you back,' and hung up the phone. He appraised me and seemed to decide that he didn't know me and didn't wish to. 'What can I do for you?' he said.

'You can tell me about Jamaica,' I said.

Panic crossed his face. 'Close the door.'

I did and sat again.

'What do you mean Jamaica?' he said.

I shook my head. 'That's a dumb question.'

'Who are you?'

'My name's William Byrd. I was a friend of Belinda Mabry.'

'What do you want?'

'I already told you. I want to know what happened.'

'You're not the police?' he said.

'I've little use for them.'

He sat quietly, his eyes fluttering as if he were looking for a way out of his office, and then he reached into the top desk drawer and pulled out a small black pistol.

I smiled. 'Are you going to shoot me here?'

'I don't know what I'm going to do.' He was sweating.

I said, 'Why don't you put away the gun and talk to me politely?'

As uncertainly as he'd held the gun on me, he set it on the desk. 'What do you know about Jamaica?' he asked.

'I know that you flew to Kingston with Belinda for Don Melchiori's party. Tonya Richmond was there. I wouldn't be surprised if Ashley Littleton was too. I know all three of them are dead.'

He paled and looked sick.

A hospital helicopter flew low over Hemming Plaza, the bass *chop-chop* of the blades pounding through the rain and penetrating the window and walls.

'Belinda was fearless,' Fowler said quietly. 'If she had an ounce of fear in her I never saw it.' There was awe in his voice, maybe love. 'We'd gone out only a couple of times and when Don invited us to Jamaica she said she was game. I knew what Don's parties were like and I told Belinda I didn't want to go. But her husband had been dead for more than a year and she was ready. I thought she would go without me so I went too.'

'Tell me about the party,' I said.

He gazed at me, hollow-eyed. 'I knew this would happen.'

'What went on at the party?'

He looked out the window as if he wished to

fly through it. Against the cloud-darkened sky the glass reflected ghost images of his face and mine. He said, 'A sixteen-year-old girl died. A messed-up kid.'

'Who was she?' I asked.

'The daughter of a man in the Jamaican Ministry of Foreign Affairs and Trade. Don said he was a regular at the parties but he was out of the country and Don had had his eyes on the girl. Her name was Tralena. She shouldn't have been at the party but Don invited her.'

'What happened? How did she die?'

'They'll kill me if I tell you,' he said.

His well-being was the least of my worries. 'What happened?'

He sighed, his eyes wet. 'She went so fast, so easily. I don't know. She had a bag on her face for twenty or thirty seconds and she went limp.'

'What do you mean "a bag"?'

'A plastic bag to cut off the air, give her a bigger orgasm. Don was screwing her.'

'He was screwing a sixteen-year-old with a plastic bag over her head?'

'We were all so high. It didn't seem crazy at the time.'

'Who put it on her? Melchiori?'

'Huh? No. Belinda and the other women.'

I felt the thick skin of my resolve split. 'Why would they do that?'

'It was part of the fun. Tralena didn't mind. We were all together, you know? Don asked Tralena if she wanted an orgasm that would crack her in two. She said, "I like orgasms," and

189

we laughed because she said it like a little girl. So Belinda put the bag over Tralena's head, and Tonya and Ashley held her arms when she tried to take if off. But only for twenty or thirty seconds. Not long enough to suffocate.'

'But she suffocated,' I said.

'Yes, she did.'

'And then what?'

'Don finished screwing her.'

'He finished screwing her after she went limp?'

'You couldn't have pried him off her with a crowbar. Afterward we put her in the shower and cleaned her as much as we could. One of the guys at the party had a boat. He carried her offshore, weighed her down and dropped her in the water. But he didn't do it right. She washed up on the beach two days later. The coroner missed most of what happened but he said she'd been raped and that she'd died before getting dumped in the ocean. On the morning that we left Jamaica it was front-page news.'

'Why didn't you go to the police?' I asked.

'You've got to be kidding.' For the first time he looked angry. 'I was *there*. I mean, I wasn't with the girl but I was part of it. Even if I'd wanted to go I couldn't have. The other guys at the party have the kind of power you don't screw with. Don brought me only because I was with Belinda and he wanted her. If I'd gone to the police I would've ended up in the ocean along with Tralena.'

'Who were the other men?' I asked.

190

He shook his head. 'If I give names I'm dead.'

'How about Tralena's father? You say he's in the government. If the papers covered the death of his daughter his name's got to be public. Who is he?'

'Godrell Graham. From what Don has said, he's on the Trade side of the ministry. Supposedly he makes things happen for a little money in his own pocket.'

'Makes things happen? Drugs?'

'That's what I'm guessing,' he said.

'Why didn't you talk to him, tell him what happened to his daughter?'

Again he was sweating. 'I did,' he said. 'More or less. I called and talked to him.'

'How did he take the news?'

'He hung up on me. I don't think he believed me. Who wants to think of his daughter that way?'

I nodded. 'How did Belinda handle all this?'

'As if it was nothing. Like I said, she was fearless.'

That both did and didn't sound like the girl I'd known. Belinda had been fearless but never cold. 'Who killed her and the others?' I asked.

Fear and sadness in his eyes, he seemed to pull into himself. 'I don't know,' he said. 'I'm sorry.'

'Yeah,' I said, 'me too.'

'What are you going to do with what I've told you?' he asked.

'I'm not sure.' That wasn't true. I planned to talk to him again, next time somewhere that no one could hear him if he cried for help. And with Charles by my side. Charles would get him to name names.

Fowler picked up the pistol from the desk and considered it like a new toy or machine whose full range of functions he had yet to learn.

'Give it to me,' I said.

'Why?' He sounded afraid.

I reached for the gun and he gave it to me. I removed the magazine, put it in my pocket and handed the gun back to him. 'I don't want you shooting yourself.'

'I wouldn't,' he said.

I looked at his hollow eyes. 'If I were you I might.'

When I turned for the door, he said, 'There's something wrong with a woman who's got no fear.'

I don't like guns. When I was thirteen my father brought home his Ruger .22 from the Best Gas station. He put it in a canvas case and kept it and a box of fifty shells on a shelf in his bed-room closet. My mother had run off to Arizona six years earlier and when I came home from school on autumn afternoons the house was mine alone and I leafed through the pictures that he'd hidden under a stack of road maps in a desk drawer or fingered the shorts, blouses and underpants that my mother had left behind when she'd abandoned us and that my father had inexplicably kept all these years in the bottom of the dresser.

One cloudy November afternoon I moved from the dresser to the closet and I felt the gun through the case. I took it to my father's bed and unzipped it. The bullets slid cleanly into the magazine the way well-tooled machine parts fit together and the gun felt solid and right in my hands as if we were tooled for each other too.

I took the Ruger into the backyard and sat in a folding chair on the pool deck. The air was cool and a solid layer of gray blanketed the sky. When a light breeze blew through the leaves of the live oak trees, a blue jay made an ugly sound and glided from a branch to the grass beside the quarry pond. I raised the pistol and looked at the bird through the sight. It stood for a full minute without moving as if it were tempting me.

I pulled the trigger and blood burst from the breast of the bird. Feathers scattered across the grass.

A gladness descended upon me, an awareness that I had power in a universe that had always seemed overwhelming. I'd killed a bird and I no longer felt lonely.

Twenty minutes later two sparrows landed on the grass. As I leveled the sight on one of them it flew away. I leveled the sight on the other and pulled the trigger. Too quick. Strangely, the sparrow didn't fly away at the sound of the gunshot and I leveled the sight again, taking my time, wondering whether the bird would have the patience to let me kill it. I pulled the trigger and the bird blasted apart. When its mate returned, I shot it too. The gray dome of the sky seemed to lower and I felt enormous. A squirrel climbed around the trunk of an oak and I aimed and fired. Bark split from the tree. The squirrel reappeared, I fired again and more bark tore away. The breeze tossed the branches. The water on the quarry pond rippled and darkened.

The afternoon slipped toward evening and I stayed perched on the lounge chair. When my father returned shortly before six o'clock, the remains of four sparrows, a mocking bird and the blue jay lay scattered across the backyard. 'What in God's name are you doing?' my father asked.

The answer seemed obvious. 'Shooting birds.'

He hit me in the face with an open fist.

As he watched over me, I picked up the birds from the lawn and put them in a plastic pail. The heart of the mocking bird was still beating when I scooped its body and its separated wing off the grass.

After I retrieved the last sparrow I presented the pail to my father.

'Inside,' he said.

In the kitchen he laid a cutting board and a fillet knife on the counter.

'Do it,' he said.

'What?'

'You'll eat what you kill,' he said. 'I'll teach you how to dress them properly. Start by cutting a line down their bellies.'

'No.'

'Goddamn it, you'll do as I say.'

I made the incisions, dug their tiny organs out of their rib cages with my index finger, plucked their feathers, removed their heads, then filleted their breasts. Tears filled my eyes as I worked but when I slowed, my father said, 'Goddamn it, finish the job.'

He sautéed the birds in vegetable oil and spooned them on to a plate which he set before me at the kitchen table. I ate the wretched meat. By the time I had finished the last bite I had come to two conclusions. Sparrow is the most revolting bird on God's green earth, and I didn't like guns.

Outside of City Hall, the rain was falling in sheets. I ran from the metal and glass awning that fronted the building, across the street and through the plaza. The drunks and homeless had abandoned the benches where they generally spent their days. The pigeons that usually toddled aimlessly were roosting elsewhere.

As I reached Susan's car, four men poured out of a van parked behind it. I reached for the door and the men surrounded me. Had the sky been clear and had I been ready I might have knocked down two of them before they'd subdued me. I clubbed one of them in the throat with my forearm and another hit me in the back with something that felt like a log. The blow knocked me sideways and I fell against the car. Someone hit me again and then my hands were cuffed behind my back and they were dragging me into the van.

No one said anything. The man whose throat I'd struck looked unperturbed. He drove, one hand on the wheel, the other resting on his thigh. All four were thick-chested and wore jeans and dark shirts speckled with rain. The man beside me didn't bother to wipe the rainwater from his cheeks.

'Are you the police?' I asked.

The man with rainwater on his face threw an elbow into my ribs, already bruised from Melchiori's kicks.

When I got my voice back, I asked, 'Do you work with Daniel Turner?'

I braced for another elbow to the ribs but it didn't come.

The van drove toward the river until we reached a brown twelve-story concrete tower. It was the PDF, which stood for Pretrial Detention Facility, but mostly we called it the county jail. The van turned into a lane that led through a large metal garage door to the Prisoner Intake. We pulled behind a squad car from which two uniformed officers were struggling to remove a Cuban man.

At the intake desk the officers unlocked my handcuffs and I emptied my pockets of keys, wallet, cell phone and the magazine from David Fowler's pistol. When I pulled out the crumpled picture that Terrence had pasted together with Belinda's face and a doubly-penetrated woman, I said, 'I need to keep this.'

'Sorry, honey,' said the woman behind the desk.

I tried to tear it but the officer whose throat I'd hit grabbed my wrists.

'What are you charging me with?' I asked.

He grinned, took the picture from me and said, 'Sorry, honey,' as though it was all a big joke.

They took me to a holding cell, a freestanding, steel-posted, wire-mesh room with a steel bench and a concrete floor. 'Welcome to the zoo,' the guard said.

I sat on the bench and wondered how the police had tracked me to Hemming Plaza and why. The officer at the reception desk on the fourth floor of City Hall had seen me pass but he wouldn't have known who I was unless he'd been given my photograph and told to look out for me. That seemed unlikely since even I hadn't known I'd be going to City Hall until a couple of hours earlier. Fowler could've called the police as I'd left his office but he'd seemed worried about involving them, so that seemed less likely, and even if he had called, the police wouldn't have been able to locate Susan's car so quickly. The van had been waiting for me and the four men inside it had known what to do and when to do it. That made me think that Fowler was right to worry about the police.

I wondered how Fowler fit into the killings of Belinda and the other women and how the events that he described did. If he'd really told Godrell Graham about his daughter's death, Graham would have good reason to come after the others at the party, but I'd have thought he'd go after Melchiori and the other men before the women. If Graham wasn't behind the killings, the men at the party would have good reason to get rid of any witnesses they distrusted.

I believed that Tralena Graham's suffocation in a plastic bag had led to the killing of Belinda and the others. But why stuff Belinda in a bag and not the others? Because she'd personally put the bag over Tralena Graham's head?

I wondered what Fowler had left out or didn't know. Belinda and her husband had been friends with Don Melchiori, and Godrell Graham had been a regular at Melchiori's parties. Could Belinda and Stilman have known Graham before the party where his daughter died? Fowler said that Graham was part of an illegal business, probably involving drugs, and Stilman had brought drugs from the Caribbean through Florida to Chicago. Supposedly he'd retired from trafficking, but he owned a thirty-eight-foot Fairline motor cruiser that could make leisurely trips to the islands. And what about his stepson? *My son.* Terrence hung out at the Little Vegas club and made obscene art out of pictures of his mother.

The guard came back and opened the door to the holding cell. 'That wasn't so bad, was it?' he asked. He took me to an interview room with a metal table and three metal chairs, told me to sit, pulled out a pair of handcuffs and told me to put my hands behind my back. 'Don't make this difficult,' he said with a sadness that I found persuasive. I put my hands behind the chair and

198

he ran the handcuff chain through the back spindles and snapped the cuffs over my wrists.

'Thank you,' he said.

The guard left and a minute later Daniel Turner came in. He set a manila folder and a clear baggie with Fowler's gun magazine in it on the table and sat across from me.

'Hi, BB,' he said.

I shook my head. 'This isn't the way you talk to me.'

'I didn't think you'd come in without some help.' He was wearing a cotton button-down shirt with the sleeves rolled above the elbows.

I shook my head again. 'Give me the picture of Belinda.'

'This?' He opened the folder and removed Terrence's cut-and-paste job. Someone had flattened and uncreased it.

I stared at it and raised my eyes to Daniel's. 'Destroy it,' I said. If my hands had been free I'd have done it myself.

He looked at the picture. 'Why did you do this? It doesn't look good, you making something like this.'

I spit on the picture. White saliva flecked the fat woman's breasts.

'That's disgusting, BB. Really.' He picked up the baggie with the gun magazine and set it on top of the picture. 'Where's the gun that this belongs to?'

'Guns scare me. I don't own one.'

'I know that and it makes me wonder why you had this in your pocket.'

'How'd you know where to find me?' I asked.

He frowned as though I'd disappointed him. 'A pistol magazine and a pornographic picture of one of the victims – that's not enough to charge you with anything. But it's surely enough to start people wondering about you.'

'Why did you pick me up?'

'Two days ago a couple of patrolmen found you with a prostitute behind the old Chevy dealership on Philips Highway.'

'Her name's Aggie,' I said.

'No. Her name's Karen Charleton but she calls herself Aggie on the street. Where is she?'

My head had started to ache. 'Ask the patrolmen. Last I saw her, one of them was getting ready to screw her in the back of the cruiser.'

Daniel reached across the table and punched me in the jaw though he didn't use much muscle. He said, 'This afternoon a car pulled up to a bus stop where three girls were hiding from the rain. One of the girls was your friend Aggie. A man waved her over. The other girls said Aggie talked to the man and then tried to go back to the shelter but he pulled her into the car.'

Something hard and heavy seemed to drop in my stomach. 'Was he driving a green SUV?'

'What if I told you that the girls identified you?'

'I'd say you're lying.'

He stared into my eyes and said, 'Maybe.'

'I haven't seen Aggie since I left her behind the Chevy dealership.'

200

'We'll see,' he said.

'How did you know where to pick me up?'

'You're worrying a lot of people.'

'Who?'

'Well, to begin with, your wife and son.'

'I've always worried them,' I said. 'Who else?'

'You send your boy out in your car and trick a rookie into following him, that doesn't mean that I won't post someone with more experience at your house so he can tail you when you leave again in Susan's car.'

I thought about that. 'So who's worried about me?'

'You were at Don Melchiori's house last night when he got shot,' he said. 'He's not accusing you. He's too dirty himself to start accusing others and you look like he gave you a beating before you gave him his.'

'Who's in this with Melchiori?'

Daniel smiled resignedly. 'I'm warning you to stop.'

'Is that why you picked me up?'

'I'm warning you, BB.'

'Are you Melchiori's message boy?' I asked.

He cocked his fist to punch me again but he held back. 'I'm releasing you now. But I'm keeping the picture and the pistol magazine.'

'You should destroy the picture,' I said.

'I'll keep that advice in mind.'

'Did your rookie arrest Thomas?'

Daniel looked mildly embarrassed. 'Thomas shook him after about ten blocks.'

SIXTEEN

At seven-thirty p.m. I ordered lamb Torinese at
Sorrento's. We'd driven to the restaurant in
Susan's car, Thomas at the wheel, Susan beside
him, me in the backseat. In my pocket, I had
David Fowler's home address, which I'd gotten
online. Rain was falling steadily but the restaurant was bright and airy, the walls painted a pale
pink that made the place look like it belonged
by a sunny Mediterranean beach.

'You've got to stop this now,' Susan said
quietly. 'Otherwise I'm leaving.'

I cut a bite of lamb chop and put it on Thomas's plate. I cut another and put it on hers.
'The lamb's excellent,' I said.

Susan stared at the meat as if it were a scrap
left over from a surgery. 'I'm taking Thomas
with me,' she said.

'OK,' I said and looked at Thomas. 'How do
you feel about that, Champ?'

He said, 'Mom's more dependable than you.'

'Yes she is.' I drank some wine.

'Why can't you stop?' Susan asked. It was a
question she'd asked before, first when I'd ridden with Charles after the rape and killing of
the six-year-old boy, again eight years ago

when I'd ridden with him once more.

I answered as I'd always answered. 'I don't know. I wish I could.'

'What was jail like?' Thomas asked. As soon as I'd arrived at prisoner intake, Daniel had called to tell Susan that they'd picked me up. The call had stopped her from scolding Thomas, who'd just returned from a seventy-mile cruise around town.

'It smelled bad,' I said. 'Like the stale sweat in a public bathroom after homeless people have been cleaning themselves.' I ate another bite of lamb and he watched me chew. I drank more wine.

'That's it?' he asked.

'That's it.'

We drove home in the early darkness. The rain had eased to a mist but as we pulled into the driveway, thunder roared overhead and it fell hard again.

Thomas kicked off his shoes and disappeared into his bedroom and Susan and I stood together in the kitchen. 'I'm serious about leaving,' she said.

'You've been gone for fifteen years.'

'You know that's not true.'

'I know how I feel,' I said.

She came to me and put her arms around me, her head to my chest. I put my hands on the small of her back. I said, 'You know that I won't stop, right?'

She held me closer. 'I know.'

'So this is it?'

'I think so,' she said.

We stood together for a while, though no matter how long we held each other the pain of being apart wouldn't diminish.

She said, 'I need a drink. You want one?'

'I could use another.'

She went to the refrigerator and I stared across the counter at the back door and the darkness beyond it. At the same moment I noticed that one of the quarry-clay bowls was missing from the counter, Susan screamed and stumbled back. On the middle refrigerator shelf, in front of a carton of eggs, Fela's head sat in the missing bowl. Her eyes were as white and opaque as congealed milk. One ear was bent inward. Her feline teeth were as sharp as pins.

Thomas heard Susan scream and he ran into the kitchen. When he saw the head he tried to stop but ran into me. I held him but he pulled away, went to the sink and vomited his spaghetti. Then he wiped his mouth on his forearm and returned to look in the refrigerator.

'I'm sorry,' I said as if I were to blame for Fela's death.

He said, 'If you stop now I'll never talk to you again.'

I looked at Susan and she shook her head, then said, 'I'm leaving and I'm taking him with me.'

I went to the phone and called Charles. 'I'll pick you up in twenty minutes,' I said and hung up.

Thomas came to me and I pulled him close in a hug. For the first time in two years he hugged me too. Susan glared. I went to her, held her head in my hands and pulled her to my lips. She didn't want my kiss but then it seemed she did and when I let go she said softly, 'You bastard.'

'I know,' I said, and walked outside into the rain.

The electronic gate at the end of Charles' driveway was open and when I pulled in front of his house he was standing under the porch light waiting for me. He stepped into the rain and climbed into the car. His calico cat was nowhere to be seen.

Charles shook the rainwater from his hands and said, 'Fuck of a night.'

'In many ways,' I agreed.

'What's up?'

I told him about getting picked up by Daniel's officers and about his warning. I told him that Aggie was missing. I told him about Fela's head. I told him that Susan was leaving me.

'Yep, a fuck of a night,' he said, as though these troubles only confirmed what the rain had already told him. 'What did David Fowler say?'

'He's scared,' I said, and I filled him in on all that Fowler had told me about Tralena Graham's death and the role that Belinda, Melchiori and the others had played in it, as well as the drug-trafficking rumors about Tralena's father.

When I finished, Charles nodded. 'It might be

a fuck of a night but you just pulled this thing together.'

'Not all the way. We still don't know who's doing the killing.'

Charles said, 'Let's go see David Fowler.'

I pulled the address from my pocket. 'I thought you might like to talk with him.'

He shook his head. 'The hell with talking.'

Fowler lived in an old, pale blue, wood-frame house on Powell Place. A single light was on in a front room and the driveway was empty. I parked on the street and we ran through the rain to the front steps. When I knocked on the door no one answered. Without saying a word, Charles went to work on the lock.

A minute later we stepped into the front hall. Fowler had spent a lot of time and money rehabbing the place. The wood floors gleamed and he'd painted the baseboards and ceiling-molding light colors to set them off from the walls. The furniture in the front room was modern with a lot of brushed nickel and bright fabrics.

I called, 'Mr Fowler?'

No one answered but something bumped against the floor in the back of the house.

'Hello?' I said louder.

Again, no one answered.

I turned for the door as soft footsteps approached from the hallway, but Charles stood where he was, then stooped and held a hand palm up toward the darkness. An old beagle with gray muzzle whiskers, its tail wagging low between its hind legs, plodded into the light and sniffed Charles' hand.

'Hey, boy,' Charles said gently, 'where's Fowler?'

The dog finished sniffing, plodded to a wall and lay down against it.

We searched the house thoroughly. Fowler seemed to live alone. The furnishings suggested that he had more money than he would make as a city events coordinator but nothing indicated that he'd gotten the money illegally. Nothing even indicated that he'd ever done anything that would embarrass him. We found no porn DVDs. We found no souvenir bag of pot from Jamaica. It seemed unlikely that anyone lived so clean.

'He scrubbed his house because he expected someone to search it,' Charles said.

Then he got two slices of bread from the refrigerator and fed them to the dog and we let ourselves out.

'What next?' he asked.

'D'you want to look around Melchiori's house?'

'Of course,' he said.

As we drove I asked, 'Did you talk with your friend at the DEA?'

He nodded. 'The lady I know says Jerry Stilman cooperated with them at least some of the time for the last three years that he was in Chicago and continued to help when he and Belinda moved here. She also says that when he left Chicago he cut himself out of most of the trafficking business but he never left it completely.'

'The DEA let him keep dealing?'

'If he wasn't in the game he couldn't tell them who the other players were.'

'Can you ask her if Godrell Graham was one of them? Did Stilman know him?'

'Sure thing,' he said.

'Did she say whether Belinda was involved?'

'They had nothing on her.'

'Terrence?' I asked.

'Him either.'

'Did she tell you anything else?'

'She said Jerry Stilman's heart attack wasn't natural.'

'What do you mean?'

He said, 'Someone shoved a shank through his chest while he was sleeping in bed.'

A few minutes after ten p.m. we broke through Melchiori's front door. A security alarm blew an electronic whistle until Charles tore the plastic facing from it and disconnected the wires. I followed him to the living room. Melchiori's blood and mine had stained the white carpet, and the room smelled of Charles' urine. Charles went to the marble fireplace and removed a steel poker from the fireplace set. He swung it and smashed the mirror that hung above the mantle. He carried it to a double set of built-in bookshelves and smashed a glass clock, a ceramic statue of a laughing Buddha and an empty vase. He inserted the tool end of the poker behind a row of books and swept them to the floor. He did the same with two more rows of books. Then he raised the poker over his head and swung down, demolishing one of the wooden shelves.

'What are you doing?' I asked.

He flung the poker at the fireplace. Its spear end penetrated the fireplace screen and the handle protruded into the room.

'I don't particularly like this man,' he said.

'It seems to me you're using more energy than he deserves.'

He shrugged. 'Seems to me just right. You want to search upstairs and I'll search down?'

'As long as you don't destroy the stairway while I'm up there.'

The second floor had four large rooms and a linen closet. Two were guestrooms with attached baths. The cabinets and dressers in them were empty though Melchiori had put a drinking glass and a new bottle of Glenlivet on the dresser in one room and a glass and a bottle of Grey Goose in the other. The third door led to an exercise room with a StairMaster, an old Cybex weight machine and a widescreen television.

The last door led to Melchiori's bedroom suite. A second fireplace, with decorative gas logs inside it, sank into one wall. A walk-in closet, filled with casual clothes and a dozen business suits, smelled of musky cologne. The bathroom had a large Jacuzzi tub. In the medicine cabinet I found a vial of Ambien and another of Lunesta, sleeping pills for a man who, it seemed to me, deserved a rough night's sleep.

I went to the dresser. There were socks, underwear and T-shirts that smelled of the same cologne as the closet. In the third drawer from the top I found a box of forty or fifty photos. They were party photos. The scenes in them could've wrecked the careers of a small group of local politicians and businessmen if they'd become public, but they showed enough wear and creasing that I guessed Melchiori kept them for private use.

The ones on top were oldest. Melchiori looked forty or so, seven or eight years younger than he was now. He was thinner then but already a big man. He was screwing a woman, also about forty and also big, from behind. They were outside on a pool deck with dark green tropical plants surrounding them, the sun shining on their sunburnt skin. They smiled into the camera with oily eyes.

The next photos showed a variety of women and girls, some younger than Tralena Graham had been when she died. In two of the pictures I recognized Ashley Littleton from a time before her final fall into drugs and twenty-buck sex. The men in the pictures were strangers to me, all except two of them. One was Melchiori, who mugged for the camera as he screwed women and girls. The other I knew only from a framed picture that I'd seen on top of Belinda's dresser when Charles and I searched her house.

But in the photo that came from this box, Jerry Stilman wasn't staring with cold, dignified eyes at a portrait photographer. He was getting a blowjob from a girl who couldn't have been older than fourteen.

I paid little attention to the photos that followed until I reached the final six. All were from the party where Tralena Graham had died. All included a naked, dark-skinned girl with long straight hair and large black eyes, almost as wet as tears. Tralena Graham, I guessed. In all of these photos Belinda also was present, along with a couple of men and, in one, Tonya Richmond. Belinda was always close to Tralena, kissing her breasts and slipping a bag over her head with an odd intimacy, as if they'd made a strange, deep connection that drew them together, and as I stared at the photos I wondered if Belinda had noticed what I was seeing now. Belinda, at seventeen, had resembled this girl. She'd had the same thin body, the same soft face, the same desire in her eyes.

The six photos from that party might enable Daniel to arrest Belinda's killer. One of the men in them might be the killer himself. But the photos also showed Belinda in a way that felt intensely private to me and giving them to Daniel would tear something vital from inside me. I took them to the bathroom, ripped them and dropped them into the toilet water where they floated in a chaotic mosaic. I flushed and watched Belinda and the sixteen-year-old girl disappear into the whirlpool.

I returned the other photos to the box and put it in the dresser drawer. When I came downstairs Charles was entering the foyer from a room that looked like a study.

'What did you find?' he said.

'Nothing,' I said. 'Nothing at all.'

He held up a white package tightly wrapped in cellophane. 'Coke. Found it in the desk in his office. Probably a half pound. Could be for personal use if he held a whole lot of parties.' He cocked his head and looked at me. 'You all right?'

I didn't feel all right. I said, 'Let's go see Melchiori in the hospital.'

We pulled down a drive lined with palms trees and into the University Hospital parking garage at ten-fifty p.m. Visiting hours in the intensive care unit had ended at nine. After checking at an information desk in the atrium, we rode an elevator to the third floor and went to the nurses' station. A solitary nurse in her late fifties sat at the counter doing a crossword puzzle. She looked up and asked if she could help us.

'We're here to see a friend,' Charles said. 'Don Melchiori.'

Her smile was pleasant, sympathetic. 'You'll need to come back in the morning. The last visits were two hours ago.'

'Officially, yes,' Charles said, also pleasantly. 'But we've driven for five hours because we heard about Don—'

'I'm sorry,' she said. 'The doctors have been

212

very strict in—'

Charles leaned across the counter and an edge of menace entered his voice. 'We understand,' he said. 'But my friend here needs to see Don Melchiori tonight.'

The sympathy fell from the nurse's eyes and she reached for her phone. I guessed she was calling security. Charles seemed to guess the same. His hand shot across the counter and held her wrist. 'We don't all have to see Don. If it's more convenient my friend can talk to him alone.' Then he smiled. 'Would you like to join me for a cup of coffee?'

'You're breaking the law,' she said but she stood and he maneuvered her around the counter and through a swinging waist-high gate.

'Thank you,' he said to her, pleasant and polite once more. He turned to me. 'We'll have a quick cup. Ten minutes be enough?'

'More than.'

He steered the nurse down the hall toward a sign that said Lounge and Vending Machines.

Melchiori's door was open and he was propped up in bed, his face bruised under his eyes, an IV tube running from his arm, a heart monitor tracking the steady pulse of his blood and a large pad of cotton gauze bandaged to his shoulder where he'd taken the bullet. He was watching television as the eleven o'clock news started.

I stepped into the room without knocking and he glanced up as if he expected a nurse. He looked unhappy to see me instead.

213

'You sonofabitch,' he said. 'How'd you get in?'

I closed the door. 'I walked past the nurse's station, turned left at the corner and here you were.'

'Well, you aren't staying.' He reached for the emergency call button.

'I saw the photos in your dresser,' I said.

His hand froze and he grimaced. He glanced at the television and hit the *mute* button on the remote. 'You realize, don't you, that you're a dead man,' he said. 'There'll be nothing left of you after I'm done.'

I said, 'I thought about that last night when I was lying on your floor and you were kicking me. And yet today you're the one who's lying in the hospital, and I'm the one who has the pictures of the party where Tralena Graham died, pictures that also include Belinda Mabry, Tonya Richmond and Ashley Littleton.'

If he was surprised that I'd learned what happened to Tralena Graham he didn't show it. 'The girl was an accident,' he said, his voice hard. 'She was at the party because she wanted to be there. She did what she did because she wanted to do it. No one made her do anything.'

'She was sixteen years old.'

'The age of consent in Jamaica *is* sixteen,' he said. 'It was an accident.'

'That's why you threw her body in the ocean?'

'That was a mistake. But her death was an accident and nothing you've got in those pictures suggests it wasn't. No one was having a better time than she was.'

'You're a sick bastard,' I said. 'You're going to jail for Belinda and the others.'

The councilman sighed. 'You don't get it. I didn't kill them. No one at the party did.'

'The pictures tell a different story.'

He shook his head. 'Listen, talk to Belinda Mabry's boy.'

'Terrence?'

'You want to see a sick bastard, look at him. He comes to Little Vegas, picks up one of my girls, takes her to a motel and does things to her that shock *me* – and I think you know how hard I am to shock.'

'Why would he want to kill them?' I asked.

A bitter laugh escaped him. 'Why not? The kid has—' Something on the television screen caught his eye. 'Ah, piss!' he said and reached for the remote.

I looked at the screen and saw a picture of David Fowler. The volume rose and caught the reporter mid-sentence, '...crossing Duval Street at six o'clock this evening when witnesses say a car struck him. Police say the driver neither slowed nor stopped. Fowler was unresponsive when emergency services arrived and was declared dead at the scene. Fowler worked for the mayor's office for the past three years and twice ran unsuccessfully for city council. Police are asking anyone who saw a green Toyota or Honda SUV near the scene of the accident to contact them.'

'Piss!' Melchiori said again. 'He was a friend of mine.'

'I know,' I said quietly.

The door to the hospital room burst open. A security guard charged in, followed by the nurse and Charles. The guard looked from me to Melchiori and back as if he'd expected to find me strangling the councilman. 'What's happening here?' he said.

Melchiori gazed at him evenly as if the guard had just disturbed a private business meeting. 'We were having a talk.'

The guard looked confused. He glanced at the nurse. 'Visiting hours are over,' he said.

I looked at Melchiori. 'We're done anyway,' I said. 'Get well fast, Don.'

He nodded. 'Be seeing you,' he said and I wondered if anyone else heard the threat in that.

The guard and the nurse stayed in Melchiori's room and Charles and I walked down the hall to the elevators, past walls scuffed by gurneys, under the cold fluorescent light.

'Sorry about that,' Charles said. 'Security decided to take a coffee break too. The nurse flagged him down.'

I said, 'A green SUV ran down David Fowler this evening. It was on the TV news.'

'Shit,' Charles said and thought about it for a moment. 'He dead?'

'At the scene.'

'Sonofabitch,' Charles said.

'Melchiori's pointing his finger at Terrence,' I said. 'Not just for Fowler. For everything.'

216

* * *

I dropped Charles at his house a little after midnight and turned toward home. But Susan had said she was leaving and taking Thomas with her. She probably wouldn't go until morning, though I didn't think I could bear watching her pack and drive away. I knew I couldn't bear watching Thomas go with her.

So I didn't go home.

The lights were off in Lee Ann's house and the wet azaleas that lined the front path clutched my legs as I walked past but she answered the door quickly as if she'd been expecting me. The front room was warm and dry and smelled like cinnamon. She took my hand and led me through the dark hallway to her bedroom.

She kissed my neck and whispered, 'You smell like bad sweat.'

'It's been a bad day.'

She kissed me again and said, 'Shower for me.'

I stood for a time in her hot shower and felt the rotten skin of heat and pain shed from me, then I dried myself with an old pink towel that smelled like Lee Ann. When I walked back into her bedroom she was lying naked on top of the bed sheet, a single bedside lamp shining dimly, the soft blonde curls of her pubic hair catching and tricking the light like electrical filaments.

I sat by her on the bed and she touched the cut on my forehead where Melchiori had butted me. 'What happened?' she asked.

As an answer I kissed her.

217

She pulled her lips from mine and put her mouth on my neck, my shoulder, my chest. She touched the bruises on my ribs where Melchiori had kicked me and didn't ask about them but kissed them softly as if her lips could suck the poison out of my life.

Then with the rain pounding the roof above us and the single dim bedside lamp burning we made love. Gently at first and then hard. And sometime during the rush of blood and muscle and skin, I wrapped my hands around her neck and she smiled a wicked smile. I tightened my fingers and a flush spread across her face and neck, so I tightened more and more until her eyes showed fear.

'I ... can't...' she rasped.

'I know.' I tightened my grip.

Her face reddened. She bucked under me, struggling to get free. Her fingernails clawed at my back. Her fists pounded against me. But I was inside her and held her by the throat and as she bucked I went in deeper and deeper until she screamed an asphyxiated scream of pleasure and pain greater than any I'd ever heard, as if she were dying from an orgasm so thorough that it was splitting her in two.

Afterward she lay panting, returning to herself. 'Jesus, that was great,' she said hoarsely and put a gentle hand on my chest. 'But never do that again. Never. Not if you want to be with me.'

SEVENTEEN

I woke at eight-thirty the next morning in Lee Ann's bed. Sunlight fell through the slats of the window blinds. I'd been dreaming of grackles, the black birds that crossed the south each fall in flocks of thousands and descended noisily on clusters of live oak trees, ate the acorn fruit and moved on. In my dream I'd been alone in my house and the grackles had darkened the sky and lowered like a suffocating blanket over the roof and walls. I'd screamed but the sound of my voice had dissolved in the *Gah, Gah, Gah* cry of the birds.

I opened my eyes, startled to find myself away from my own bed. Outside the window, a steady drip of rainwater from last night's storm fell from a branch or a roof eave and plinked against something metal. No birds cried or sang.

Lee Ann lay beside me. Her face had the soft fleshiness of sleep and death. She opened her eyes when she felt mine on her and she smiled sleepily. 'Since when do you spend the night?'

'Since Susan left me.'

Her eyes opened wider. 'Did she?'

I gave a half nod.

'Did she cut your forehead and kick you in the ribs on her way out?' she asked.

'She took Thomas with her.'

'Oh. I'm sorry.' We lay for a while and listened to the plink of water on metal and I wondered how many minutes or hours we could lie in bed before the dripping stopped. 'What does this mean for us?' Lee Ann asked.

I thought about it. 'It means I can spend the night sometimes.'

'I'm not sure I want you to,' she said. She smiled sadly and kissed me, got out of bed and went into the kitchen. This is what the world must come to when the love of one's life died, I thought – the solitude of lying alone in a strange bed that reeked of sweat and sex but not love. For some reason, that thought comforted me, as if I'd lived my whole life moving toward this inevitable moment, and now it was here and it was bearable, or nearly.

We drank coffee at the kitchen table, the windows open to the storm-cooled morning, and Lee Ann said, 'Are you going to tell me about it?'

'What?'

'All of this. What's been happening the past few days.'

'It's my whole life,' I said. 'Are you sure you want it?'

'I'll stop you if I don't.'

I told her about the past four days and about the moments that had led to them and I felt like I was confessing but that the confession wouldn't lighten the burden, and when I finished I said, 'I've told other women I loved them but Belinda's the only woman I've ever really loved. I know that makes me a bastard.'

'I don't know what it makes you,' she said.

We ate breakfast together silently and when I stood to go she said, 'Come back tonight.'

Susan's car was gone from the driveway and the house was empty when I let myself in. I wandered into the sunroom. She'd made her bed and cleaned the room before leaving, stacking magazines on the bedside table, lowering the blinds halfway. I resisted an impulse to tear the covers from the bed and ravage the room and instead wandered through the house to Thomas's bedroom. He'd taken clothes, his laptop computer and his stash of comic books. He hadn't made his bed. But he'd left a gift for me. Tacked to the wall above the bed was a new drawing. A female character stood against a white background in leather lace-up boots, her thin muscular legs rising to short shorts, her breasts bulging from a bustier. She raised her arms above her head. One hand shot sparks into the air and in her other hand she held the severed head of a cat. A word bubble that rose from her mouth said: *Kill the asshole!*

'Well,' I said, and wandered back through the house.

A quick search on the computer brought up the phone number of the Consulate General of Jamaica in Miami and a call to the Consulate

221

redirected me to the Jamaican Embassy in Washington. The Embassy gave me a United States phone number for the Ministry of Foreign Affairs and Trade. The woman I talked to at the Ministry, sounding more British than Caribbean, said that Godrell Graham was on a business trip but gave me a cell phone number where I could reach him.

One of Graham's assistants answered my call. He hesitated when I asked to speak with his boss until I said that my call concerned a party that Don Melchiori hoped to hold in his honor.

Graham picked up the phone and asked angrily, 'Who is this?'

'My name's William Byrd, Mr Graham,' I said. 'I think we share some concerns.'

'What's this about Don Melchiori?'

'He's one of the concerns,' I said. 'I know what happened to your daughter. I've seen pictures of the night she died. I know who was there.'

He was quiet for a moment. 'What do you want?'

'Nothing. Just to talk.'

'About what?'

'A friend of mine was also at the party where your daughter died,' I said. 'My friend's dead too.'

'I don't understand.'

'Where are you?' I asked.

'Why?'

'I'd like to meet with you and talk.'

'We're checking Florida port facilities. I've

been in Miami but we're heading north to JAXPORT this morning.'

'I can meet you by the port,' I said. 'How long have you been in Florida?'

'Two weeks – why?' he said.

Two weeks brought him to Florida just before the killings started.

'And what do you drive when you're in the States?' I asked.

He said, 'I have a driver. Why?'

'Does he drive a green SUV?' I asked.

'What's this about?'

'What does he drive?' I said.

'A limousine.'

I said, 'A place called Blackeye's Fish Camp, a couple miles from the port, has a restaurant. Can you meet me?'

'I can be there at two,' he said. 'Bring the pictures of my daughter.'

I hung up.

An ugly job awaited me in the kitchen. Susan had made her bed and adjusted her shades but she hadn't dealt with the real mess. I figured she must have seen Fela's severed head as a fair reminder of what I'd done to our family.

When I opened the refrigerator, the gamey smell of rancid meat poured into the room. I picked up the bowl but Fela's blood had softened the unfired clay and the sides crumbled in my fingers, so I scooped up the pieces as well as I could and ran into the backyard, past the pool and down the slick grass to the quarry pond. I dropped them on the mound where I'd buried Fela's body. Then I returned to the kitchen, unloaded the refrigerator of milk, juice, a bag of oranges, a slice of pizza – everything that the stink of Fela's rotting head could contaminate – and carried it all outside to the garbage.

The morning sun was high and hot but a cool breeze crossed the quarry pond as I shoveled Fela's head and the pieces of clay bowl into a second hole. Afterward, I scrubbed my hands and arms in the shower, though I knew that the stain was deep. I didn't get dressed. I climbed into bed naked and lay with my eyes wide, staring at the white ceiling, shaking with a guilt and sadness worse than cold.

I needed to decide whether to call Charles before going to see Godrell Graham. When I'd told him about my conversation with David Fowler he'd said that the information Fowler had given me pulled this thing together. But I'd still been a long way from knowing what had happened or why. Melchiori's Jamaica pictures explained a lot. Belinda had died because she was at the party. Someone was angry about what had happened to Tralena, or someone wanted to get rid of the women who had witnessed her death, or Tralena's death had tipped someone's mental balance and turned him into a killer. If I followed Melchiori's hints and the implications of the cut-and-pasted pictures that fell from an S&M magazine, that someone was Terrence.

What if Godrell Graham gave me information

that pinned the killings on Terrence? Would I kill Terrence? Would I hurt him? My own son? I didn't feel the blood between us, not as I felt it with Thomas. But still I was uncertain what I would do.

Charles wouldn't hesitate to kill or hurt him though. If I called Charles now and Graham made us believe that Terrence had killed Belinda and the others, Terrence would be dead or so badly injured he'd never fully recover. Not because Charles loved or cared for Belinda. But because there simply was no alternative for him. He fixed what needed fixing, broke what needed breaking.

Eight years back, when I'd suspected Susan was having an affair with that real-estate agent, I'd called Charles and asked him to help find out whether I'd lost her for good. We'd followed the man to work. We'd watched him meet Susan for lunch. We'd sat in Charles' car as they stood together in a park. Then one morning while we waited for him outside his house, Susan arrived and went inside.

'Go in after her?' Charles asked.

'No,' I said.

We waited for two hours and Susan came out again and the man, wearing a bathrobe, walked with her on to the driveway. They stood together and Susan looked happy in a way I hadn't seen since before Thomas was born and they kissed and then she got into her car and drove away.

The man stood alone on his driveway, enjoying the breeze – happy, too, as far as I could tell – and so I got out of Charles' car and went to him.

He seemed to recognize me – Susan must have shown him pictures – but he didn't seem to fear me. I could have killed him then. I felt the strength in myself to do it. But I talked to him instead. I told him he needed to end the affair. I might have threatened him but I didn't touch him.

He looked at me calmly. He was shorter than I was and thick around the middle, a friendly-looking man. 'OK,' he said.

'You'll end it?'

He nodded. 'Sure.'

'OK,' I said and went back to Charles' car and climbed in. 'He said he would end it,' I told him.

'I'm unconvinced,' Charles said.

'He said it.'

'And I'm unconvinced.'

He reached into the backseat and got out of the car with a wooden bat. He went to the man and swung it so hard against the man's knees that they buckled backward and the bat shattered. The man screamed with the purest pain you would ever want to hear.

Charles climbed back into the car as the man lay broken on his driveway. He started the engine and said, 'Now he'll end it.'

'That was unforgivable,' I said.

He nodded. 'That's why I did it.'

I would go see Godrell Graham alone, I

decided. I shaved and got dressed. My meeting with Graham wouldn't start for another two hours but everything in the house spoke to me of all that was gone or leaving, so I got my keys and stepped out the front door.

Charles' Dodge Charger was parked at the curb. Charles was getting out of it. I forced a smile. 'Hey ... Good morning.'

He glanced at the sky as if he hadn't noticed. 'You didn't answer your home phone when I called. Or your cell.'

'I was burying Fela's head,' I said, 'and then I showered. What's up?'

'I found your hooker friend, Aggie.'

'Where?'

'Come on,' he said and climbed into his car.

We drove to a stretch of Philips Highway lined by cheap motels. Rusting late-model cars stood in the sun-bleached parking lots. Charles pulled into the lot of the Luego Motel, a dirty-brown two-story strip with an attached diner.

'*Luego*. What kind of name is that for a motel?' I said.

'It's a good name. *Hasta luego*. Makes you want to come back and stay again.'

'It doesn't make me want to come back.'

Charles parked at the far end and went up a set of concrete stairs to the second-floor landing and stopped outside the first door.

'Is she alive?' I asked.

'Depends on your definition of *alive*,' he said and opened the door.

The room was a wreck. A metal chair was
227

bent, the seat torn off. An easy chair that looked as if it had been in bad shape to begin with was toppled over, its cushion gone from the room. The television, ripped from its metal mount, lay face down on the carpet. The covers and sheets were stripped from the bed. Aggie was in the middle of the bare mattress, naked, her knees pulled to her chin. Her back had cuts from her shoulders to her thighs – thin lines of blood, as if someone had sliced her carefully with a razor blade. She didn't move. As far as I could see, she didn't breathe.

I asked, 'Is she...?'

'Not quite,' Charles said and nodded at a couple of syringes and a rubber tourniquet on the floor. 'But whoever did this to her pumped her up with so much coke and heroin that she's not feeling a thing.'

'Who did it?'

'He was gone by the time I got here.'

'What did he cut her with?' I asked.

'He didn't. He whipped her.' He pointed to a long strip of plastic next to the bed. 'With the electric cord from the TV.'

I looked around the room. There were no large plastic bags and there was no clothesline. This didn't look like the work of the man who'd killed Belinda and the others.

'What do you want to do with her?' Charles asked.

'What do you mean?'

'D'you want to get rid of her?' he asked.

'I want to get her to a hospital.'

'She could cause problems,' he said.

'What kind of problems?'

'The police already connect her to you.'

'I was with *you* when they say the man forced her into his car.'

'Sorry, but they won't see me as a very good alibi.'

'Let's get her to the hospital,' I said.

He nodded. 'I'll take her. But I'm dropping you off first. You don't want to be around.'

We wrapped the bed sheets around her as well as we could, carried her downstairs to Charles' car and squeezed her into the backseat.

'How did you find her?' I asked as we pulled on to the highway.

'Same way I find anyone. I asked questions and asked them the right way.'

EIGHTEEN

I'd exaggerated when I'd told Godrell Graham that Blackeye's Fish Camp had a restaurant. It was a roofed-in bait-and-tackle shop that also sold cold sandwiches that you could eat at the picnic tables they kept out back. Pauly, the owner, kept a shotgun behind the counter though he said he'd only shot it once and that was at a mullet jumping near the riverbank on a drunken afternoon. You could launch a boat or for a dollar a day you could fish from the pier. My dad had taken me there to catch redfish when I was a boy and I'd taken Thomas to do the same.

When I pulled into the parking lot at a quarter to two a black stretch limousine was idling by some empty boat trailers.

I knocked on the driver's window and a young black man in a white cotton shirt and a black chauffeur cap rolled it down. 'Are you with Mr Graham?' I asked.

He stared at me with amused slate-green eyes. 'You're late. He's already inside.'

I went into the shop. It was packed with fishing rods, reels and lures, and you could buy fresh baitfish and shrimp from coolers by the cash register. I got a Miller and a ham sandwich out of the refrigerator case and took them to the counter. 'Hey, BB,' Pauly said and rang up the total.

'You know if there's a Jamaican man who might be looking for me?' I asked.

'Three of 'em. In back.'

I went outside to the river. Two large men in navy-blue suits stood watching the water from an embankment of sand, broken concrete and tar paper that had blown off a nearby roof when the remnants of a gulf-coast hurricane had blown through. The men were Graham's body-guards, and I wondered how a mid-level Foreign Ministry employee justified them to his bosses. Graham, in a charcoal suit, was short and thin with graying hair and was as soft-featured as his daughter had been. He stood by the building, talking on a cell phone which he hung up as soon as he saw me. The bodyguards eyed me, seemed to decide I was no threat and went back to watching the water.

'Mr Byrd?' Graham extended a hand to shake. I nodded. 'You don't want a sandwich?'

He curled his lips for a moment as if I was telling an unfunny joke.

We sat at a picnic table in the afternoon sun.

'Show me the pictures,' he said.

'I don't have them any more,' I said.

'What happened to them?'

'I destroyed them,' I said. 'I didn't like what was in them.'

'I don't understand.'

'As I said this morning, a friend of mine was at the party with Tralena. She was in the pictures too. They were terrible pictures. I destroyed them.'

His eyes sparked with anger but his voice remained calm. 'Then what are you trying to sell me?'

I unwrapped my sandwich and took a bite. 'I found the pictures in Don Melchiori's house,' I said. 'They're probably also on his camera or on his computer. If you want them you can send your men for them. All I want is to know what you're doing about Tralena's death. She died four months ago and you told me you've been in Florida for two weeks. That's when people around here started dying.'

'We grieve in our own ways,' he said and

231

folded his hands on the table. 'I understand business, Mr Byrd. Give me numbers and I'm in heaven. I find comfort in such things. If I can buy an answer to what happened to Tralena, I'll do so. The other work I'll leave to the police and men trained to handle this kind of thing.'

'I've heard you were a regular at Don Melchiori's parties,' I said. 'Who else was there?'

He smiled faintly and I suspected he was covering anger. 'Did Don tell you I was a regular?'

'Does it matter?' I asked. 'Who else was there?'

He looked annoyed. 'You say your friend is dead? Was that Belinda Mabry?'

I nodded.

'I knew Belinda,' he said. 'She was an attractive woman and very smart. Her husband and I did business.'

'Cocaine.'

He laughed at me and said, 'I wasn't surprised when I heard that Belinda was at Melchiori's party with my daughter. Belinda was adventurous. But my daughter wasn't. She was sixteen years old. Still a child. They got her high and assaulted and killed her. Belinda Mabry, this smart and attractive woman who still apparently holds power over you, did that to Tralena. There's nothing you can do to change that.'

'I'm aware of that.'

'Then please explain again what it is you want from me.'

I asked, 'How well did you know Belinda and

her husband?'

'Well enough. Stilman had family. I had family. We invited them and their boy down to visit twice in the last year that they lived in Chicago.'

'What did you think of Terrence?' I asked.

'What about him?' For the first time I thought I heard the calm in his voice break.

'Did Stilman involve him in his business?'

'I don't think he trusted him,' he said.

'It sounds like you didn't either.'

'The last time they visited was three and a half years ago,' he said. 'Terrence was twenty-one. Tralena was twelve. She saw this good-looking young man from Chicago and she liked what she saw. Terrence didn't put her down. He treated her like her love was real but never crossed the line. That's what I thought. But one afternoon, my wife came home and found him in bed with Tralena.' His voice was level again though I heard the strain in it.

'I'm sorry,' I said.

'That's how it sometimes happens. But no, I don't trust him.' A motorboat cut toward the fishing camp dock, banked and ran back toward the middle of the river. The wake lines swelled behind it and washed slowly toward shore. 'If you want to know what real obsession looks like you should've seen Tralena when they left. She was crazy for that boy. Crazy. And Stilman told me his son was crazy for her too.'

'Do you think Terrence found out how Tralena died?' I asked.

'I don't know.'

'Melchiori thinks he's responsible for the killings here.'

He eyed me with interest. 'I wouldn't know about that. I'm a quiet man. I do my business without hurting anyone. But God knows Jerry Stilman could be violent when he needed to be. Living in a house like his, Terrence would have learned violence.'

'He seems soft,' I said.

Graham shook his head. 'Nothing soft about that boy.'

I looked at the river. A single palm tree threw a shadow that intersected the embankment. I said, 'So your daughter dies and you're just going to let things play out however they do?'

'Seems like the problem's taking care of itself, I think.'

'So far, three women who were at the party and one of their roommates have died and a man who didn't even want to be there has been run down by a car. If Terrence is doing this, why wouldn't he go after Melchiori and the other men first?'

'Maybe he did. I hear that Melchiori got shot.'

Graham didn't need to know the details. 'But he's still alive,' I said.

'When they put the bag over my little girl's face, she didn't die right away. She had time to become afraid. Time to know that she was dying. If Stilman's boy is doing this, he might want Melchiori and the others to have time to be afraid too.'

When Graham and his bodyguards drove away in his limousine, I called Charles.

He answered, 'Hey, where are you?'

'I decided to go fishing.'

'Ha.'

'I tracked down Godrell Graham,' I said.

'Good for you. What did he tell you?'

'He's definitely tied to Melchiori and the parties. I think he knows who's behind the killings and he's probably encouraging him. But he's not the killer himself.'

'No,' he said. 'The killer is Terrence.'

'Huh?'

'Aggie woke up and started talking,' he said. 'She was ripped up pretty bad but I could understand what she was saying.'

'Terrence did that to her?'

'None other.'

A chill ran down my back. 'I want to go after him on my own,' I told him.

'You sure?'

I was never less sure of anything. He was my son, and I felt his closeness to me as though he'd been an unseen ghost whose presence I'd never sensed until he'd suddenly materialized and told me he'd been haunting me all my adult life. 'He's mine,' I said. 'He needs to be.'

'I guess so. If you want help you know how to find me.'

'Thanks, Charles. Did you get Aggie to the

hospital?'

'No. Too complicated with her talking like that.'

'For God's sake, Charles. Take her to the hospital.'

'Too late,' he said.

Another chill ran down my back. 'What do you mean "too late"?'

'Jesus Christ, don't be an asshole. What do you think I mean?'

NINETEEN

I didn't know what to do with Terrence. Kill him? Turn him in to Daniel Turner? Save him?

There was no saving him, no more than there was saving myself.

Kill him? This part of me that I hadn't known about for twenty-five years and had appeared in my life as a fiend. This man who had destroyed a woman I probably had never fully understood though I'd loved her ever since I'd met her and she'd made my blood course even in her absence. Could I kill him?

I drove toward downtown on a road that skirted marsh, river and a field of petroleum storage tanks. An egret soared across the road, its long wings staggeringly white in the afternoon sun, so white that it dizzied me and hurt my eyes. Too much white. Too much sun.

Terrence. My boy?

Would I try to save him even knowing the impossibility of his redemption? How could I try? Hold him from behind, my hands over his mouth and nose so that he couldn't breathe? Hold him until he felt the pain and orgasmic pleasure of suffocation, until he knew what it means to die in another's arms, a father's arms? Hold him against my chest until he wept tears that washed him and me clean?

He had no such tears inside him. I felt certain of it.

Would I turn him in to the police? No. That I wouldn't do.

The white cable-stayed Dames Point Bridge rose in front of the car like a bleached skeleton of two enormous wings, wings of a huge angel that had crashed or fallen into the old river.

Whose wings?

Belinda's?

Belinda was dead.

Aggie's?

Aggie was dead too.

Don't be an asshole, Charles had said. She was dead and that knowledge burned in me. What had Charles done? What had I done? Aggie was still breathing when she was in the room at the Luego Motel. *What do you want to do with her?* Charles had asked. Had he ever planned to take her to the hospital? *Too complicated.* Charles was protecting me. Allowing me to get Belinda's killer. Charles knew how to move from point x to point y. Use no more energy than necessary, no more force. *Just enough to do the job*. Charles' motto. Not that he always lived by it. Get rid of Aggie and get to y. What did she matter in the bigger scheme?

Why not get rid of her if getting rid of her meant I could stop Terrence?

Would I kill Terrence? Would I save him? I drove to Belinda's house hoping that when I came face-to-face with him my next step would become clear.

The highway cut across an area that until the early 1980s had been uninterrupted pine forest and wetlands and where, even fifteen years ago, I sometimes saw wild boars and deer and, every now and then, a black bear. But now there was a shopping mall and strip after strip of high-way-side apartments, though I still heard stories of water moccasins slipping from the creeks and shading themselves under cars in the parking lots.

I drove over the Intracoastal Waterway, its surface gleaming under the low concrete bridge, cruised past condominium developments and turned on to the dead-end street where Belinda had lived.

I stopped the car.

Emergency lights, muted by the glaring sunshine, flashed in the cul-de-sac. Thick black smoke rose from Belinda's house. Neighbors were hurrying from their driveways toward the house. I drove down the street and parked behind a police cruiser. Four fire trucks, a paramedic van and three more police cars had pulled into Belinda's driveway and were parked on the lawn.

Flames poured upward from the second-floor windows. The fire made a low roar. As three firemen steadied a hose, the flames died back and black smoke disgorged from the openings. Then the tile roof above one of the windows buckled inward and flames flared into the sky.

I joined a loose crowd that the neighbors had formed about fifty yards from the house, far enough to keep out of the way of the firefighters. Terrence was on the lawn talking to one of the police officers. My heart froze as I realized the officer was Daniel Turner. Did he suspect Terrence of the killings? Terrence pointed at one of the second-floor windows. If I remembered right from our search, it was Bobby Mabry's room. I looked from face to face in the group near the house. Bobby wasn't among them.

Daniel yelled something to one of the firemen, and Terrence looked up at the billowing smoke, then out at the yard. A man in the crowd gave him a sympathetic wave and Terrence waved back. Then he seemed to see me and he panicked. What he saw in my eyes or face I couldn't guess. He backed away from Daniel and ran toward the burning house. No one stopped him until he started up the porch steps, where a fireman put a hand on his forearm and spoke to him. Terrence shook the hand off and continued, and when the fireman seized him again and held him, Terrence stared at him a moment, then swung his free fist at him. It connected and the fireman stumbled backward off the porch steps. Terrence ran inside.

I yelled, 'Terrence!'

He kept going. But my yell got Daniel's attention. He looked at the crowd and found me, then went to two uniformed policemen, talked to them and pointed in my direction. The policemen unholstered their pistols and ran toward me.

I was stunned. What had Terrence and Daniel seen in my face? What had they heard since I'd last seen them?

There was an explosion of wood and metal. The garage door to Belinda's house burst outward, and the Nissan SUV that Charles and I had seen while searching the house came through the shattered door, spun on the driveway and headed for the street. Terrence was at the wheel.

The two officers who were coming for me turned and watched, uncertain whether to go back to the house. Then three firefighters emerged from the front door, holding Bobby, his shirt and shorts darkened by soot, his face covered with an oxygen mask.

I ran.

I was halfway across the yard when Terrence drove out of the driveway on to the street. I got into my car and jerked from the curb. Terrence had reached the end of the street, and I followed him, expecting police cars to follow us. None did. There's no law against plowing through your garage door when your house is on fire, and the officers who were coming after me had gotten caught in the confusion.

Terrence drove north and then west toward the Interstate. We flew up the bridge over the Intracoastal and accelerated down, my Lexus shaking from the speed. We shot past sound-damping walls that protected neighborhoods from the highway noise, stands of oleander bushes with pink flowers that lit up the air like candle flames and leaves so poisonous that eating just one could kill a man, and a billboard for a surgeon who removed varicose veins. Traffic thickened and Terrence slowed as the downtown buildings rose in front of us. We snaked over the bridge across the river and as we came out of downtown Terrence opened up again and headed toward the airport and the Georgia border.

We passed highway-side churches and a large industrial park and drove into the heavily wooded land north of the city. As we neared the airport we passed another industrial area and Terrence moved into the left lane and then whipped across the highway into the exit lane. But the exit was a tight cloverleaf and Terrence was going ninety miles an hour. He seemed to realize that he would never make it and jerked the wheel so he skidded on the shoulder gravel and returned to the highway.

He sped up but I moved in close behind him. We drove north to the next exit and Terrence slowed, veered down the ramp, cut around a car at the stop sign, and turned. He was heading to the airport by the two-lane back road.

The road passed some farms and sank back into thick pine forest. I hit the gas, cut into the oncoming lane and moved alongside the SUV. If I turned the wheel, I could end the chase for him and me both.

A sign on the shoulder indicated that to get to the airport we needed to take a hard left at the next crossroad. We were moving too fast, but Terrence hit the brakes and I flew past. I watched in the rearview mirror as he tried to make the corner. The SUV slid sideways on to the roadside gravel, spun once and rolled down the embankment.

When I turned around and pulled to the spot where the SUV had left the road, Terrence was still inside, spinning the tires, setting the car deep into the mire, so I got out and started down toward him. He got out and ran to the edge of the pine forest. I yelled after him. 'Why are you running from me?'

He stopped for just a moment and yelled, 'Why are you trying to kill me?' Then he ran into the woods.

The ground was soft from yesterday's rain. I slid down the embankment and followed him over a ditch, through a brake of switch cane and into the trees. The air was warm and dark. The forest floor was thick with pine needles, and fallen leaves blanketed wind-felled branches and sandy soil. Live oaks, scrub pines, bay trees and palms blocked out the sun. Terrence leaped over a fallen log about fifty yards in and disappeared. I ran after him, tripped over a branch, caught myself and ran again.

We went for twenty minutes or more, tripping, sliding on damp leaves and running. When sweat soaked my shirt and blurred my vision, I slowed and yelled at him to stop.

He kept going.

I ran after him.

The only sounds in the woods were our breathing and the swishing of our feet through leaves and pine needles. After a half hour Terrence finally slowed but when I got close he ran hard again so I slowed too and soon we were walking and running both, him fifty yards in front of me, never out of sight and never within reach. An hour passed and we went into a grove of scrub pine, planted years ago for a paper mill, then crossed the old logging road, now thick with saplings and weeds.

We ran for a way along the road and then I stopped, unable to continue. I yelled, 'I'm done,' and sat on a spot of grass. He kept going another twenty yards or so and stopped too. I could see him panting. I could hear him. He eyed me warily and lowered himself to the ground. We sat apart, breathing heavily, sweating. Mosquitoes and deer flies hovered like a halo around my face. I yelled, 'Why?'

He sat silent for a long time, watching me. 'Why what?'

'Your mother, for Christ's sake!' There were

tears in my eyes.

'Fuck you!'

'Yeah,' I mumbled. 'Fuck me.' I got to my feet and stumbled toward him.

He pushed himself up and ran again.

I ran after him.

Another mile in, the ground dipped and the soil became soft and wet. We slogged forward. He stopped once and leaned against a tree but as I neared he moved onward. Once, I stopped and he put thirty or fifty more yards between us but I never let him out of my sight. Never.

We came out of the mire on to a dry grassy space as the afternoon light fell toward evening.

'No more,' I yelled. I sat down, close to despair, my clothes soaked with sweat.

I expected him to keep going but he sat.

I was hot and thirsty and knew he was too. There was no breeze, no sound but the high whining of a locust.

Then my phone rang in my pocket. I jumped, fumbled for it, looked at the display and answered, 'Hey.'

'Hey,' said Charles. 'Are you anywhere that the police can find you?'

I looked at the woods around me, looked at Terrence sitting across the clearing. 'I don't think that's likely.'

'Good,' he said. 'They're looking for you. They're convinced you did Belinda Mabry and the others.'

I felt empty and exhausted. 'How did this happen?' I said.

'They've placed you at Melchiori's house two nights ago and in his hospital room last night. They've also placed you in Aggie's room at the Luego Motel.'

His words made me light-headed. 'How did they do that?'

'Someone saw us carrying her out of the motel room and called it in.'

'They after you too?'

'Not that I know of,' he said. 'You're the only one they named. The caller recognized you from the TV coverage of Belinda's death.'

'You should've taken Aggie to the hospital,' I said.

'Belinda Mabry's house also just burned down. They think you lit it.'

'Huh?'

'Where are you?' he asked, as if he could help.

I mumbled to him about chasing Terrence across the city and into the woods.

'Are you still with him?' Charles asked.

'He's sitting fifty yards from me.'

'Let me talk to him,' he said.

'He won't let me get near him.'

'Tell him I want to talk.'

I called across the clearing. 'I've got someone who wants to talk to you!'

Terrence laughed derisively.

I told Charles, 'He's laughing at you. Or me. Or both of us.'

'I heard. Tell him again.'

I said, 'Charles wants to talk!'

Terrence seemed to think about that. 'Bring the phone halfway here, leave it and go back where you are.'

I said to Charles, 'Hold on a minute.'

'Good man,' Charles said.

'Don't stir him up,' I said.

I put the phone where Terrence told me to and went back to my spot in the grass. Terrence approached as if the phone were a trap, spoke into it and listened. Then he broke the back from the phone and threw the pieces in my direction.

'Damn it!' I yelled at him.

He walked away.

I started after him. 'What did Charles say?'

He kept going.

TWENTY

The ground beyond the grass clearing became soft and dropped into a shallow black-water swamp. We trudged ankle-deep past cypress knees, over roots, sludge and God knows what as the sun dipped low and the woods darkened. Night birds whisked through the branches.

'You know what lives in this swamp?' I yelled. Once or twice a year, visiting north-erners, men hunting without permit, or hikers found themselves deep in the wetlands and got bitten by a snake or something else invisible and poisonous, and the sheriff's department airlifted them out – those who had cell phones. Those without cell phones crawled out themselves or didn't.

Terrence kept going.

I stepped on something hard – a branch, a bone, something. Terrence disappeared in the shadows and reappeared.

'We'll die out here!' I yelled.

Silently he arced to his left. For ten minutes he turned through the darkening woods before I realized he was taking us back to the clearing. A three-quarter moon was rising as we climbed, legs caked with swamp mud, back on to the grass. He crossed the clearing and sat facing me. I sat too. For a long time we stayed silent as the sky turned black and insects, frogs and birds began to make a low nocturnal hum. The moon cast a yellow light. Thirst and hunger gnawed at my throat and belly.

I said, 'When your mother and I met we were just kids but I'd never seen anyone like her and I've never seen anyone like her since.'

He said nothing.

I said, 'She had no limits. There was nothing she wouldn't do. That's how it seemed to me then. And that was freeing to me because until I met her I was ... cautious. Overly. I grew because of her. I lived. Do you understand?'

For a while he was quiet. Then he said, 'You screwed a girl when you were a teenager and

you never got over it. That's what I understand.'

'It was love,' I said.

'It's pathetic.'

'Is there a difference?'

'Between love and being pathetic? Yeah,' he
said. 'There's a big difference.'

'I don't think I want your opinion.'

'You're insane,' he said.

I laughed at this man, whose blood I shared,
who'd killed his own mother and trussed her
and wrapped her in a plastic bag like she was
supermarket meat. I laughed, surrounded by
miles of forest, sitting across a grass clearing
from him – this man who I wanted to kill and
save.

When I stopped, we sat quietly again, eyes on
each other in the moonlight. The sounds from
the trees ebbed and flowed and the woods
seemed to tighten on us. I was thirsty and
hungry and felt a bone-deep fatigue. The moon
cocked high in the sky and, although the night
was clear for as far as I could see, distant
thunder rumbled.

I wondered about Terrence. What if I hadn't
been his father? Would that make any difference? I'd told Charles that he was *mine*, that he
needed to be, and I felt that the past few days
had made this much true.

I called to him, 'When I first met you, I didn't
recognize myself in you. I didn't see it.'

He said nothing and we fell back into silence.

The heat, humidity and darkness clung to me.

The moon shone, a single dull eye, three quarters open. It was nothing like the single eye of light on the approaching train engine on the last afternoon that Belinda and I spent together. She'd let her blouse fall between the railroad tracks. She'd unhooked her bra and let it fall too. I'd told her I loved her. She'd told me she loved me too. As the train had closed on us, its whistle blowing, she'd come, bucking like a terrible muscle. I'd ripped away and crawled down the embankment and she'd lain between the rails, her legs open, and waited for the train to take her. I'd opened my mouth to scream, and when it had seemed too late, when the train was yards or feet from her, she'd rolled off the tracks and on to the other embankment. Away from me. Away. With a freight train between us. Because – I knew then and still knew – there was no other way to divide from each other.

No other way. Terrence knew nothing about the past.

The night flaked away. The forest noises rose to a high pitch, then lowered as animals found mates or prey, and for a while all was silent except our breathing and our beating hearts. The moon hung overhead and began to descend to the west and sometime I drifted into an unpeaceful half-sleep in which the darkness and moonlight and the noise and silence blurred and left me in a spot between the world and unconsciousness.

Soft footsteps woke me. I opened my eyes and saw Terrence a few yards from me. The moonlight shined on his face. He held a heavy branch. I leaped up and he dropped the branch and ran back to his spot in the clearing. It happened, it seemed, without a sound.

I stood in the night. 'You were going to kill me.'

He asked, 'What did you expect?'

A good question. What did I expect? I still didn't know what I would do to him when I got my hands on him. I'd chased him across the city and through the woods all afternoon and into the night. That was more than enough to make him think he needed to defend himself by crushing my head while I slept. But he'd run from me as soon as he'd seen me outside his burning house, and he'd already seemed to think that I was dangerous to him. He would've heard the stories about me beating the men who'd attacked the Honduran students and breaking the ribs of the man who was riding with a Garfield doll after the rape and killing of a six-year-old boy. But those were old stories and they hadn't seemed to worry him when I'd first talked with him.

What had happened since then? Mainly, as far as he was concerned, I'd talked with Don Melchiori who'd all but told me that Terrence had murdered Belinda and the others – and then I'd talked to Godrell Graham who'd told me the same thing and then had warned me to keep my hands off Terrence and let everything play out. Would Melchiori or Graham tell Terrence that I was coming after him? If Graham was to be believed, he had no love of Terrence. But he might use him to punish the men and women who'd killed his daughter. Would Graham call Terrence to warn him about the conversation we'd had? If so, Terrence's fear of me would make sense.

A phone call from Graham would also explain the house fire. If Terrence thought that I was coming after him, he might think the best way he could clean the house of evidence would be to burn it.

I called across the clearing, 'Why did you light the house on fire?'

No response.

'Did you burn your collection of pictures?' I asked. 'Or did you bury them in your backyard? I'm guessing you hid them. I'm guessing you couldn't give them up.'

After a long silence, he said, 'I see why my mom was afraid of you.'

The words hit me like a boot. 'She wasn't afraid of me.'

'Did she call you when we moved back south?'

'No,' I admitted more to myself than him.

'She didn't tell you about me and when we moved back she didn't let you know. I wonder why, unless she was afraid.'

'I hurt her a long time ago,' I said. 'I let her down. She didn't get over it. Neither of us did.'

'That's not all of it.'

'You weren't there,' I said.

'But she told me about it. I know what you

251

did to your friend Christopher with the stone. Was he the first person you tried to kill? It took my mom a lot of years to forgive you for that.'

'I did that for *her*.'

'I know all about you,' he said.

'You're confused, Terrence.'

'Hell, I probably know more about you than *you* do,' he said.

'You know nothing.'

Hours passed. The moon set in the west and the sky turned black except for faint light from the stars. I couldn't see Terrence across the clearing. But now and then he made a noise in the dark, and the trees and the swamp absorbed the sound. I couldn't see my own feet or legs and felt myself dissolving into the dark as if by morning the swamp surrounding the grass clearing would suck in all that had ever been of me. I no longer felt I knew who I was, no longer felt it was important that I should know.

I stood in the darkness and went after Terrence, determined to kill him or die at his hands. The turf was soft under my feet. Swamp mud had dried on my pant legs and clung to my ankles like boots. I moved slowly and silently and smelled my own vinegary sweat and nerves. I crept closer, looking for a deeper darkness. Then I realized I was standing on a spot of trampled grass and Terrence was no longer there.

I spun.

He was swinging the branch at me. I raised my arms too late. The branch clubbed me below the ear and for a moment afterward the shadow of Terrence stood in front of me, panting. Then I fell through the dark.

I landed face down and waited for the club to drop again and crush my skull. I waited, powerless to get up, and I didn't beg Terrence to spare me and didn't pray to God to take me when I died. The idea of dying in a clearing of the woods gave me no peace and I waited for the inevitability of it.

But a killing blow never came. I listened. Terrence was splashing through the swamp. My eyes cleared. His branch lay by my side. I pushed myself to my hands and knees, got up and staggered, sick to my stomach. My head spun. I stumbled across the turf to the edge of the clearing, grabbed a tree and stumbled into the swamp after Terrence. My throat burning, I ran, following the sound of Terrence's splashing footsteps. Branches raked across my arms, body and neck. Oily leaves pressed against my cheeks. There was life in the swamp that could poison me or tear me apart and I didn't care.

Another night seemed to pass in the swamp before a gray dawn began to brighten the trees. Wisps of fog hung above the black water. Leaves and scum floated on the surface. The branches of sweet gum trees, cypress and loblolly pines dripped with dew. I stepped into a hole, tumbled forward and got back to my feet, slick and filthy. The fat waists of the swamp trees, blistered with lichen and pink fungus, funneled outward into the water. Terrence ran and stumbled as though the devil were after him.

The swamp became shallow and we crossed a muddy flat, dropped into knee-deep water and climbed a sandy bank. Terrence ran through the trees until he came to a chain-link fence, after which lay an RV park, a flea market and then the Interstate. He climbed the fence and as he jumped to the ground I caught up and we stared at each other for a moment with only inches of air and interlaced wire between us, and in his scratched, filthy face I knew I was looking at an image of my own. A small laugh escaped from my throat and seemed to scare him. He ran and I climbed the fence and went after him,

No one was outside in the RV park. We ran down a concrete aisle past quiet campers, bicycles, potted palms and plastic tables littered with beer bottles. At the end of the aisle a deteriorating sign said *Welcome – Pecan Park Flea and Farmers' Market*. Three yellow-and-blue metal sheds, each a city block long, were closed, their metal garage doors pulled down, blue plastic tarps tied over the openings. When the market opened, *J&J Blades* would sell cane machetes and Samurai swords and other vendors would sell boiled peanuts, bootleg martial arts videos and automobile tires shined with Armor All until they gleamed like hot, wet asphalt. On weekends a Ukrainian immigrant would set up a table display of hollow-glass swans filled with colored water.

Terrence ran between the sheds and out on to

a grass parking lot. Another chain-link fence stood between the lot and an embankment to the Interstate. He scrambled over the top and up to the highway shoulder.

Cars and semi-trailers shot past. To the east the sun was rising, orange and enormous. As I climbed over the fence and started up the embankment, Terrence tried to cross but a Landstar truck blasted its horn and he dodged back to the side. He ran toward the oncoming traffic, tried again and got to the median, where he climbed between the guard rails.

'No more running,' I yelled.

He climbed over the other rail.

'You've got to face me sooner or later,' I yelled.

A gap appeared in the traffic between us. I ran toward him. He stepped into the highway on the other side. A car blew its horn and shifted lanes to avoid hitting him. I cleared the first guard rail and he tried again. He got across the first lane and most of the second. Then a red convertible, its roof down, its headlights on as if to focus on a target, clipped him. He flew twenty or twenty-five feet and landed on the roadside gravel.

The convertible pulled to the side and other cars and trucks stopped. Terrence wasn't moving. Men and women dressed for the workday surrounded him, two calling 911 on their cell phones, and I walked over and joined them. Terrence lay face down, his left arm stretched beside him, a broken bone sticking through the skin. I watched his back for breathing and saw none. My stomach turned.

Then he moved his good arm and the crowd gasped. He pushed himself on to his knees, the fabric of his pants torn and bloody, and rose unsteadily to his feet. The driver of the convertible, a blonde woman in her twenties, wearing beach shorts and a bikini top, cried and reached for him, and others moved close as though he were a hatchling who might need their help to stand, but he stumbled away from the circle until he reached a blue sedan that was idling on the roadside. He leaned against the trunk and everyone moved toward him but he stood on his own and stepped back into the highway. He went to the driver's door and climbed in. The owner of the car seemed uncertain what to do and, by the time he decided Terrence didn't belong in the car, Terrence had locked it, shifted into drive and hit the accelerator.

I looked around frantically for another car but none had been left running. 'I need a car,' I yelled, and everyone backed away from me as if I were the monster who'd made the morning bloody.

Some got in their cars and drove away. Others waited for the police. I sat on the highway shoulder and wept.

TWENTY-ONE

I lay on an exam table in the ER at University Hospital. A young black nurse had cleaned my cuts and abrasions and a Pakistani doctor was checking me a second time for the concussion Terrence had given me with the branch. Two uniformed police officers stood outside the exam room. They hadn't arrested me but they'd ridden in the ambulance and had stayed within a few feet of me since arriving at the scene on the Interstate.

The doctor shone a pen light into each of my eyes and asked the questions you ask when you think someone might have a brain injury. 'Do you know your name?'

'Yes.'

'What is it, please?' he said.

'I'd rather not tell you.'

'Why?'

Because, from what Charles had told me before Terrence had broken my phone, the officers outside the room would slap handcuffs on me, but I still hoped I could walk out of the hospital and pursue Terrence. I said nothing.

The doctor's expression remained neutral. 'How old are you?'

'Forty-two.'

He nodded. 'Your birthday?'

'I'd rather not say.'

'Well, would you like to tell me what hit your head?'

'A large tree branch,' I said.

'And how did your head meet this large tree branch?'

'Sorry.'

He sighed. 'I believe this is a mild concussion, not that you're helping me to be sure. You should avoid drinking alcohol for three or four days and of course avoid any illegal drugs. Take it easy, rest, sleep well.'

'May I leave?' I asked.

He smiled, tightlipped. 'If you can persuade the police officers to let you go.' He left without another word.

The nurse appraised me. My legs were caked with mud, my clothes soaked with swamp water. I smelled like sulfur and decay. 'Honey, you're a mess,' she said. 'Don't you have someone you can call to bring you clean things?'

'If I can get to a cab I'll be all right.'

The exam room door swung open and the nurse said, 'Sorry,' and seemed to mean it.

Daniel Turner stepped in. He looked at me for several seconds and said, 'Jesus, you're a sight.'

'Morning, Lieutenant,' I said.

'What the hell've you been crawlin' through?'

'Worse than you can imagine.'

He shook his head. 'You look it. Smell it too.'

258

'Are you here to arrest me?' I asked.

A faint smile appeared on his face. 'Now why would I do that?'

'Because you think you've placed me at Melchiori's house and Aggie's room.'

'Yeah, I want to hear about all that,' he said.

'And because yesterday at Belinda's house you sent two deputies after me.'

'That was when I thought you were responsible for all kinds of nastiness that I now know you had nothing to do with.'

'So you finally figured out who did it?'

He looked at the nurse. 'Do you mind?'

'Not at all, honey,' she said, but in her eyes I saw a disdain for Daniel and a protectiveness for me that neither of us had earned. 'Make yourself at home,' she said and left the room, closing the door behind her.

Daniel turned to me. 'Terrence Mabry blamed you for the fire. He said you and Charles Tucker threw Molotov cocktails through the windows. But when he left through the closed garage door I decided we should take a closer look. We found the remains of some bottles of gas but anyone could've thrown them, including him. We also found clothesline that matches the line that the killer used on Belinda and the other women. We found plastic bags that match. And we found some of the filthiest pictures you'd ever want to see, including one of Ashley Littleton. We've issued a warrant for his arrest.'

I considered all he'd told me. 'So I'm free to go?'

'There's still the matter of who shot Don Melchiori,' he said.

'You know it wasn't me,' I said. 'I'm afraid of guns.'

'So you say. What about Aggie?'

I looked him in the eyes. 'What about her? I haven't seen her since your fellow officers talked to us behind the old Chevy dealership.'

'What worries me is no one else has seen her either. But we've got a motel room with blood on the mattress and an eyewitness who saw you going into the room.'

'I don't know about a bloody mattress and I'm betting that any eyewitness you found at a motel where Aggie would be staying wouldn't be worth much.'

'So you say.'

'What's happening with Terrence?' I asked.

'We found the car that he stole in the parking lot at the Avenues Mall. There was plenty of blood. We're guessing he took another car though we haven't received any reports of one stolen.'

'He took the owner with him?'

'That's the worry right now. But all the witnesses say his arm's in bad shape. He'll need to get help for it sooner or later.'

I thought about him enduring the pain and fears of trudging through the midnight swamp. 'He may take some time before popping his head up.'

'We'll be waiting for him when he does,'

he said.

The air conditioning and bright lights of the exam room made me shiver. I asked, 'So why did you come here to tell me all this?'

'I figured I owed it to you.'

I didn't think anyone owed me anything. 'You had good reasons to suspect me.'

'But I did more than that,' he said. 'I told Susan she should leave you. For her own safety and Thomas's.'

I knew that Susan would've made the same decision on her own but anger flooded my belly all the same. So I changed the subject. 'How's Bobby Mabry?'

'Second- and third-degree burns on his arms and legs. The doctors say he'll survive.'

'He's had to survive a lot in his life.'

Daniel nodded. 'Some men seem to be born that way,' he said and he seemed to be including me. 'Susan and Thomas are outside. You want to see them?'

'What are they doing here?'

'I called them,' he said. 'I thought I owed you that too.'

I wasn't ready to face them but I said, 'I'd like to see them.'

He stepped into the hall and waved them over, then left with the two police officers who'd stood sentry.

Susan wore a blue floral-print cotton dress and carried a small duffel bag. Thomas wore khaki cargo shorts and a white T-shirt. They looked freshly bathed. Thomas came to the exam table and though I was filthy I pulled him to me in a hug. Susan stayed by the door. 'Hi,' I said to her.

'Hi.' She sounded almost shy. 'I brought you new clothes.'

'Come here,' I said.

She did. 'I'm sorry,' she said.

'Don't be. Why?'

'I thought you did it,' she said.

I felt a weight in my stomach. 'Why would you?'

'You go out at night while we're sleeping. You aren't ... normal.'

I looked at Thomas. 'What do you think?'

He shrugged.

'Did you think I was killing these women?' I asked.

'No,' he said.

I said, 'I think I'm normal.'

Thomas laughed – at me, with me, I didn't know which – and then Susan laughed too. She put her fingers tenderly on one of the scratches on my face. 'How are you feeling?'

My head ached. My arms and legs were sore. I was exhausted in body and spirit both. 'Hungry,' I said.

We went to the Metro diner and I ordered eggs, bacon, toast and pancakes. After my night in the woods, sitting and calmly eating break-fast with Susan and Thomas, surrounded by men and women dressed in clean clothes and having polite conversations, felt dizzying, a scene from another life. When I pushed back

262

from the table Susan said, 'Are you going to tell us about it now?'

I gazed at her. She looked like she had nothing to lose from me any more and that made me think I had nothing to lose either. I turned to Thomas. 'To begin with,' I said, 'you've got a brother. Or a half-brother. His name's Terrence Mabry.' I asked Susan, 'Did Daniel tell you about that?'

She shook her head though the news didn't seem to shock her.

So I told them more than I'd ever told anyone other than Charles. I told them about falling in love with Belinda when I was just two years older than Thomas was now. I told them that my friend Christopher had assaulted Belinda's brother Bobby, that I'd failed Belinda by letting Christopher walk away from what he'd done, and that I'd lived with that knowledge for all my adult life. I told them about meeting Terrence for the first time after Belinda's death and of coming to think that he must be responsible for his mother's and the other women's deaths. I told them about chasing him through a waking nightmare in the swamps and woods north of the airport.

When I finished I looked from Thomas to Susan.

Thomas said, 'Wow.'

Susan said, 'Yes.'

'I love you,' I told them both.

Susan raised her eyebrows. 'You've said that too often.'

'I want you and need you,' I said. 'Both of you. Like no one else in the world.'

Susan and Thomas dropped me off at home and left again to get their bags from the hotel where they'd stayed the previous night. Inside the house, the motors on the air conditioner and refrigerator hummed like insects. They were familiar sounds in a familiar place, but in my exhaustion I felt out of sorts, out of myself, a man wearing another man's clothes, an impostor in his house. I walked down the hall and stopped at the kitchen door. Through the back windows the sun was glinting off the swimming pool water and the quarry pond beyond. The grass was dark green and cool to the eyes.

I forced myself to smile. Susan and Thomas were coming home. For better or worse, they were coming. Probably worse but they would be with me and that was good and I hadn't needed to ask. They were coming because they'd chosen to come. Thomas would draw obscene comic books. Susan would sleep in the sunroom. I would make my rounds to my gas stations and spend occasional nights with Lee Ann. We would try not to infuriate each other.

But first I would sleep.

When I stepped into the kitchen, a shadow moved from beside the door. I stepped to the side, spun and saw Terrence – wild-eyed, his broken arm in a sling, a knife in his good hand. He lunged at me. The knife slashed at my chest but missed. I moved toward his bad arm and the

264

knife slashed again. It caught my sleeve.

I kicked at him and missed. I kicked again and connected and he hollered and the knife clattered to the floor.

He scrambled after it but fell and rolled on to his back. Somehow he got the knife and held it up at me. I kicked his legs and went for his ribs but he slashed again.

He lay on the floor, panting. He was filthy from the night in the swamp. Blood from the exposed arm bone stained his sling and shirt. He smelled like death and decay. His wild, glassy eyes locked on to me.

'I spend all night chasing you,' I said, 'and as soon as you escape you turn around and come after me. Why?'

'Because you'll never leave me alone if you're alive,' he said. 'I don't want to run anymore. Sooner or later you'll come after me. You know that's true.'

He was right but I said, 'I didn't want to know you to begin with. If you'd kept your hands off your mother and the others I would've left you alone.'

'You're sick,' he said.

'You're lying on my kitchen floor like a dying animal and you tell me I'm sick?'

He lunged sideways and swept the knife toward me. But he moved too slowly. I side-stepped him and booted him in the ribs. Something cracked inside him and the knife fell from his hand and slid across the floor.

'You motherfucker,' he gasped. 'I'm your

265

son.'

'You're nothing.' I stepped over him and picked up the knife.

He slid away from me until he reached the refrigerator and pulled himself to his feet. His cracked ribs bowed him at the waist. 'Motherfucker,' he said again and stumbled toward the French doors. Sunlight danced on the pool and quarry pond. The green grass looked like a cool shadow. As he reached for the doorknob I sank the knife into his back. His body arched and he spun and faced me. I stuck the knife into his chest and left it there.

He found enough life only to cry once before he slid to the floor, his shocked eyes locked on mine.

'You're nothing,' I said and I kicked him again.

When Daniel arrived, Terrence was dead, hunched against the French doors. The room smelled of swamp, sulfur, and the urine that had streamed from Terrence on to the floor as he died.

Daniel asked, 'What was he doing in your house?'

'He came to kill me,' I said.

He stooped in front of Terrence. 'After running away from you all night?'

'He tried to kill me last night. He hit my head with a branch.'

'But this time he tried to stab you with a knife.'

'Yes.'

'Which you took away from him.'

'It wasn't hard,' I said.

'And you stabbed him in self-defense.'

'I suppose.'

'In the chest,' he said.

'Also the back,' I said.

'I see that.' He looked at Terrence's body. 'And the caved-in ribs?'

'Self-defense.'

'Uh huh.'

A bald man in a khaki shirt with a patch that said *District Four Medical Examiner's Office* went to work on Terrence. An evidence technician bagged the knife. A uniformed police officer stood at the door to the hallway and tried not to look at the body. I went to the thermostat and turned it down.

Familiar voices came from the front of the house. Susan and Thomas had arrived and a police officer was telling Susan that she could not come in. I went to see them. Thomas was sitting on the front porch steps facing the street, his head in his hands. Susan was trying to get past the officer. 'BB,' she said when she saw me, 'will you tell this man to let me into our house?'

I shook my head. 'You really don't want to come in here right now.'

'Yes,' she said angrily. 'I do.'

She pushed past the officer and headed down the hall.

'Stay where you are,' I said to Thomas and

followed Susan into the kitchen.

She stood a few feet from Terrence and gazed at him as if his corpse might hold the answer to an old, painful question. She said, 'This is him? This is your son?'

'It's Terrence Mabry,' I said.

'Terrence Mabry,' she repeated and she spit on him.

TWENTY-TWO

Daniel gave me business cards for Decontamination Specialists LLC and Dririte, two companies that cleaned violent crime scenes, but I found a roll of paper towels and a bottle of Fantastik and got down on my hands and knees. Thomas refused to come inside until late in the afternoon and then steered wide of the spot where Terrence had died. Susan pretended normalcy. She made us a late lunch and after delivering a plate to Thomas on the front porch we sat together at the dining room table. But the orange scent of Fantastik and something more permanent and terrible hung in the air.

In the afternoon I swam in the pool and then lay on a lounge chair with my eyes closed and let the sun beat against my eyelids. A breeze breathed across the lawn from the quarry pond.

Susan lay beside me, wearing opaque sunglasses.

The phone rang inside the house.

I waited for Thomas to get it.

He was still on the front porch.

I waited for Susan to get up.

She'd either fallen asleep or was pretending.

I went inside and answered on the sixth ring.

It was Charles. 'You're not answering your cell phone,' he said.

'I don't have one anymore. Terrence broke it after talking with you last night. What did you say to him?'

'I told him you were going to kill him.'

I said, 'You upset him pretty well. That didn't help.'

'But I understand you've done the job now. Put a hole in back and a hole in front.'

It didn't please me. It was something that had needed to be done and I'd done it. 'Why are you calling?' I asked.

'Just like that? You kill him and it's *Why are you calling*?'

'As you said, the job is done.'

'Almost done,' he said. 'We need to take care of Aggie.'

'What do you mean? When I asked if you'd taken her to the hospital you said it was too late.'

'It *was* too late. But I've still got her. We need to put her in the ground.'

The thought of it nauseated me. 'I'm exhausted, Charles.'

'*You're* exhausted? You know how old I am?'

'No, I don't,' I said. 'But I'm not coming, Charles.'

'Fine. I'll dump her body on your porch and you can take care of it after you rest.'

'Charles...'

'What?'

'Jesus Christ, I'll be there in a half hour.'

'Bring a shovel,' he said.

We buried Aggie in the woods in front of his house. He'd sponged the cuts that she'd had when I'd seen her at the Luego Motel and wrapped her in a clean white sheet before stowing her in a backyard shed. As we dug, the shovel blades kept striking the hardwood roots of oak trees and red maples as if the soil didn't want her. The afternoon was hot and thick with humidity and Charles worked as hard as I did but after we lowered Aggie into the hole and covered it, his shirt was still white though mine was soaked with dirty sweat.

I asked, 'You won't be bothered knowing she's buried outside your front door?'

'No,' he said. 'Should I be?'

'Maybe.'

'Come inside and clean up.'

I showered in his bathroom and he put my clothes in his washing machine. Then I wore his bathrobe and sat drinking beer with him in his screened porch. A blood-red cardinal and his brown mate pulled something from the pine needles, disappeared into the trees and returned for more. A horse fly had become trapped inside the porch and buzzed furiously against the screen. Charles watched it with mild interest.

He said, 'Not a lot of men could do what you've done.'

'Thank God.'

'Takes a special kind of man to do that,' he said.

'That's what you told me the first time we met.'

He nodded. 'Worman's Deli. After you beat up the Honduran kids.'

'It was the other way around. I beat up the men who were attacking the Hondurans.'

'Whatever. It's still true. It takes a special kind of man. I'm proud of you.'

'I don't want you to be proud of me.'

'I know,' he said. 'That's good too.'

We sat silent for a while. The horse fly buzzed.

'I'm leaving town,' he said. 'In a few days.'

'One of your mysterious trips?'

He shook his head. 'This time I won't be coming back.'

The news shouldn't have surprised me. Charles had always seemed to exist on the edge of the city even if he knew more about the place than anyone else, and he'd always seemed impermanent even if he hadn't changed in twenty years. I should have been glad to see him go though I knew he'd become a part of me. 'Where are you going?'

He gave me a look that said I should know better than to ask.

'I'll miss you,' I said.
'Yeah, I'll bet.'

Over the next three days, Susan, Thomas and I tried to put together the fragments of our lives even though the cracks were twenty-five years old and older. The scratches on my hands and face healed. The split on my forehead where Don Melchiori had butted me mostly vanished, and the bruises on my ribs where he'd kicked me were fading. The concussion where Terrence had smacked me with a branch still gave me headaches but they would pass. The newspaper and nightly news cycled through the story. They started with Terrence's death in my kitchen, and by day three they had long biographical accounts of him with high-school photographs, remarks from high-school friends, comments about his visits to the Little Vegas Gentlemen's Club, and insinuations about his sexuality. I made the rounds to my gas stations and when the slow-witted day manager at my Best Gas station said nothing about my troubles I felt generous and told her I was giving her a raise. Thomas swam in the backyard pool and drew obscene superhero comic books. Susan showed houses to clients without selling any, saw friends and ate meals with Thomas and me. At night I stayed home instead of going to see Lee Ann.

On the third evening, as we sat for dinner, there was a knock at the door. Christopher stood on the front step. His face was flushed and slack. He was drunk. He held a rock in his hand, about the size of the ones we flung through the Mabrys' windows before they moved into the neighborhood.

'Hey, Christopher, what's up?' I said, though I was sure that I didn't want to know.

He stepped inside smelling of gin and beer and handed me the rock. 'I was going to throw this at your house,' he said.

'Thanks,' I said, as though he'd given me a bottle of wine.

He looked into the living room. 'This place looks just like it did when we were growing up.' It was a criticism.

'Some things don't change,' I said.

'Ain't that the truth.'

Thomas joined me at the doorway.

I asked Christopher, 'What are you doing here?'

He gestured at the rock in my hand. 'Like I said.'

'Why?'

'My wife's leaving me,' he said. 'She took her daughter and she's staying with her parents. For a week. But it's her house. I'm to move out before she returns.'

'I'm sorry,' I said, 'but I don't see—'

'I can't get Belinda out of my head,' he said.

I laughed. At him. At myself. I couldn't stop. He stared at me with uncertain anger. 'What?'

'You want to have dinner with us?' I asked.

The idea seemed strange to him. 'No.'

'What can I do for you then?'

Again he looked uncertain. He asked, 'How did it feel to kill Terrence?'

'Honestly?'

'I mean, *your own boy.*'

Thomas looked at me for an answer too.

I nodded. 'I didn't feel it at all. It was just something that needed to be done.'

The next morning there was a service for Belinda, though her body remained at the morgue pending final disposition. The service was held on a rolling lawn between an ocean-side beach and the third fairway of a golf resort south of the city. The sun had risen from the ocean but a soft sea breeze nudged at the heat. There were white broad-board lounge chairs and unlighted gas lanterns on metal posts. The minister said that Belinda had loved to come to this spot and the service would celebrate her life, not mourn her death. With a put-on laugh he said he would return to this spot later in the week to conduct a wedding.

Christopher was there in a blue suit, looking mostly sober. He sat by himself and talked to no one. Bobby Mabry had arrived from the hospital in a special van, and a nurse pushed him on to the lawn in a wheelchair. Already a small man, he seemed hunched inside himself. A white sheet was draped over his burned and bandaged legs. His short beard, neat and clean the last time I'd seen him, looked matted, and the skin on his cheeks glistened with a pained sweat. He kept his eyes to himself.

Daniel Turner sat next to another man who looked like a police officer. Charles sat at the back of the crowd looking as content as a man with tearstain scars on his cheeks ever could look. He chatted quietly with the strangers next to him. Tralena Graham's father showed up late in a dark suit with his two bodyguards. When he caught me watching him he nodded in my direction.

In the crowd of forty, only two women attended. One of them was the nurse with Bobby and the other looked like a plainclothes police officer. Four police cars had parked in the resort lot and a couple of uniformed officers stood behind the rows of folding chairs. I wondered what loose ends Daniel was still investigating.

I looked out at the ocean. Seagulls soared ten or fifteen feet above the waves, plunged into the water and emerged, their beaks empty.

The minister said, 'The pain that Belinda Mabry suffered in death is nothing when compared to the pleasure she brought to others when she was alive.'

Sitting next to me a gray-haired black man wearing a bolo tie called out, 'Got that right.'

There was no music and there were no testimonials from friends or family – just the minister's voice, the breeze, the roar and hush of breaking ocean waves and children laughing on the beach. When the service ended, the minister was the first to go and most of the others followed him. Daniel and the police officers stayed and studied the crowd. I wandered over to Charles.

'I thought you were leaving town,' I said.

'Soon.'

We watched Christopher join Bobby, who stared at him, slack-jawed with medication.

'Twenty-five years ago,' I said, 'that man raped him.'

Maybe Christopher was apologizing. Bobby raised a hand a few inches off the sheet and Christopher took it in his own hands and held it. He stooped so that he looked at Bobby eye to eye and held his hand as if he were trying to pass strength to him or take strength into himself.

'Funerals are hilarious,' Charles said.

I went home and lay by the pool with a pitcher of margaritas, and Thomas swam lap after lap like a metronome counting the slow beat of our existence.

That night, Susan, Thomas and I ate a late dinner on the pool deck with the pool filter chugging reassuringly in the dark beside us and then I went inside to my bedroom, climbed into bed and turned on the ten p.m. news. A *Breaking News* banner appeared across the screen and the anchorman announced a tragic development in an ongoing story and cut to a reporter on the street.

The reporter, a young man in short shirt-sleeves, stood outside University Hospital. The yellow-orange glow of streetlights cast weird shadows over him. Police and paramedic emergency lights flashed behind him. He said,

'According to hospital officials, a little after nine tonight City Councilman Don Melchiori was attacked violently in the room where he was recovering from a gunshot wound sustained earlier this week. We learned minutes ago that Melchiori has died. Police haven't named or apprehended a suspect. The mayor's office has issued the following statement: *Don Melchiori was a dedicated public servant and civic supporter. His contributions to historical preservation will be felt for generations to come. We offer condolences to Don's family.* We'll be back with more details as this story develops.'

I was out of bed and mostly dressed by the time that the camera cut back to the anchorman. The phone rang as I headed for the front door, and I went back to the kitchen and answered.

'You see the news?' Charles said.

'Just turned it off,' I said. 'What do you make of it?'

'The man I've talked to says it was strangulation by ligature,' he said. 'Clothesline. They haven't matched it yet but I'm guessing it's the same line as the others.'

My stomach fell. 'Which means Terrence Mabry didn't do the killings?'

'Which is something I'm thinking the police already suspected since they showed up at Belinda's funeral in big numbers,' Charles said. 'Maybe he was in it with someone else who's continuing alone. But if I had to guess, these are one-man jobs.'

'No one saw Melchiori's killer go into his room?' I asked.

'The security camera in the corridor was disabled and the nurses at the station apparently saw no one suspicious.'

'Do they have any idea who did it?'

'That's why I'm calling,' he said. 'I'm hoping that around nine o'clock you were surrounded by friends and neighbors who can testify that you weren't at University Hospital.'

'I was home with Susan and Thomas.'

'That might not be enough,' he said. 'If I were you I'd get out of your house fast.'

'I was leaving when the phone rang.'

'Yeah? Where were you heading?'

'I was going to find Daniel Turner to see what was happening.'

'I wouldn't do that. He thought you were the man before. He probably thinks it again.'

I closed my eyes and breathed deep.

'You still there?' he asked.

'Can I hide out for a while at your place?'

'Any time,' he said.

I said, 'I'll be there in a few hours.'

'Where are you going now?'

'I need to check on a couple things.'

'You need help?' he asked.

'I need a hell of a lot of help. But I'll see you in a few hours.'

I hung up, turned and saw Thomas in the doorway.

'What's wrong?' he said.

'Nothing,' I said. 'It's all right now.'

'Are you in trouble again?'

I started to lie but instead said, 'Yeah,' and tried a smile. 'It seems to follow me.'

'What can I do?' he asked.

'You can lend me your cell phone.'

TWENTY-THREE

The moon hung in a wispy veil of clouds over Don Melchiori's house. The windows were dark, the building heavy in shadow. Only the leaves of an orange tree growing against the front wall glimmered vaguely, like fish in shallow water. Someone had boarded up the door that Charles and I had kicked in on our last visit. The police would arrive soon, as they investigated Melchiori's death.

I pried a sheet of plywood from the door and stepped inside.

I felt my way up the dark stairs, went into Melchiori's bedroom and flipped on a bedside lamp. The box of party photos was in the third dresser drawer where I'd left it. I thumbed through the pictures, trying to remember which of the men had been in the party photos I'd destroyed. Belinda, Tralena and the two other women from the photos were dead, buried in Jamaica or lying in the morgue. Two of the men

– David Fowler and now Melchiori – were also dead.

In the photos that remained now I saw two other men who might have been in the pictures I'd destroyed. I knew neither of them, though one – a middle-aged white man with a paunch and a stoned grin – looked familiar enough to make me think he was a city politician whose face appeared occasionally in the paper or on the news. I slipped a couple of pictures into my pocket.

The photos in the box had been a select collection from Melchiori's parties, and Melchiori usually starred in them. But there had to be more. He would want others within easy reach for nights when the greatest-hits photos weren't enough to get him off. But he would also want them well enough hidden that a cleaning woman or visitor wouldn't find them. I fanned my fingers through the suits and shirts on the closet bars. I opened three shoeboxes that were stacked on a shelf. I removed two clear plastic sweater bins from the next shelf. One of the bins was heavier than it should have been, and when I dug through it, I found two albums that Melchiori had wrapped in cotton sweaters.

On the bed, I paged through the first of them. It covered early parties which looked innocent in comparison to what they would become. Melchiori started with girls who appeared in various poses and positions with or without him. He moved on to groups that included other men. One early party had six girls and just one other man.

The second album was hardcore. The girls got younger, the sex more violent, the drugs more plentiful. I recognized a city councilman who was licking the asshole of a sixteen- or seventeen-year-old. I recognized an Asian television anchorwoman. I recognized but couldn't name three other faces.

The last pages contained pictures from the party with Belinda and Tralena. The first covered party preparations. Melchiori and David Fowler appeared again, as did the two men whose photos I'd taken from the dresser box. Fowler was shown cutting lines of cocaine. Tralena was shown sitting on a couch in panties and a bra, her head thrown back laughing. Tonya Richmond was shown with her tongue between her lips and her fingers plunged inside her skirt. Belinda was shown taking Melchiori's penis into her mouth.

I turned the page and the photos wrenched my stomach. They showed the next stages of the party, after the first hits of coke, after the undressing, but before the binding and suffocating. They showed Melchiori, David Fowler and the other two men switching partners. But they also showed a fifth man.

In the first, Tralena mounted Lieutenant Daniel Turner as he sat on a dining-room chair.

In the second, Daniel took Tonya Richmond from behind on a living-room sofa.

In the last, he sat on the same sofa alone watching David Fowler screw Ashley Littleton on a rug.

I yanked the final pictures out of the albums and stuffed them in my pockets with the others. My breath felt thin and insufficient and the darkness outside the bedroom windows seemed to press against the house as though it meant to crush it. How was Daniel involved in the killings? Could he be the killer? His presence in the pictures made no sense. He'd pushed the investigation hard, as though his own life depended on it. Maybe it did. He was at the party and everyone at the party was dying. I needed to talk with him. He might shoot me. He might put me in jail. But we needed to talk.

I wanted Charles by my side when we met. I dialed his home number on Thomas's cell phone. It rang a half-dozen times and I hung up. I dialed his cell. It rang four times and kicked to voicemail. I said, 'Hey, Charles – call me,' and hung up. Day or night, the only times I'd known him not to answer his phone had been when he was on one of his mystery trips. He'd told me he was preparing to leave town but less than an hour ago he'd given no sign that he was ready to go.

I put the albums in the sweater bin, returned the bin to the closet shelf and turned off the bedroom light. But as I stepped out of the room I heard footsteps downstairs. I went back into the closet but realized as the footsteps came up the stairs that I had nowhere to go, so I slid out and stood against the wall.

The footsteps moved past the door, stopped

and returned. A hand touched the wall beside me and found a switch. The room filled with light and a tall black man stepped in and spun to face me with a black pistol in his hand. He was the manager of Little Vegas, the man who'd led me at gunpoint to Melchiori's and then accidentally shot his boss. I knew him as Darrin.

He looked almost relieved to see me. 'Man! I almost shot you.'

'You're not going to?' I said.

He smiled disdainfully. 'Hell, no. Why would I do that?'

I moved cautiously from the wall. 'Why are you here?'

'Same reason you are, probably.'

I considered his possible motives. 'You going to rob the place?'

'No, you stupid fuck. I'm not going to rob the place. I'm trying to figure out who's killing these folks.'

'Why?'

'To save my ass, why else?' he said. 'Everyone from the party's dead, just about. I made the travel arrangements for Tonya and Ashley. I booked most of the tickets. I figure this crazy bastard's coming after me too.'

'How do you know I'm not the crazy bastard?' I asked.

'I heard they cleared you this morning.'

'Tonight they're saying I did it again,' I said.

'In that case...' He pointed the pistol at my chest.

'I didn't,' I said. I went to the bed and laid out the photos that I'd taken. 'As you say, most of them are dead.' I named each of them. 'D'you recognize the others?'

He pointed at one of the two men whose names I didn't know and said, 'He's Phil Lingren. He does computers at the mayor's office. I booked his ticket.' He pointed at the other man. 'Him I've seen around but I don't know his name.' Then he pointed at Daniel Turner. 'And him I've never seen.'

'He's a police officer,' I said. 'Homicide squad. He's leading the investigation into the killings.'

He whistled and said, 'That sucks.'

'He used to be a good man. I don't know what he is now.'

He gestured at the picture in which Tralena had mounted Daniel. 'Looks like she thinks he's good.'

'What were you looking for when you broke in?' I asked.

'Anything,' he said. 'These pictures ain't a bad start. I came in once before and searched downstairs. When I heard about Melchiori getting killed, I figured the cops would beat me to the search if I didn't move fast.'

I pointed at the picture of the man whose name Darrin didn't know. 'D'you think you could find out who he is and go watch him?'

Darrin narrowed his eyes at me. 'What're you thinking?'

I gestured at the picture. 'You find the man

with no name and I find Phil Lingren. We stay on them until the killer arrives.'

'And then?'

'You've got the gun. Use it. Or bring him to me. I don't care which.'

'What about you? You got a gun?' he asked.

I shook my head.

He smiled disdainfully again. 'You've got rocks in your head. What happens if the killer doesn't come?'

'You think that's a possibility?' I asked.

'No,' he admitted. 'What about your cop friend?'

'If he's the problem, we'll see him when he comes after Lingren or the other guy. If he's not the problem and the killer goes after him, he's got a gun too.'

We went downstairs together in the dark. I gave him the number to Thomas's cell phone and he gave me the number to his. He gazed at the ceiling of the big front hall and said, 'Mr Melchiori had funny habits but he was all right. Overall.'

When he stepped through the broken doorway on to the darkened front porch, I noticed that the night sounds that I'd heard when entering the house – the high singing of tree frogs, the rustle of birds and insects in the branches – were gone. Then a gunshot cracked not far away and Darrin stumbled back into my arms.

I held him, the warmth of his body heavy against me, then let him slide to the floor and pulled him from the door. His chest was wet and spongy.

'Darrin,' I whispered.

He was already dead.

I huddled in the dark, afraid to move, and waited for the killer to come for me. Five minutes passed. Ten. A single frog trilled in the bushes outside the door. The air smelled of the closed-up house and the sweat and blood of death. Darrin's pistol, lying in the doorway, gleamed in the moonlight.

Another five minutes passed. I listened for footsteps. The frog trilled.

I stretched my leg into the doorway and scooted the pistol toward me, then huddled against a wall, waiting, clutching the grip of a gun I doubted I would use. Darrin's dark body lay beside me more silent than any object I'd ever known. I pulled out Thomas's cell phone and dialed Charles again. Voicemail picked up.

Another five minutes passed. A warm spot spread under my leg. I touched it and my fingers came away wet and slippery. A pool of blood was expanding across the tile from Darrin. I wiped my hand dry on my shirt, tucked Darrin's pistol into my belt and crept along the wall away from his body, staying in the shadows, moving into the hall and then the living room. Two sets of glass doors with metal lattices looked out toward a backyard garden. The shooter might be covering the back of the house, or he might not.

I unlatched a door and stepped on to a stone path. When no one shot, I stepped again. A moonlit garden surrounded me. The air smelled like roses and damp earth. I waited for a gunshot.

Then I ran.

The grass was slick with dew. A short stone garden wall loomed in front of me and I jumped over it, cut around the side of the house and sprinted toward my car. It stood on the driveway next to Darrin's blue pickup. A deep shadow fell between the truck and the driver side door of my car, and I ran into the gap as though it were a chasm that could drop me into either life or death.

No one was waiting to kill me.

I climbed in and jammed the key into the ignition, whipped the car down the driveway and pulled on to the street. A half mile from Melchiori's house, I rolled down the window and chucked Darrin's pistol into a hedge of holly bushes.

TWENTY-FOUR

Phil Lingren lived in a lowland rural area on the northwest side. A limestone gravel driveway stretched into the trees from the road. I parked on the shoulder and turned off the car. Moonlight filtered through live oak branches. Insects hummed and a raccoon shuffled through the

287

scrub and fallen branches. After a hundred yards the driveway opened into a clearing with several brightly lit sheds and outbuildings and a brightly lit house. It was one-thirty a.m. and the place looked as though Lingren were getting ready for a party.

The first outbuilding was a wooden work shed with an open front wall. On a grimy workbench there were darkly oiled table vices, a metal mallet, a hacksaw, metal tongs and a propane blowtorch – heavy tools that could bend or fashion metal. On the back of the bench stood plastic gallon milk jugs of gasoline, engine coolant and oil. The metal shavings on the floor were caked with grease.

Next was a storage shed, its door open, a fluorescent light buzzing brightly over rakes, a lawn mower, a leaf blower, an edger, shovels and a pail of garden gloves. An outside lamp threw a cone of light on the driveway. I called into the yard, 'Mr Lingren?'

A detached two-car garage stood next to the storage shed. The doors were up, the lights on. An old Plymouth Fury was parked on one side. On the other, there was a Yamaha motorcycle and beyond it a dozen stacks of boxes that reached to the ceiling. I stepped inside, glanced under the car and moved toward the boxes. Lingren had arranged the stacks a couple of feet apart from each other as if the boxes needed breathing room. I stepped into a gap between them and eased myself through the maze.

No one was there.

A gravel path led from the garage to a brown ranch-style house. The front door was open, though a screen door was shut. Every light seemed to be on inside.

I rang the doorbell and called again, 'Mr Lingren?'

When no one answered, I stepped into the house.

The lights suddenly went out over the yard, from the sheds and garage to the house, dumping me into blackness. The night birds and insects quieted and all was silent.

Slowly the sounds started again, first a cricket, then a rustling in the leaves near the house, and my eyes adjusted to the moonlight. I knew I should back away and go to my car. I should call Charles and we could search the place together. If Charles still wasn't answering his phone I should drive away.

I went deeper into the house. Moonlight through the living-room windows cast shadows over worktables that were stacked with old radios, televisions and stereo components. The family room had a couch, an easy chair, a wall-mounted large-screen television and a long table strewn with computer parts. I didn't want to know the man who lived this way.

The kitchen had only a small window, which faced away from the moonlight. I stumbled over a chair, then felt my way along counters until I reached a pantry. When I tried the door it resisted as if someone were holding the knob.

I pulled harder.

The door pulled back.

I should walk away. I should run. I should call Charles. I should stand aside and let the earth turn until it ground its old axis to dust.

I yanked the knob.

The door blew open and knocked me to the floor. A man stepped past me. I reached for him but missed, then scrambled to my feet and went after him. He ran through the house as if it were on fire. By the time I reached the living room he was out the front door. When I reached the door I glimpsed him disappearing into the trees alongside the driveway.

'Lingren!' I yelled.

The man didn't slow or answer.

I went to the kitchen, groped along the wall until I found the pantry and ran my hands past the shelves until I found a circuit breaker box. The main breaker had been thrown. I flipped it and the house and yard lit up.

The house looked thirty or forty years old and had touches of the rustic. A coarse-grained chair rail lined the kitchen walls and hand-hewn beams crossed the ceiling. Electronic components littered the counters, tables and chairs. In the bedroom, clothes lay on the floor. The bathroom smelled like stale urine.

I went out the back door into the yard. Floodlights, planted in the ground, illuminated the branches of three huge live oaks. At the rear of the property, backing against a wooden fence, there was another shed. Unlike the rest of the buildings, it was dark.

I crossed the yard and tried the door. It swung open freely. A sickeningly sweet smell swelled out and I stepped away and caught my breath.

I reached inside, found a switch and flipped it.

A man was hanging by his neck from a steel support bar, a plastic bag over his head. He was a small man and wore only underwear and a white T-shirt, as if he'd awakened from sleep for this. The noose was made of clothesline. Except for the dead man the shed was empty.

I hoisted him into the air, loosened the line, got him down, laid him on the floor and pulled the bag off his face.

Phil Lingren's dead eyes stared at me.

The man in the kitchen pantry must have killed him. I'd arrived at the house too late. A half hour. Five minutes. Thirty seconds. I didn't know when Lingren had taken his last breath but now there was nothing left of him.

Everything was moving too fast. The killer was getting rid of the last of the partiers before anyone could focus. With Lingren dead, there were only two left – Daniel Turner and a man whose name I didn't know and who might already be dead.

I pulled out Thomas's phone and dialed Charles but hung up after two rings. Even if he answered he could do no good. I dialed another number and after four rings Daniel's wife said, 'Hello.'

I'd awakened her. 'Hey, Patty, this is BB. Can I talk to Daniel?'

'Christ, BB. He's working. You can get him at

the station or on his cell.'

Phil Lingren's head tipped to the side and for a moment I thought he was alive but his body was only giving itself to the gravity that would pull it deep into the ground.

'You still there, BB?' Patty asked.

'Yeah,' I said. 'This will seem like a strange question but what kind of cars do the two of you drive?'

She sighed. 'It's two in the morning.'

'I know.'

'A Honda Pilot and a Buick LaCrosse.'

'What color is the Pilot?'

'BB...'

'Please.'

'Blue. They call it *blue pearl*.'

'Is that a greenish blue?'

'No, BB, it's blue. Pearl blue, whatever that means. I'm really tired.'

'Just one other thing,' I said. 'When Daniel comes in, do me a favor and ask him about his trip to Jamaica.'

Her voice came awake and angry. 'You know something? You're a damned hypocrite, BB.'

'You already know about Jamaica?'

'It's none of your business what I know.' She hung up.

Why had the man in Lingren's pantry run away instead of attacking me? Why had the shooter at Melchiori's house allowed me to escape? I wondered about Daniel's involvement. He'd been at Melchiori's last party. He'd called me right after a homeless man found

Belinda dead on an empty lot on Blue Avenue. He'd played me in and out. Had Daniel set me up to fall from the beginning? When I wasn't working out as a fall guy, did he set up Terrence? And now that he had problems with Terrence, was he setting me up again?

I dialed Daniel's cell number. When he answered I said, 'I know you were in Jamaica.'

He said, 'You know nothing, BB. Come in now and you won't get hurt.'

'I don't think so.'

'What are you going to do?'

'Try to figure you out,' I said.

'Yeah? What's to figure?'

'With all the people who've died after attending Melchiori's party, why are you still alive?' I asked.

'I was hoping you would tell me,' Daniel said. 'Maybe you're afraid to go after a cop. Maybe you're my friend and can't get yourself to kill me. Maybe another reason altogether. Why don't you come in and talk about it?'

'Not a chance,' I said. 'Who were the other men at the party?'

'I don't like your games,' he said.

I'd known Daniel for most of my life and I listened to his voice for signs that he'd turned vicious or worse but I heard neither innocence nor guilt. 'I've got pictures of everyone who was there,' I said. 'Phil Lingren was one of them.'

'Yeah, Phil was there.'

'Melchiori too, and David Fowler and you.

293

And one other man. You tell me who that other man is and I'll tell you something interesting about Lingren – unless you know it already.'

'What's that?'

'Who was the other man?' I asked.

'You've got his picture too?'

'In my pocket.'

'His name's Steve Perkins,' he said.

'If you really think I'm responsible for the killings, why would you tell me that?'

'With his picture you could identify him anyway.'

'Or you're setting a trap to bring me in,' I said.

'Or I know that Perkins is already in hiding and safe.'

'Could be,' I said. 'D'you know where he lives?'

'What's this about Lingren?'

'You sure you don't already know? You can find him in his backyard shed. He got hung by his neck from a steel bar with a plastic bag over his head.'

'Jesus, BB! Did you...' His shock sounded real.

'No,' I said. 'I didn't. But I'm thinking that you might've.'

'You there with him?'

'Regrettably.'

'Wait there for me,' he said.

'Yeah, right.' I hung up.

Flies were buzzing around Lingren's mouth and eyes. A couple of mosquitoes were making a strange Eucharist of his cheeks and forehead.

As I stepped out of the shed Thomas's phone rang. I flipped it open, thinking Daniel was calling back. 'What?' I said.

'BB?' It was Susan. She sounded confused.

'Yeah. Hey. What's up?'

'Why do you have Thomas's phone?' she asked.

'I borrowed it from him.'

'Is he with you?'

'No, of course not. What's going on?'

'He's gone.'

'What do you mean?'

'I mean he's gone. I woke up and he wasn't here. He took my car.'

'Damn.' The news shouldn't have surprised me. I'd left the house hundreds of times when I should've stayed locked in my room and he'd watched me go. Now he'd left in the middle of the night and the thought of it terrified me.

'He's worried about you,' Susan said. 'He wants to be with you.'

'I'm the last person he should want to be with.'

'Come home,' she said. 'Let him find you here.'

'I can't,' I said.

'He's your son, BB.'

'Call me if he comes back.'

'BB...'

'I love you.'

'Don't say that.'

I hung up. Thomas would have no idea of

where to search for me. He would have no idea what to do. But I knew too well the urge that got a man out of bed in the middle of the night and made him drive through dark, empty streets whether or not he knew where he was going.

I cut across the lawn, around the side of the house and on to the gravel driveway. Daniel had talked as if I was the killer. He could probably make a case against me. Thanks to him, forensics would be able to show that I'd been to the site where Belinda's body was found. I'd also been to the house where Ashley Littleton's roommate died, in the room where Aggie had taken a beating, in Melchiori's house when he got shot, and now in Phil Lingren's shed.

The insects buzzing in the bushes seemed to mock me. I yelled, 'Fuck,' and the sounds stopped but there was no echo and by the time I reached my car they started again with new urgency.

I called 411. They had numbers and addresses for three men named Steven Perkins. No one answered at the first number, and at the second the man's voice sounded too old for weekend orgies in Jamaica. At the third the man sounded fatigued but right and so I hung up and drove toward his house.

Perkins lived in a neighborhood of neat single-story bungalows with well-tended lawns – houses that rested back in the shadows as if they were hiding from the glare of the street-lights. I parked in Perkins' driveway behind a silver Prius, my headlights shining on a brick house with a red door. A wooden fence extended from either end of the house and circled into the backyard. Despite the rain, an irrigation system was on in the yard next door, the sprinkler heads hissing as they sprayed the lawn. The sound of semi-trailer trucks rumbling over a highway a half mile away drifted through the still air.

It was a quarter to three in the morning and Perkins' house was dark when I climbed the front porch stairs. A glazed pot of plumbago stood on each step. A wreath of dried wildflowers hung on the door. The place looked like a cardboard cutout of a kind of happy normalcy that I'd never known personally, and standing on the porch sent a tremor of discomfort through me.

A voice answered my knock immediately. 'Yes?' I'd awakened no one.

'Mr Perkins?'

'What do you want?'

'I need to talk to Steve Perkins.'

'About what?'

'Jamaica.'

Several seconds passed, then two lock bolts clicked and the door swung halfway open. The lights remained off inside and out.

'Come in,' the voice said.

I stepped over the threshold and a pistol barrel pressed against my jaw. I was shoved to the side and frisked from front and back. 'Come on,' the man said. He led me into a windowless kitchen, closed a door and turned on a light. As I expected, he was the man in Melchiori's party photos. He was about thirty, a little short of six feet tall, and had the build of an ex-athlete who'd eaten and drunk too much. He held the pistol firmly and had a second gun tucked into his belt. A bottle of Smirnoff, the cap off, about a third full, stood on the counter next to three butcher knives.

Perkins went to the counter, lifted the bottle to his lips and asked, 'Why are you here?'

I glanced around the kitchen. On the refrigerator, magnets held photographs of two blonde-haired girls, about three and five years old, and the crayon art that the girls had made. A large, framed professional portrait of the Perkins family – Steve himself, a blonde woman and the girls, all dressed in jeans and red shirts – hung on the wall between a spice rack and another wildflower wreath, this one shaped into a heart. The inside of the house, like the outside, felt clean and corrupt.

I scratched my cheek and said, 'My name's William Byrd. People call me BB.'

'I know who you are.'

'Then you know why I'm here. Did you know that Phil Lingren died tonight?'

Fear flashed in his eyes but he said calmly, 'I'm not surprised. Killed the same way as the others?'

'Close enough. You're one of the last alive. You and Daniel Turner.'

'I have the feeling I'm next on the list,'

he said.

'Whose list?'

'The girl's father said he'd get us.' He drank again from the vodka bottle.

'Godrell Graham?'

He nodded. 'When everyone else left Kingston I stayed for an extra day because I couldn't change my flight. Graham came to my hotel room with a couple of men. He threatened me. I told him I didn't touch Tralena. I was there when it happened but it wasn't me and I couldn't stop it. I said I had daughters too.'

'Did you tell him the names of the others at the party?'

'I had to. He said he'd kill me.' He spoke with a deep sadness but no guilt that I could hear.

'You deserve to die then,' I said.

'I've got two girls. I was thinking of them.'

'You put them on the line the moment you got on the plane to Jamaica.'

'I know.'

I asked, 'Where are they now?'

'I sent them with my wife to her mother's house up in Savannah.'

'Good.'

'I'll kill Graham if he comes after me,' he said.

'He's not coming himself,' I said. 'He arrived in town two days ago. He must've hired out the killings.'

'To who?'

'Daniel Turner?' I said.

'I don't think so.'

299

'Daniel also has a wife,' I said. 'He might think he has no choice.'

The idea seemed to worry him. He said, 'Twenty minutes before you arrived there was someone else outside. He tried to come in the front door but I said I had a gun.'

'I saw no one,' I said. 'Did you call nine-one-one?'

'To say what? Someone's trying to kill me because I saw a sixteen-year-old killed in Jamaica?' He drank from the Smirnoff bottle. It was nearly empty. He offered it to me.

I shook my head and said, 'You need to get out of here.'

'I'm not running away.'

'If you stay, you'll die. That won't do your daughters any good. Check into a motel in Gainesville for a few days. Go to Alabama. But don't stay here.'

'How about you? What good are you doing anyone?'

I tried to smile. 'I'm already past hope.'

Without much more persuasion, Perkins turned off the kitchen light and went to assemble a travel bag. When he returned he had a third pistol.

We went out the back on to a patio. A clothesline stretched from the patio to a fence, and a plastic playhouse stood in the moonlight like a magic cottage. Next to the fence, there was a sandbox with pails.

We stayed in the shadows and worked our way around the house, Perkins carrying a pistol in one hand and his travel bag in the other. When we reached the fence gate to the front yard I stepped into the moonlight.

A gunshot rang and a bullet slapped into the gate.

I ducked to the wall.

Another gunshot rang.

'Shoot your gun,' I said to Perkins.

He was wild-eyed. 'I can't see him,' he said.

'Doesn't matter. Shoot it.'

He pointed his pistol over the back fence and pulled the trigger four times and in the fury of sound I opened the latch and yelled, 'Run.'

We pushed through the gate and sprinted across the front lawn. Gunshots trailed us.

We got into my car and I pulled back on to the street and shifted into drive. As we drove away, a large SUV that had been parked against a curb two houses down flipped on its headlights and a set of blindingly bright post-mounted spot-lights. As the SUV closed on us, I stepped on the accelerator. In the rearview mirror, through the brilliant light, I recognized the silhouette of the driver.

It was Charles.

TWENTY-FIVE

The SUV followed a half block behind us, never closing the gap. When we accelerated, it accelerated. When we slowed, it slowed. When we crossed through an intersection as a stoplight changed, it rolled through the red as if it were green. A newspaper delivery van pulled from behind a stand of crepe myrtle trees on a side street and the SUV cut casually into the oncoming lane and back behind us as if an invisible tether held us together. The post-mounted spotlights glared in the humid night air, two terrible balls of brilliance.

What happens when the monster you know becomes a stranger?

We drove on residential streets lined with oaks and magnolias. In another two hours the sun would rise, cars would fill the streets and the sidewalks would come alive with people walking their dogs or jogging through the neighborhood. But now the moon was setting and the deepest dark of night blanketed the city.

Perkins sat nervously beside me, hunched forward, glancing over the headrest at the SUV, cradling a pistol in his lap.

I asked, 'What was Belinda Mabry like?'

He leaned toward the passenger's side window, peered in the rearview mirror and answered distractedly. 'She was insane.'

'What do you mean?'

He looked at me. 'I never met her before the party but that was enough. She put the bag over Tralena Graham's head and wouldn't take it off even when the girl started screaming. Fowler and I tried to pull her away but she locked on to Tralena and wouldn't let go. They had a weird connection the whole weekend. I've been thinking about it a lot.'

'Belinda killed her?'

'We all did, I suppose. Belinda put the bag on her head and held it until Tralena stopped kicking and screaming and fighting. But we were all together.'

We rolled through a stop sign and, a block later, rounded a corner toward the Five Points district of restaurants and shops. The SUV followed a half block behind.

If the monster that you depend upon turns on you, then what?

Perkins rolled down his window and peered at the SUV.

'What're you doing?' I asked.

He raised the pistol to the window. 'I'm going to shoot this guy.'

I hit the brakes and we slammed to a stop. 'Out!' I said.

'What?'

The SUV closed on us and stopped too.

'Out,' I said. 'No shooting from my car.'

'All right, all right,' he said and put the gun down. 'Go!'

The lights from the SUV brightened the interior of my car. I looked in the rearview mirror. The driver's door of the SUV swung open.

'Go!' Perkins yelled.

I did.

'You're insane too,' he said.

'You don't realize how easy it is to kill a man like you,' I said. 'You're all dressed up with your three pistols – and you've got butcher knives on your kitchen counter, for God's sake. But the man in that SUV knows exactly what you are. He's toying with you and when he's finished he'll break your neck. I've half a mind to do it myself.'

Perkins looked at me nervously and his hand floated back toward his pistol.

'That would be a bad idea,' I said, and he rested his hand on his knee.

In Five Points we rounded a corner by a Mexican restaurant. The SUV followed us. I floored the accelerator to widen the gap and we swung into a nearly empty parking lot shared by a grocery store, a barbershop and a pizzeria.

A wide alley ran along the side of the grocery store and connected with a side street behind it. We slipped into the alley as the SUV entered the lot. Halfway along the store, for a space of three car widths, the wall jutted inward toward a loading dock. I hit the brakes and we backed into the space. A moment after I flipped off the headlights, the SUV spotlights shone into the alley and on to a chain-link fence and a trash dumpster across from us.

'What are we doing?' Perkins asked.

'Shut up,' I said.

The spotlights approached. If I'd parked far enough behind the corner of the wall we wouldn't be visible until the SUV was nearly past us.

'I'm getting out,' Perkins said.

'Another bad idea.'

He reached for the door handle as the SUV lights flashed upon us and I revved the engine and took my foot off the brake. We shot across the alley.

The front end of my Lexus smashed into the side doors of the SUV. The SUV veered and slammed into the dumpster.

I yanked the gearshift into reverse, backed away, shifted into drive and hit the gas. The SUV remained dead against the dumpster as we rounded the corner from the alley into the parking lot. We sped up, cut to a side street and turned again.

We left the SUV behind us but I thought I heard Charles' laugh.

It wasn't an evil laugh. It was a laugh of surprise and pleasure, the kind you hear from a teacher whose student has shown a moment of accidental brilliance that the teacher had never imagined possible.

We cruised toward downtown under the glare and shadows of streetlamps. I said, 'I can take you to the airport but they won't let you on a plane with the guns.'

Perkins seemed to have considered the problem already. 'Can you get me to a taxi?'

'I can,' I said and turned west.

The Checker Cab Company depot was in an industrial strip on Old Kings Road and ran taxis from dawn until midnight and by request during off hours. A man was reading a paperback book in the dispatcher's booth when we pulled up.

Perkins climbed out and asked, 'Do you want to know where I'm going?'

'I wish I'd never met you,' I said, 'and since we've met I'd prefer to know as little about you as possible.'

He nodded. 'Thanks for pulling me out of my house.'

'Have a safe trip,' I said.

'Yeah,' he said. 'You too.'

I turned and drove toward downtown. The lights on the office towers glimmered in the humid air. I drove slowly and thought about my options. It seemed to me that I had only one.

I dialed home on Thomas's cell phone.

Susan answered, her voice full of fear.

'Hey,' I said. 'It's me.'

'Oh.' Disappointment that it wasn't our son. Relief that it wasn't the hospital or worse.

'You haven't heard from Thomas?' I asked.

'No,' she said. 'Can you come home now?'

Only one option. 'I might not be coming home for a while.'

'What do you mean?' she said, her voice as close to panic as I'd ever heard it. 'How long is a while?'

'I don't know what's going to happen to-night.'

'It's almost morning,' she said.

'I know.'

'Come home.'

'I can't,' I said.

'What are you going to do, BB?'

I hung up.

What happens when the monster inside you cuts teeth and chews its way out?

Two semi-trailer trucks barreled past, their headlights searching the dark. I dialed Daniel's cell phone. When he answered I told him, 'I'm ready to talk.'

'OK. You can turn yourself in at the station.'

'I'm not turning myself in,' I said. 'I want to talk with you. Alone.'

'What's there to talk about?'

A long red light stopped me. No traffic came from either direction. No cars were parked along the curb. No one walked on the side-walks. I waited anyway.

Daniel said, 'I'm at University Hospital, wrapping up the reports on Don Melchiori. We can meet here. Inside or outside, whichever.'

'Outside.'

'Fine.'

I said, 'I'll be on the third floor of the parking garage in twenty minutes.'

'I'll be there,' he said. 'You want me to bring you a cup of coffee?'

'Don't fuck with me.'

'Just trying to be friendly,' he said.

'Don't.'

Ten minutes later I parked across the street from the hospital, jogged across an outside parking lot, crossed through a memorial garden and walked up the ramp into the garage. A security camera, mounted above the garage entrance, eyed me. I no longer cared.

On the ground floor about ten cars were parked in spaces reserved for doctors and clergy. Orange sodium lights threw long shadows on the floor. A yellow arrow, painted on the wheel-polished concrete, pointed deep into the garage. I walked up the incline past a stairwell, around the first two bends, past an elevator and on to the second floor.

A helicopter hovered in the far distance, its rotor ticking through the walls of the garage.

I passed the second entrance to the stairwell, rounded two more bends and stopped at the third floor. A motorcycle and five cars were parked in various spots, and three more cars and a pickup were clustered by the door to the stairwell. The air smelled of concrete, oil and the muggy night. A pipe was dripping somewhere, as softly and persistently as a clock hand chipping away at time.

No one else seemed to be in the garage. I went to the top of the third floor, stopped and listened to the pipe dripping and the silence around it, and returned to the stairwell door. The pickup was parked next to a black VW Passat. I stepped between them and sat on the oil-stained floor.

Fifteen minutes had passed since I'd called Daniel.

If he'd alerted hospital security early enough and they'd been watching the video feed from the garage security camera, he would know I was waiting for him. If not, I would have the advantage of surprise.

A vehicle approached from the lower levels of the garage and as it rounded the bend to the third floor I crouched out of sight behind the pickup. It was a yellow-and-white sheriff's department van. It stopped about ten yards beyond the elevator, the side door slid open, and a man dressed in black and carrying an automatic rifle stepped out and silently disappeared behind a parked car.

Daniel was stupid.

The van continued up the incline and stopped next to the pickup. The door slid open again and two men, also dressed in black and carrying automatic rifles, climbed out. One stepped into the stairwell and closed the door. The other, a compact Hispanic man with a moustache, stepped between the pickup and the VW, spit on the floor and crouched. I could hear him breathe.

The van drove around the bend, stopped, drove further, stopped again and then turned around and drove down toward the garage exit. We were alone – me and five SWAT officers Daniel had promised not to bring.

The pipe dripped softly.

The Hispanic officer spit again.

I unbuttoned my shirt, slipped it off my shoulders and arms, and twisted it into a thick rope. The Hispanic officer shifted, got comfortable and repositioned his rifle. I moved silently behind him. He cleared his throat. I slipped the roped shirt around his neck and tightened it. I whispered, 'If you make a sound I'll break your neck.'

He tensed for a long moment and relaxed.

'Put down the gun,' I said.

He did.

I shoved it under the pickup and got his handcuffs from his belt. 'Behind your back,' I whispered.

He put his hands where I wanted them and I cuffed them. I gagged him with the shirt and knotted it behind his head, pulled him toward the garage wall and said, 'Lie on your belly and stay quiet.'

He did.

The pipe dripped. The man breathed. Two minutes passed. Three. The third-floor elevator chimed and Daniel got out.

'BB?' he called.

He walked part way up the incline, past the first SWAT officer. He showed no sign of seeing him. The orange sodium lights made his face look jaundiced. He stopped and checked his watch. He looked up and down the incline and continued walking, his footsteps echoing off the concrete walls. Far in the distance a freight train sounded its horn.

The man on the floor behind me grunted when Daniel stepped past but he alerted him too late. I yanked Daniel toward me and threw him against the roof of the VW. The other officers, all but the one in the stairwell, sprang from their hiding spaces, rifles ready. I held Daniel close from behind, pulled his head back and said, 'Tell them to stay away.'

'Back off,' he yelled.

None of them moved.

'Now,' he yelled.

They backed away.

I pulled Daniel toward the door to the stairwell, holding him between me and the other officers. 'Tell them to stay where they are,' I said.

He did.

'Tell them I'll kill you if they follow us.'

'No.'

I yelled the warning myself, then said to him, 'Now turn the doorknob.'

He turned it.

I spun and kicked the steel door and felt it hit the weight of the officer on the other side. He fell on his back and his rifle clattered down the stairs.

'Go,' I said to Daniel and he stepped over the officer.

The officer looked up, surprised to see me.

'Don't get up,' I said.

He tried to sit.

I kicked him in the chest.

At ground level, I held Daniel tight to myself

and forced him through the door, expecting more officers with more guns.

No one was there.

'You did a bad job of this,' I said.

'You didn't give me a lot of time.'

I dragged him through the memorial garden and across the parking lot toward my car. Officers followed fifty yards behind, fingers on their triggers. When they realized we were heading to a car, three of them ran toward the hospital yelling into radios.

I got Daniel into the passenger seat and veered to miss a man who'd run into the street. We blew through a red light and another before the sound of sirens reached us. I turned on a side street and we circled behind the hospital, zigzagged through a residential neighborhood and arrived at Springfield Park, a mile-long strip of grass and trees that flanked a sanitation canal. I pulled the car off the road, over the curb, and into a stand of palm trees.

'Give me your shirt,' I said.

He shook his head but unbuttoned it, and I dressed myself as a helicopter flew over, its spotlight shining through the palm fronds.

Daniel watched through the windshield as it passed to the south. 'You've really fucked up, BB,' he said.

'That's the story of my life.'

He spoke calmly, slowly. He seemed to force himself to. 'It's time to give up.'

'Why would I do that?'

'We know what you've done,' he said.

'Yeah? What's that?'

'We've got Aggie's body. Cut up but scrubbed clean like the others. Wrapped in plastic. Lying in some weeds on a vacant lot on the Northside.'

That made my head spin. 'But...'

'But what, BB?'

'Did Charles...?'

'He's been helping us. Since the beginning. Since before the beginning. We talked to him when Jerry Stilman died with a shank in his heart. He hinted at you then with your obsession with Belinda Mabry, but it was only hints. Ashley Littleton's neighbors didn't report men outside her house when her roommate got killed. Charles told us. Aggie too. Charles said you were at the Luego Motel.'

I felt lightheaded. 'He told you where to find Aggie's body?'

'He told us where you put her.'

I almost laughed but Daniel looked at my grin as if it validated his worst suspicions about me. I asked, 'Did you ever look at him as the killer?'

'Of course we did. But face it, the man is eighty-four years old. He can't do much more than get up to pee four or five times at night.'

'I don't think you know who he is,' I said.

'I know everything there is to know, BB. He's a wannabe. No threat unless he hangs around someone like you. He grew up in Maryland. Dropped out of high school his junior year. Was married for five years in the early fifties. No children. Moved here in seventy-three. Got into occasional trouble with us since then, mostly in connection with you. Drove long-haul trucks for a living until retiring eleven years ago.'

'Jesus, Daniel, who told you that?'

'He did. And our background check verified it.'

'You don't get teardrop scars from driving a truck,' I said.

'You do when a battery explodes. Happened in seventy-five. Except for safety glasses he would've been blind.'

'No, Daniel.'

'How do you explain it then?' he asked.

'I don't. But he's the most violent man I've ever known.'

'In your imagination he is, BB. But really? He's an eighty-four-year-old retired truck driver. And he's the bad excuse you use for the terrible things you've done. At most he's been your cheerleader. That's all he's ever been.'

'I've done nothing,' I said.

'You killed Terrence Mabry. Your own son. Would killing the rest of them be any worse?'

'He was coming after me with a knife,' I said.

'You'd chased him all night. He was scared to death of you. Your son.'

'I didn't make things the way they are.'

'Yeah, BB, you did.'

'Did Terrence say I lit his house on fire?'

'He didn't see who did it. But he thought it was you or Charles.'

'Charles,' I said.

'You know what? I wouldn't be surprised. That old man loves you and would do just about anything for you. But not protect you when you've done what you've done. It's too much.'

Daniel's words dizzied me. A moth batted its wings against the windshield. A police cruiser flew past on the street, its lights flashing but its siren off.

I asked, 'But how would I have found out about Melchiori's party and why would I want to kill everyone there?'

'I've got no idea, BB. But I know you did,' he said. 'It would take a smarter man than me to figure out your motives. Why did you beat those men when you were in college just because they were teasing a couple of Mexicans? What was the motive there?'

'Hondurans. The men were attacking them.'

'And why did you beat an innocent man after that six-year-old boy got killed?'

'He wasn't innocent,' I said.

'He didn't kill the child, BB.'

'He wasn't innocent.'

'You've spent your life lying to yourself,' he said.

'Get out of the car.'

'It's time to give up, BB.'

'Get out!'

'It's time,' he said, and climbed out into the night.

TWENTY-SIX

I drove to Charles' house, wondering if Daniel was right that my life was a lie and wondering how much it mattered if it was. Living a lie or not, I would do what I needed to do. The electronic gate was open at the end of Charles' driveway but a green light showed that the closed-circuit camera was on. I got out of my car, picked a branch out of a ditch by the mailbox and smashed the camera. I drove up the driveway, the headlights reflecting off the trunks of old trees and the palmetto undergrowth. Spanish moss hung in gray webs from the branches.

It was time.

To kill and heal.

If that's what it took.

Charles' house was dark. The spot where he usually parked his Dodge Charger was empty. I got out and walked toward the place in the woods where we'd buried Aggie. In the deep darkness a narrow trail in the dead leaves traced our steps but no loose soil or evidence of a grave remained.

It was time.

I climbed the front steps and knocked on

the door.

No one answered.

When I tried the knob the door swung open and Charles' calico cat sprang into the night as if something were chasing it and disappeared into the brush at the side of the driveway.

A switch inside the door lit up the living room. Charles had set up a long wooden work-table and laid out a series of photographs. They were before-and-after shots. Tonya Richmond before Charles had put his hands on her and after. Ashley Littleton before and after. Belinda before and after. Ashley Littleton's roommate before and after. There was a photo, taken through a windshield, of David Fowler leaving City Hall and another of the SUV hood, dented and streaked with blood. There was a picture of Aggie lying unconscious in the Luego Motel room and another of her after Charles had dug her up from his yard, bathed her and stuffed her into a plastic lawn bag. A little Canon digital camera stood at the end of the table. I threw it across the room into the fireplace and the pieces splintered on to the floor. I looked again at the before picture of Belinda. It showed a woman in her early forties with a tight, graying afro. She was smiling, one side of her mouth turned upward. Charles had gotten her to smile before he'd killed her. Something of the seventeen-year-old girl I'd loved remained in her eyes but I realized that I didn't know the woman.

I gathered the pictures. Charles had left them

for me, I felt sure. He'd *taken* them for me.

In the bedroom, Charles' bed was made and the dresser top was clean. But he'd left scraps of clothesline on the bathroom floor and a sheet of twist ties on the back of the toilet. He'd scrubbed the bathtub and left an empty bleach bottle by the garbage can. In the medicine cabinet a toothbrush lay next to a tube of Colgate. A half-dozen white shirts hung on the rod in the closet next to a half-dozen pairs of faded blue pants. Charles hadn't left town. Not yet.

I went into the kitchen. Plates and glasses were neatly stacked in the cabinets. The sink and counters were wiped clean. A half-gallon carton of milk stood on the top shelf of the refrigerator above a long, plastic-wrapped slab of pork loin. On the bottom shelf a rotting cantaloupe smelled like death.

I went to the garage and flipped on the light. A green Mercedes SUV stood in the parking spot, its hood crushed by the impact with the dumpster outside the grocery store. The metal still radiated warmth and the engine clicked as it cooled. Inside the driver-side door, a spot of blood and phlegm stained the dashboard and a gleaming white front tooth lay on the carpet. I picked it up. It weighed in my hand like a pearl or a gemstone. I put it in my pocket.

Damn Charles. Where was he? I called his cell number though I guessed he wouldn't answer.

He picked up on the third ring.

'Where are you?' I asked.

'I'm gone.' He sounded cheerful. 'Long gone.'

'Your clothes are still in your closet.'

'Ah, good. You made it to my house.'

'Your toothbrush is still in the medicine cabinet,' I said.

'Can always buy a toothbrush and clothes.'

'I found your tooth,' I said.

He laughed. 'That was a sweet move you made behind the store.'

'You're out of control,' I said.

'You know better than that, BB. I assume you found the photographs too.'

'Yeah, I found them.'

'That's one of the sets. I'll place the others carefully. The police'll think you shot the pictures. Did you see the camera too?'

'I threw it in your fireplace,' I said.

'I didn't think you'd be able to keep your hands off it. The memory card's inside. They'll match the prints on the camera to you.'

'You're a bastard.'

'I know.'

'Why did you do this to me?'

'Why not?' he said. 'You were perfect. I turned down the job when I found out that your old girlfriend was at Melchiori's party. But then Godrell Graham told me how much he'd pay and I thought, hell, I'm not getting any younger. At that point picking you was logical and also a practical necessity. I knew that you'd never rest until you caught Belinda's killer and I knew that when she died you would be an obvious suspect to Daniel Turner.'

'But we're friends.'

'I'm not your friend, BB,' he said. 'I've been many things to you but never a friend.'

'Did you kill Jerry Stilman?'

'Of course. Graham paid me to. He found out that Stilman was working with the DEA. Later he found out that Melchiori and his friends had killed his daughter. He has enough money to buy the kind of justice that courts don't understand.'

'*Your* kind of justice.'

'Yours too, BB. Don't forget that.'

'I'm not the same as you, Charles.'

'The biggest problem with you is that you've always lied to yourself,' he said. 'You think you're better than me. That makes you vulnerable. I once had high hopes for you.'

'I'm not done yet, Charles.'

'Actually you're wrong. You were done before you even knew this had started.' He hung up on me.

I went to the living room, kneeled on the hearth and picked up the metal, plastic and glass from the camera. I removed the memory card and broke it in half. There was a Bic lighter in a kitchen cabinet. I brought it to the fireplace and burned the photographs, then held the flame under the pieces of the memory card until the plastic dripped on the hearthstones. Charles said he had other copies of the pictures. Undoubtedly he knew how to plant them so that they would look like I'd taken them.

Do just enough to do the job. His motto. I hadn't done enough. Probably never would do.

As I stood, Thomas's cell phone rang.

The screen said the call came from my house.

I answered and Susan said, 'BB?' She sounded upset.

'Yeah. Did Thomas come home?'

'There's someone outside.'

'Thomas?'

'No—' Something slammed. 'Jesus, BB—'

'Who?'

The line went dead.

I had no doubt. Charles was inside my house.

I sped across town. The sun was rising and the sky hung thin and gray as if it hadn't yet sorted itself out from the blackness beyond. Cars began to appear on the roads, driven by men and women in business suits, drinking coffee from travel mugs or wearing exercise clothes as they headed to the gym before work. I yelled and steered around them, shot into the oncoming lane and on to the shoulder. I leaned on the horn and punched the accelerator to the floor. The car lifted over the railroad tracks a half mile from my house. I slowed for a commercial strip, blew through a red light in front of a pickup truck and turned on to my street.

A car was parked in front of the house. A blue Honda Pilot. My heart slowed and I eased my foot from the gas. Daniel Turner's wife had said that was one of their cars. Maybe Susan had heard Daniel outside, not Charles. But the illogic struck me at the same moment as the hope that Susan was safe. Daniel wouldn't have broken in. The phone wouldn't have gone dead.

I looked farther up the street. Another car was parked four houses away. Charles' Dodge Charger.

Daniel was lying on the front porch with blood on his chest. Next to him lay a plastic-sheathed morning newspaper. He was alive. His belly heaved with each breath. His eyes were glassy and bloodshot. I reached toward him but he shook his head and muttered, 'Inside.'

'Charles?'

A bitter, gruesome smile formed on his lips. He clenched his teeth and closed his eyes.

I stepped over him, turned the doorknob and threw my shoulder into the door. It swung open into the dark, empty living room. I went inside and yelled, 'Charles!'

'Up here,' he called.

I ran up the stairs. On the stairway walls he'd tacked copies of the pictures of the women he'd killed. On the landing he'd left more.

He sat on an armchair in my bedroom, a large pistol resting on his lap. Susan lay next to him on the bed, wrapped in a clear plastic bag, naked, her legs tucked over her head, her mouth gagged, her ankles lashed behind her neck with clothesline, her wrists bound beneath her. The bag heaved as she struggled to breathe.

'Jesus, Charles, what are you doing?'

He shook his head. 'Sometimes you say the dumbest things.'

I rushed toward him.

'No,' he said distractedly and he held the pistol to Susan's head.

I froze.

The window shades were down and lamps burned on the two bedside tables.

Charles said, 'The police will find you here beside your wife. Dead. Self-inflicted gunshot.'

'I don't like guns.'

'Susan will be dead too,' he said, 'raped by you, a man who, as everyone in town knows, couldn't get his wife to do him. With your background they'll know what you did. They'll know you're the killer. They'll find Daniel Turner dead on your porch where you killed him. Too bad Thomas isn't here. I had ideas for him. But I'll hunt him down later. Loose ends and all.'

'Why me?' I asked again.

He stood up. 'You let me down.'

'This won't work,' I said.

He smiled. 'It's already done. I'm already gone.'

'What about the car in your garage? What about the little things that you've left behind?'

'I leave nothing behind. Ever. If they look for the car they won't find it. Or if they do they'll connect it to you.'

Susan was struggling inside the bag. Her breath had fogged the plastic over her face. I couldn't see her eyes and for that I was grateful.

'What now?' I asked.

He offered me the chair he'd been sitting in. 'Why don't you take a seat?'

'I'll stand.'

He pushed the pistol against the plastic so that its muzzle pressed into the skin on Susan's forehead. 'Please,' he said.

He tied my wrists and ankles to the chair with clothesline. He cut another length, wrapped it around my throat and tied it to the chair back so that I would garrote myself if I leaned forward.

When he was done he asked, 'You keep a toolbox in your garage?'

'Why?'

'Do you or don't you?'

'Go to hell.'

He left the room.

I spoke to Susan. 'If there was a way that I could...' I stopped. There wasn't a way and never had been. But for a moment she ceased struggling and I felt that in that moment there was forgiveness.

Charles returned from the garage with a long-shafted screwdriver. He sat on the foot of the bed opposite me and looked me in the eyes. He touched the sharp tool-end to my chin and forced my head up. Sweat formed on my brow and ran down the back of my neck.

'Now, say you're sorry for failing to live up to my expectations,' he said.

'They were unreasonable,' I said.

He increased the pressure so the straight steel edge pushed into my skin. 'Say you're sorry.'

'I'm sorry,' I said, 'for failing to live up to your expectations.'

He removed the screwdriver from my chin.

'Ah, that's all right,' he said, then flipped the tool and punched a hole through my right hand.

I screamed.

He yanked the screwdriver out and punched another hole.

I screamed again and blood splattered his white shirt. He regarded it and said, 'Now that makes me mad.' He plunged the screwdriver again.

Tears and sweat erupted from my face. 'Don't!'

He looked sincerely perplexed. 'Why not?'

And suddenly I didn't have a good answer. Why not stick a tool into my hand? Why not? I said, 'The police will wonder why my own hand.'

He yanked out the screwdriver and plunged it into my other hand. 'I'll leave a note for you that explains it,' he said. 'It's an act of expiation. Four hundred years ago sinners did it all the time. Margaret Mary Alocoque carved the name of Jesus into her breasts when she was younger than Thomas. Not many people do this kind of thing anymore, which is a shame.'

He yanked out the screwdriver and plunged it again. It hit bone.

When I stopped screaming, Charles shook his head. 'Be a man, BB. Nothing more. Being a man is enough.' He yanked out the screwdriver, leaned back in his chair and surveyed the room like a bored child looking for a new toy.

Susan had stopped struggling. She breathed slowly. The bag heaved gently. Charles smiled.

'You've got yourself a smart wife, BB. She's conserving her breath. Not that it'll do any good in the long run.'

She grunted through her gag and struggled again.

'Or maybe she was just in shock,' he said.

Outside the room, footsteps climbed the stairs – slow, heavy footsteps, pausing, persisting. 'Now who the hell is that?' Charles said.

Daniel appeared in the doorway, his chest bloody, his skin pale.

'Hey,' Charles said happily. 'You're still alive.'

Daniel stepped into the room, his face haggard but his eyes furious.

'Oh, stop,' Charles said.

Daniel shook his head. 'You ... can't...'

Charles casually lifted the gun from the bed and casually pulled the trigger. The report shook the walls. Daniel spun and fell on his face.

Charles shrugged, then looked at me level. 'Should we finish this? Do you want to do Susan? Or d'you want me to do her after I kill you?'

I spit at him.

'I can't believe you did that,' he said and he held the gun barrel to my head. 'But things are as they are.'

A figure stepped into the bedroom doorway. Thomas.

His eyes were wild and terrified and innocent. He wore green shorts, a brown soccer shirt and white tennis shoes. He held the shovel that I'd used to bury Fela.

'Well, hello,' said Charles.

'Run,' I yelled.

Thomas walked into the room. He glanced at his mother on the bed and me in the chair. His eyes turned to Charles.

Charles seemed pleased to have him join us. 'Come in, come in,' he said. 'I'd been thinking I would need to go out to find you. I was just offering your dad a final shot at your mother. He wasn't interested. How about you?'

Thomas lifted the shovel above his head and swung it at Charles.

Charles threw an arm up and grabbed the shovel. He pushed it and Thomas stumbled back. Thomas looked startled but then he grinned at Charles and Charles laughed. Thomas swung the shovel again, and again Charles grabbed it. Then he aimed his pistol at Thomas's chest.

I begged. 'Run.'

Charles grinned. 'Did you hear him, boy? Your daddy said to run.'

An anger arose in Thomas's face that I'd felt course through my own blood but had never seen in another man. Not even Charles. A terrible anger that transcended all impulses of fear or weakness.

Charles saw it too and for just a moment he loosened his grip on the shovel. Thomas pulled it from him and drove the blade into Charles' chest. As the blow punched the air from

327

Charles' lungs, a look of surprise crossed his eyes and he tumbled over the end of the bed and landed on the floor.

His pistol fell from his hand and Thomas picked it up and pointed it at him.

'Get help, Thomas,' I said.

He let Charles pull himself to his feet.

'Get help,' I said.

Charles looked at the floor. He looked at Thomas's white gym shoes and green shorts. He looked Thomas eye to eye. A grin crossed his lips again. 'Well, I'll be damned,' he said and took a step toward him.

Thomas didn't back away. He aimed the pistol at Charles, and Charles hesitated.

'No,' I said to Thomas.

'No,' Charles agreed. 'I don't think so.' He stepped toward Thomas again.

Thomas shot him in the stomach. The roar of the gun shook the walls.

Charles looked at his belly, at the stain of blood that soaked through his white shirt, and he started to laugh but the laugh became a wheezing whine and he took another step.

Thomas shot him again.

Charles looked perplexed. He nodded and stepped again.

Thomas shot him in the chest.

Charles stumbled toward him.

Thomas pulled the trigger but the gun didn't fire. He pulled it again. Nothing.

Charles reached for Thomas as if he would choke him but he just patted him twice on the shoulder. 'You're a good boy,' he managed to say, and he stumbled out of the bedroom into the hall.

TWENTY-SEVEN

That afternoon Lieutenant Denise Nuñez led a squad of seven cars to Charles' house. They'd picked me up in a Percocet daze from the ER, saying they wanted a friend of Charles to negotiate with him to come out. I wore bandages as thick as mittens on my hands.

A large police officer snapped the chain on the security gate with bolt cutters and we rolled up the driveway to within thirty or forty yards of the house. The window shades were down. Charles' Dodge was parked on the spot in the driveway where he usually left it. Locusts hummed in the trees. A single cardinal flew across the driveway and landed in the branches of a cypress.

More police cars were parked a block away on streets facing houses whose backyards touched Charles' property. Officers had rushed to the neighbors' houses and explained that they would need to evacuate, then accompanied them to vans that took them to wait at a community center. Only then did Denise Nuñez speak into a megaphone telling Charles to come out.

No sound came from the house.

The shades remained down.

The front door remained shut.

For an hour and a half Nuñez spoke into the megaphone and made telephone calls into the house, all to the same silent response. An officer received word that Daniel Turner had lived through surgery and probably would survive, and happiness surged through the crowd. Then Nuñez ordered tear-gas canisters to be shot through the windows. Glass broke and gas filled the house and spiraled into the yard.

More silence.

Another forty minutes passed.

A tactical helicopter rattled the air overhead.

Nuñez told a group of four SWAT members to break down the front door. They approached the front steps behind handheld ballistic shields, one of them carrying a hydraulic battering ram. They stopped and spoke to each other. Nuñez talked to one of them on a radio. He climbed on to the porch and removed something from the front door and all four backed away.

It was a white envelope. Nuñez looked inside and brought it to me. 'A gift for you apparently,' she said. Inside the envelope was a photograph of me twenty years ago as I sat inside Worman's Deli on the day that Charles introduced himself. He must have taken the picture as he'd entered, though I couldn't imagine how without my seeing him do it. I looked young and sure of myself though I didn't remember myself that way.

I gave the photograph back to Nuñez. I said, 'I don't want to look at it.'

The four SWAT officers crept toward the house again. They climbed the front porch steps, and the one with the battering ram positioned it so that its bolt would strike the door lock. They gave a silent count, the lead man triggered the ram and two of the others kicked the door off its hinges. The fourth covered them with an automatic rifle.

For a moment nothing happened. Then Charles' calico cat leaped over the threshold, dashed down the front steps and darted across the driveway. The man with the automatic rifle spun and shot it dead.

The house was vacant. The furniture was gone. The kitchen cabinets and refrigerator were bare. The green SUV was missing from the garage. The counters and bathrooms smelled like bleach and industrial cleaners. The floors gleamed as if no chair had ever scraped across them. Our footsteps and voices echoed in the empty rooms and every echo told us that Charles was gone and never would return.

'Damn,' Nuñez said and turned to me. 'Who was this guy?'

'I don't know,' I said. 'Ask Daniel Turner when he wakes up.'

She shook her head. 'If.'

An officer approached. 'What about the car in the driveway?'

Nuñez looked at me.

'I gave it to him eight years ago,' I said. 'He might've decided he no longer wanted it.'

'Check it out,' Nuñez said to the officer. 'Carefully.'

The officer left and two evidence technicians approached. One of them said, 'At first look there's no trace of him. Not a drop of blood. Not a hair.'

Nuñez smiled grimly. 'Why am I not surprised?'

The technicians went to make a second sweep. I gazed out the front window and discovered that Charles had left a second gift in the Dodge Charger. As the officer opened the door a fireball rolled from the hood across the front yard. It lit up the trees and sky. The explosion rocked the walls. The heat of it washed over my face and arms. A deep, slow silence followed the blast and then the screaming, crying and sirens started. When those sounds passed too the whole world rang in my inner ears and kept ringing.

A week of wetland searches turned up bloody rags but no Charles. The police issued a national and then an international alert and newspapers and magazines featured Charles' tear-scarred face. How do you hide a face like that? The best lead had him holed up in the Hillside neighborhood of Laredo, Texas, but when the police raided the house they found a one-eyed Mexican immigrant with an old knife wound on his cheek in bed with his fifteen-year-old wife. The police arrested him out of pure spite on charges of statutory rape.

Charles was gone, as he'd said he would be, but without a body buried or incinerated I felt his presence always behind me and expected to hear his voice each time the phone rang. I put his broken front tooth in a dish on my desk at my Best Gas station in case he came looking for it. After the bandages came off, my right hand had three puncture scars and my left had two. Everyone in town knew how I got them. But when children or visitors asked, I said I burned myself with battery acid.

Daniel Turner improved to fair condition after two weeks in intensive care. I visited and we sat together quietly in his room because there was nothing we could say that would do any good, but Charles had wounded us both and we'd wounded each other before saving each other and so sitting together quietly seemed fine. After a month the hospital released him and we promised that we would get together for dinner though the idea turned my stomach and from the sound of his voice I knew it turned his too.

After I got back from Charles' house late in the evening of the day that Thomas shot him and after the ringing dulled in my inner ears, Susan came to me in my bedroom. She'd bathed and put on a yellow cotton dress as if insisting furiously that Charles' attempt to violate her and our family could do nothing to change who she was. I leaned against a pillow on my bed where Charles had stripped and bound her and she sat beside me and kissed me on the forehead as if I were a child. 'I'll be leaving you,' she said.

'I understand,' I said, though that was a lie. 'Are you going tonight?'

'Tomorrow,' she said. 'In the morning.'

Then she stood and unfastened the dress hooks behind her neck, and her dress slid to the floor.